Miriam Raftery
LOVE IN ITS FLIGHT

"You did it!" I pulled off my goggles and shook my hair free, giddy with excitement. "You broke the Wright Brothers' record!"

Nathaniel lifted me out by the waist and spun me around, then pulled me into his arms and hugged me with the exuberance of a conquering hero. My arms closed around his neck in return as I savored the intoxicating taste of victory and the protective feel of his embrace. I buried my head against his chest, unable to catch my breath.

He lifted my chin with his fingertip to meet his gaze. Suddenly there was no laughter, no celebration in his eyes, but only one unmistakable emotion—desire. "No," he corrected me, his voice husky. "We did it. I couldn't have done it without your help."

"I—it was nothing."

"You're wrong." He brushed a stray lock back from my cheek with his hand and leaned forward, his mouth hovering a hairbreadth above mine. "It was everything."

MIRIAM RAFTERY

APOLLO'S FAULT

LOVE SPELL   *Love Spell*   **NEW YORK CITY**

LOVE SPELL®

March 1996

Published by

Dorchester Publishing Co., Inc.
276 Fifth Avenue
New York, NY 10001

To my friend, Cheryl Becker, who inspired *Apollo's Fault;* my husband and children, for their infinite patience; the writers in my critique group, for sharing their wisdom; and the members of Romance Writers of America's San Diego chapter, for their support and encouragement.

"A few days after the main shudder, they told us the quake had lasted only 15 seconds. But that is in real time. Earthquake time isn't real time. Or maybe the truth is, earthquake time is the most real time of all, a time when...the preciousness of life is understood most acutely."
—Stephanie Salter, *The San Francisco Examiner*, in an article written after the 17 October 1989 earthquake

Exellent

good book

Chapter One

I should've listened to Apollo.

He tried to warn me that we were in for trouble, but I didn't pay attention. I accused him of concentrating on his love life instead of my concerns, but the truth was just the opposite. I couldn't have known it then, of course, but Apollo was about to lead me straight into the adventure of a lifetime—and the romance of the century.

Not to mention a one-way road to danger.

If only I'd trusted Apollo's instincts, I could've prepared myself for the big upheaval that was about to turn my life upside down and backward. I might've taken some photos or tapes or letters—anything to prove to Nathaniel Stuart that

11

I was telling the truth. At the very least, I'd have packed a makeup bag and some decent clothes. I might even have turned tail and run from that crumbling old mansion, though in hindsight I know that would have been a big mistake.

But I'm jumping ahead in the story. It's getting to be a bad habit, this hopping around in time. To be honest, I never felt quite in step with the rest of the modern world. I guess that's why I escaped into the make-believe world of the theater, then later into history, as a graduate student. I've always felt more comfortable in the past—or thought I did, before.

Now I've really got to start at the beginning, if there is such a thing as a true beginning point in time. Personally, I believe time flows in circular motions, ending up ultimately where it began.

The trouble started the day Apollo first came into my life. I remember it in detail; the images haunt me as clearly as if I were looking into a mirror.

"He's just the thing for you, Taylor," Victoria Stuart decreed in her brittle, dried-leaf voice, thrusting the Shar-Pei puppy into my arms as a thank-you gift the day I agreed to write down the memoirs she was determined to dictate.

I stared down into the wrinkled, puglike face of the ugliest dog I'd ever seen. Frankly, I wasn't sure whether to feel honored or insulted by Victoria's words.

She's nearly blind, I reminded myself. Be charitable. She probably can't tell what the creature looks like.

Or maybe she can, a voice inside me nagged as I watched her gnarled fingers caress deep folds in the Shar-Pei's velvet skin. I lifted my gaze to the timeworn creases and grotesque scars on her nearly century-old face, scars inflicted by the tragedy that had robbed the sweet old spinster of her future. The dog, I saw in a flash of clarity, reminded her of herself—ugly and unloved. I felt a wave of pity for both of them and tightened my grip around the awkward bundle in my arms.

"I'll name him Apollo," I said impulsively, thinking of an illustration I'd seen of the handsome Greek god who represented youth and beauty. Also prophecy, though I didn't think of that at the time.

The old woman nodded, never ceasing a slow forward-and-backward motion as she perched on the edge of her battered rocking chair, staring through rheumy eyes into the dimness of her drab apartment in the Mission District. A corner of her mouth lifted in approval. "A godly name," she replied in a fading reedy voice that I had to strain to hear.

"It seems fitting." I shrugged. "I've been reading a book on Greek and Roman gods, and—"

"Yes," she murmured as her eyes slid shut. A smile of contentment lent her face the illusion of a woman years younger. "I know."

At the time, I dismissed her strange remark as the ramblings of a half-senile old woman, since I hadn't told her about my reading habits. She was often like that, drifting in and out of lucidity the way the sun slips among the clouds. But later

I came to believe she said exactly what she meant.

True to his name, Apollo behaved like a little deity. It was unsettling at times. He quickly claimed my wicker peacock chair as his own, sprawling on its cushion, wrinkles of fat rolling out beneath him—a decadent sultan lounging on his throne. He had a gourmet palate and refused to bend to my will, towing me on long walks at a pace that he and he alone determined. Equally stubborn, I refused to consider obedience school, knowing intuitively it was a prospect doomed to fail.

Apollo's constant demands pushed my patience to the limit. It was impossible to leave him at home, where his constant barking made the neighbors complain until the landlady threatened to evict us. So it was that I came to have Apollo with me wherever I went, a four-footed albatross with suedelike fur and a lopsided grin.

We started our morning that infamous day with our usual routine: guzzling orange juice and jelly-filled junk food at our favorite doughnut shop before jogging over to the Historical Society office where I worked as a student intern, preparing my master's thesis on potential restoration of the city's few surviving nineteenth-century mansions. It was through my research interviewing survivors of the 1906 earthquake that I'd met Victoria Stuart. I'd spoken with quite a few of the old-timers, yet there was something about Victoria that intrigued me, compelling me to become drawn into the intricate web of her past.

I pushed open the heavy door and stepped inside. "Any progress yet on Stuart House?" I asked Wilma, my mentor, who looked even more ancient than the musty office in which she sat.

Wilma pushed her bifocals low on her nose and peered over the top. "None, I'm sorry to say. The state won't declare the place a historic landmark—the house is just too dilapidated."

My stomach did a backflip. "There must be something else we can try."

Wilma shook her blue-haired head. "Unless we can come up with a miracle, Stuart House will be bulldozed this Friday."

I swallowed hard, dreading the prospect of breaking the news to Victoria. "What sort of miracle?" I inquired.

Wilma lifted her shoulders and flipped her hands palms up. "Archaeological relics, historic documents discovered, that sort of thing. Or a wealthy benefactor. Know any millionaires?"

I shook my head glumly. My mind rebelled against the image of a wrecking ball smashing Victoria's childhood home, the only place she'd ever known happiness. Not to mention the fact that it was once one of the grandest mansions in all of San Francisco—no small feat in a town where keeping up with the Joneses is practically an Olympic sport.

Wilma patted my hand. "You'd do best just to forget about that old place. Save all that youthful energy of yours for a battle you might win. Like rooting for the Giants." She grinned. "Say, my grandson's coming over tonight to watch the World Series on TV. Why don't you join us?"

"No thanks," I said quickly, envisioning a blind date with Delbert, the ultimate computer nerd. "I've got homework."

I knew she was right about the house, but somehow I just couldn't let it go that easily. I slunk into my office and tethered Apollo to a leg of my desk. He teethed on the chair leg, then curled up in the king-size doggie bed at my feet. Soon he was snoring contentedly.

Meanwhile I poured a cup of Wilma's industrial-strength coffee to brace myself before pulling out my accordion file on Stuart House. I laid the "before" pictures out until they covered the scarred surface of my desk, took a long sip of the coffee, and studied the sepia-tone photos, as though some clue lay hidden in their depths to help me save the home.

It was awesome, a magnificent Queen Anne–style Victorian built on Van Ness Avenue in 1885 by Josiah Leonidas Stuart, a sea captain who made his fortune importing goods during the gold rush. Josiah founded Westwind Shipping Company, the fleet that built the family fortune inherited by his son, Nathaniel. But after Nathaniel's demise in the 1906 earthquake, the empire crumbled. Nathaniel's widow remarried a "foppish dandy with no more business sense than a gnat," or so Victoria claimed. "I tell you, it's positively criminal the way Quentin Fenniwick swindled the Stuart family out of their own company," Victoria would often say, her spine stiffening. "And what he did to that house . . ." Here she would grow misty eyed and often incomprehensible.

The mansion itself was an inspiration, a monument to Josiah's dreams, built for his bride who died when Nathaniel was a small boy. Years later, over his family's heated objections, Josiah remarried an actress, Jessica, who abandoned the stage temporarily to give birth to Victoria a scant eight months after the wedding.

But the mansion itself had a grandeur which could not be diminished by the taint of scandal or the passage of years. The home and its grounds occupied almost a whole city block. It was three stories high with white fish-scale shingles, gingerbread trim the color of a Blue Willow plate, a wraparound spindled porch, and a widow's walk on the roof lined by a wrought-iron railing. Two rounded turrets stood like sentinels at each front corner, their curved windows reminding me of eyes watching all that transpired before them.

Since Nathaniel had a fascination with photography, among other things, the interiors of most rooms were documented with photos—the elegant ballroom where some of the city's most gala events were held, the parlor with rose-printed wallpaper and windows draped in velvet, the music room that held a pianoforte and a harpsichord, and my personal favorite, the turret room library that was home to hundreds of leather-bound books.

The family photos weren't at all like those embarrassing candids my own father used to take when he was sober enough to hold the Polaroid steady. You know the type—me as a baby smearing oatmeal on my high chair; my brother, Alex, yanking my hair as I practiced my lines before my first audition, and so forth. Thank goodness Dad couldn't afford a camcorder or we'd never have had any peace.

The photos of Josiah and his wife were much more dignified, as were those of their son, Nathaniel, at various ages, ending with a wedding picture of Nathaniel and his bride, Prudence. I saw Victoria as an infant in an elaborate baby carriage. Oddly, there were no photos of the infamous Jessica. Torn in rage from the family album by a furious family member, perhaps?

But it was the formal portrait of Nathaniel that made me stare, mesmerized. He was an imposing man, tall and powerfully built, with a mustache set amid the craggy planes of his face and a confident stance that reminded me of some nineteenth-century explorer. He wore a pin-striped morning suit with a starched collar and a gold pocket watch suspended on a chain. His thick black hair gleamed from the macassar oil popular in his day, yet his eyes were what drew me to him like magnets—dark, riveting, commanding my attention.

I closed my eyes, savoring the vision of what Stuart House must have been like in its heydey, its ballroom filled with guests waltzing to an orchestra beneath that glittering chandelier. I suppose a shrink would say my fantasy was understandable for an emotionally repressed woman from a dysfunctional family, the product of a teenage mother and an unemployed alcoholic actor. No way was I going to repeat Mom's mistakes. Still, I'd have given my first-edition copy of *Joy of Sex* for just one waltz across that dance floor with the incomparable Nathaniel Stuart.

Nathaniel was a man ahead of his time, Victoria loved to boast. Frankly, I thought he sounded a bit eccentric, always dabbling with various inventions. The man kept a workshop, sundial, windmills, darkroom, and even a weather station behind the house that he loved so much. Also a stable and carriage house, storage shed, Victoria's dollhouse, and a prim white gazebo standing regally in the midst of an English-style garden.

Gone, all gone. Only the house itself still stood, and it was a miserable shell of its former self. Ironically, it survived the great earthquake and fire only to be destroyed by human greed and neglect. Prudence, Nathaniel's ill-fated bride, remarried Quentin Fenniwick, "a gambler with no sense of business," according to Victoria. Prudence died a year after her second marriage and her grieving widower promptly ordered the home's turrets, scorched by fire after the earthquake, sawed off at the top. I recalled how Victoria shuddered when she told me of watching those splendid turrets crash to the street below, and felt a rush of anger. What kind of man could do such a thing?

Fenniwick had a fourth story built, destroying all but a small section of the widow's walk, then hired a contractor to divide the home into fractured cubicles for rental as apartments. During the post–World War I boom, he prostituted the house further by stuccoing over the wood exterior and extending the front facade out nearly to the street to squeeze in more tenants. After his death, his equally greedy heirs sold the neighborhood eyesore to a slumlord who rented rooms to drug dealers and pimps. Transients moved in; thieves stole everything not nailed down and some things that were. By the late 1980s, the city had declared it unfit for habitation.

There was a sadness about the house that moved me almost to tears as I stared at the recent photos. Windows were boarded up; graffiti artists had defiled once-proud walls with territorial sprays. Now, finally, a developer had purchased the lot and rezoned it commercially. In a few days, the worthless old home would be torn down and replaced by a pizzeria and video arcade.

Barring a miracle.

I closed my eyes, unable to look at the photos anymore. After a moment I shoved them back into the accordion file and returned the whole thing to the drawer. Nudging Apollo with my toe, I elicited an annoyed grunt. "Time to go, lazybones," I cajoled. "Victoria is waiting."

* * *

We sat on her threadbare sofa sipping tea. Or rather, I sipped, while Apollo slurped his from a chipped china bowl. He'd seemed unusually agitated ever since we arrived, pacing back and forth and pawing at the door as though to hasten our departure. So Victoria offered him a bowl of chamomile tea "to soothe his nerves."

"Well," sighed Victoria, folding her hands across her lap as she rocked. Blue veins showed through the skin on the backs of her hands, skin as delicate and nearly transparent as onion paper. "I suppose it's time."

"For what?" I asked.

"The end of the story, of course."

I was confused. Over the past few weeks Victoria had spoon-fed her story to me in rambling scraps with no coherent order. I'd heard about her childhood in Stuart House and the events since—how she'd been parceled off to an elderly aunt and uncle after the earthquake, a couple who locked the child in a closet so that her disfigured face wouldn't frighten visitors. Her real mother turned up after the quake and tried to claim her, but was prevented when Victoria's uncle went to court to have the woman declared an unfit mother.

Victoria tried to get a teaching job when she turned 18, but no school would hire her because of her scars. She wound up teaching Braille at a school for the blind, but never married and had no children. I suspect she thought of me as a surrogate daughter; she coaxed me into accepting an antique heirloom locket along with her pathetic life history. What more could there be to her story?

"I'm referring to the earthquake, of course," she went on, oblivious to my confusion. She lifted a hand to trace the corded scars on her face and neck. "You must wonder how I got these. Oh, you needn't look surprised. I wasn't born this way, you know."

I felt myself redden. "I didn't think you wanted to talk about it."

Her lips grew taut. "I must, now. It was the day of the earthquake. Not long after his wedding . . ."

"Your brother's?"

She smiled wistfully and nodded. "Nathaniel was handsome as a rake in his morning suit, tails, and top hat. Mark my words, he could have wedded any woman in the state. The country, probably."

I smiled indulgently. Victoria's perception was often filtered by rose prisms when she spoke of her older brother.

She shook a finger at me reprovingly. "It's the truth, I'm telling you. Nathaniel was a man who dominated the space around him. When he entered a room, people ceased talking to turn and stare; when he sat down, he filled the chair. Not that he was a man of great physical girth; he was not. But there was an air about him that commanded respect."

I turned up the volume on my tape recorder as she pursed her lips and continued. "Such a shame he up and married Prudence. She wasn't

a bad woman, really. But she was a foolish one—
a vain, empty-headed chit with less sense than a
child. But Nathaniel was determined to find a
suitable mother for me after my real mother ran
off."

"Jessica, the actress."

"Father loved her, you know. He told me he fell
in love with her the instant he first saw her tread-
ing the boards, as they said in the old days. She
broke his heart, and he died a year after she left
us. To this day, I'll never understand how my
mother could abandon her own daughter. I think
deep down Nathaniel was afraid I'd turn out like
her, and he wanted to save me from my true nature." She sighed deeply. "I've often thought how
different things would have been if only that
marriage had never taken place."

I glanced up from my notes and saw her wipe
the moisture from her eyes. "Because Prudence
didn't take you under her wing after your brother
died?"

A veiled expression came over her face. "Did I
say he died?" She shook her head as though per-
plexed. "My memory must be worse than I
thought. He didn't, you know."

I raised my eyebrows in surprise. "But—"

"He disappeared the night of the earthquake.
Four days after his marriage to Prudence."

"Weren't they off on a honeymoon?" I asked.

"The wedding trip was postponed because Nathaniel was involved with Mr. Spreckels on some
urgent business—Nathaniel was very secretive
about the whole thing." A hint of a smile formed

23

on her lips. "Prudence was in a snit, but Nathaniel promised her the delay was only for a few days. I recall quite clearly how relieved she seemed when Antonio Giuseppe, Nathaniel's business manager—lord, he was a strapping young fellow, handsome as a bull! As I was saying, Antonio burst in late the night before the earthquake with news about the business transaction being completed. Prudence was enthralled; she made Nathaniel promise that the two of them could sail for Honolulu the very next day aboard one of his ships."

"How did he disappear?"

She glanced downward. "I was the last one to see him. I'd risen early and was in my bedroom— I had the second-story turret room with the lovely floral paper—reading." A dainty flush stained her withered face. "It was a shocking novel for its day, and I didn't dare risk letting Nathaniel catch me perusing it, you see. I was reading by candlelight so as not to be found out."

"Go on," I said, suppressing a grin.

"I heard footsteps. I peeked in the door of my brother's room—that is, the one he shared with Prudence." She sniffed haughtily. "I saw Nathaniel disappear into the attic, telescope in hand. He fancied himself an amateur astronomer, you see."

"And that's the last anyone heard from him?"

She nodded. "The earthquake jolted the rest of the household awake a few moments later. It was just after 5:00 in the morning. Oh, it was a dreadful calamity, wrath of God, some said. . . ." She paused to wipe her eyes with a faded lace handkerchief.

"Nathaniel's body was never found," she went on. "A few gossips whispered that Prudence drove him away. But most theorized he must have opened the door from the attic to the roof, then fallen off the widow's walk."

"But wouldn't someone have seen—"

"The workshop and carriage house below were destroyed, you see. The earth below just crumbled away and everything collapsed . . . a body might have been swallowed up beneath the rubble without anyone knowing. But I never believed a word of it."

I shuddered at the thought of a skeleton somewhere on the Stuart House grounds and promptly changed the subject. "Were you still in bed when the earthquake struck?"

She paused to pick up a teapot and refill Apollo's bowl. I frowned; next the spoiled animal would be demanding crumpets.

"I was curled up under the covers in my bedroom. What a lovely comforter it was, embroidered with blossoms to match the wallpaper," she said, adjusting the crocheted tea cozy as she set the pot down. "Did I tell you it was in the second-story turret, all done in roses and violets. . . ."

"Yes," I interrupted, trying to keep her focused.

"Ah. Well, as I was saying, I was in bed reading when the earthquake hit."

"And?" I prodded gently.

She closed her eyes. "There was a terrible rumbling noise. I was frightened, so I huddled under my covers and prayed it would stop. The trembling grew worse; a porcelain doll fell from its shelf and shattered. I started to cry—I was afraid the roof would collapse and I'd be buried where I lay! Finally, the room stopped shaking. I grabbed the candleholder and leapt out of bed, then ran out onto the landing to see if anyone was hurt. Who could have known another quake would hit? The stairs lurched beneath my feet; there was a twelve-foot-high Tiffany chandelier suspended from the third-story ceiling above the ballroom below. I saw it sway toward me just before it crashed. Thousands of glass slivers everywhere reflected the chaos. . . . I grabbed for the rail to keep from falling, but the candle tipped and set my hair on fire."

"You must have been terrified," I whispered, spellbound.

Her face scrunched with the pain of remembrance until she looked like a dried apple. "I screamed—over and over again. Somehow I found the good sense to blow the candle out, but by then the flames were upon my face. The smell of burning hair and flesh was horrible. . . . I thought I was going to die."

I took her hand in mine. "You don't have to do this. It's okay." It wasn't, but I didn't know what else to say.

"Mrs. O'Hara, our housekeeper, reached me first. She pulled off her robe and threw it around my face to smother the flames, but the damage was done."

"How awful," I murmured, recalling the photos I'd seen of Victoria as a vibrant, beautiful child. "To lose your brother and your youth all at once."

"Yes. Well." Victoria settled back into her chair and resumed rocking. "We can't change the past, can we?"

She looked at me thoughtfully. "You know," she observed, "I think on Saturday I should like to have you to take me by the old house. No matter how much a shambles it appears, something about that place never fails to make me feel young again. Father felt it too, I think. Perhaps that's why he chose that spot to build his home. Did I tell you that no compass would work in the home? Drove Nathaniel to distraction trying to come up with a logical explanation for it. He concluded there must be a magnetic force of some sort beneath the earth, causing interference."

I looked away. I couldn't tell her about the house. Not now. I glanced at Apollo; even he looked depressed, as though reading my thoughts.

Then my gaze traveled back to Victoria, and I had the eerie thought that she knew what I was keeping from her. Her breathing was shallow, almost trancelike, and her eyes stared straight ahead. A strange look flickered in their depths. Not quite grief; if I hadn't known better I'd have sworn it was . . . ecstasy. I spoke to her, but she withdrew inside herself, rocking faster as though driven by some unseen force. She mumbled something incoherent and would not respond when I tried to address her again.

Apollo and I had finished our late-afternoon workout at the gym and started jogging home when I had a strong urge to detour by Stuart House. I told myself I had to get over this obsession I was developing for the old house, especially since it was going to be sawdust soon. Still, I had this crazy idea that if I'd just poke around the premises long enough, maybe I could find a hidden compartment under a floorboard or someplace where some long-ago Stuart might have stowed papers or anything of value. It would provide only a temporary stay of execution at best. But Victoria was fading, on the brink between two worlds, it seemed lately. How much time could she have left? Maybe only days or weeks. If I could just postpone the inevitable until after she was gone, to spare her the pain. . . .

Apollo barked as we passed the California Street trolley and turned onto Van Ness Avenue. I felt a flash of annoyance; if it wasn't for the darned dog I could ride home. Occasionally I'd considered giving away the troublemaker, but the thought of hurting Victoria's feelings made me stop. Like it or not, I was stuck with Apollo.

Together we jogged a few blocks, passing rows of restored Victorian homes converted to retail shops and boutiques. We passed the usual sights—yuppies out shopping, punk rockers with safety pins in their ears, a panhandler hitting up a lady in a fur coat outside a trendy hair salon, a drag queen walking a fluffed and dyed-pink poodle with a matching bow.

Apollo panted after the poodle, slobbering on my shoes as I jerked on his choke chain. "C'mon, Romeo," I scolded. "We've got work to do. This is no time to start a love affair."

Famous last words. Truth be told, we were standing on the threshold of the one great love of my life. Literally. I looked up then and saw the boarded-up Stuart House, perched like a mad aunt in the attic, awaiting us to set it free. The late-afternoon sun cast looming shadows that darkened the walkway in front of me. Frankly, the old place gave me the creeps. But for Victoria's sake, I held my imagination in check and forced myself to ignore the prickling sensation on my skin as I climbed the massive cracked steps to the porch.

I didn't even have to jimmy the lock, a feat I wasn't sure my credit cards and hairpins could accomplish. We found a windowpane broken by a beer bottle that lay inside on the faded carpet, so I simply removed the glass shards and climbed inside. Or rather, I hoisted Apollo through first, ignoring his whimpering and clawing, even when he snagged my spandex tights.

It was darker than I'd expected inside. I reached into the fanny pack at my waist and pulled out a penlight. It was a ridiculous tool for even an amateur archaeologist, but it was all I had.

"Hello!" I called out, flashing the beam around the room. I didn't want any surprises. Sure, I always carried a can of Mace in my fanny pack, just in case. But who wants to put that stuff to the test? If some transient was camped inside, I'd get out of there and forget the whole idea.

But there was no one. I probed around on the ground floor for a while with no success, then forced myself to ignore the way my hair was standing straight up on the back of my neck and climbed the stairs. It was stuffy up there, so I shucked my oversize sweatshirt and hung it over the banister.

Clutching Victoria's locket around my neck, I completed a search of the second and third levels with equally frustrating results. Outside of a few beer cans and cigarette stubs probably left by some neighborhood kids, I found nothing to indicate that people had ever lived here. Anything of value had long ago been stripped and sold for drug money, I concluded, depressed.

By this time Apollo was becoming an unbearable pest. He wound his leash around my ankles; I untangled myself and scolded him for thinking more about his love life than my immediate problems. He gnawed at my shoelaces, whimpering pathetically.

His behavior was bizarre, even for Apollo. He was usually such a levelheaded tyrant, growling only at strangers he didn't like. It was uncanny how that animal knew right off who could be trusted—and who couldn't.

Stupidly, I ignored his desperate actions—until he yelped and bolted up the stairs, towing me behind him as I fought not to bump my head in the darkness.

"Whoa—slow down," I yelled to no avail. We bounded through what must have once been a bedroom on the third floor. Skidding across the splintery floorboards, I yanked on Apollo's chain in a futile attempt to stop him. On the far side of the room, the dog halted at a small door on a triangular-shaped wall. I tried it; it was locked.

"The attic," I concluded, feeling a shiver of excitement. If anyone wanted to hide something where no one would find it easily, it would be in the attic.

The door, coated with generations of peeling paint, had a rusted old lock with a large keyhole. My credit cards were useless; I tried a hairpin with no luck. Impatiently, Apollo whined and pawed at the door. I unfastened his leash, shoving it in my fanny pack to keep him from wrapping it around my legs again. Then I shoved my weight against the door and felt it give. The wood was rotted and after a few more tries it gave way. I pushed it open and we stepped inside.

It was pitch black in the attic, except for the narrow beam from my penlight. I squinted, hoping my eyes would adjust to the blackness, but still couldn't make out a thing. There were cobwebs everywhere, I discovered when I walked face-first into one. I pried the sticky fibers off my face, shuddering as I removed one from my tongue.

Apollo whined at my side, rubbing his head against me. I patted him reassuringly. "I don't blame you. This was a dumb idea—we'll never find anything up here, at least not without more light. Let's go ho—"

Before I could finish, I heard a deep rumble that seemed to emanate from all around. The room began to tremble; my heart leapfrogged to my throat. "An earthquake," I gasped, realizing that the tumbledown house had probably never been reinforced to meet the city's seismic safety codes. The shaking grew stronger, until the walls around me trembled. A rafter crashed to the floor, narrowly missing my head but causing my heart to thump against my rib cage.

The penlight slipped from my hand; the bulb shattered as it struck the floor. Apollo clawed at my ankles; I reached for him but he slipped away. Darkness closed in.

No one even knows we're here, I thought disjointedly. A vivid image flashed in my mind, causing me to tremble from head to toe. The vision of Victoria's brother danced in my brain: Nathaniel, who vanished up here without a trace over 80 years ago—during an earthquake just like this.

Chapter Two

I scooped Apollo into my arms and raced for the door, stumbling over an object in the darkness. The floor pitched and rolled in undulating waves, as though someone were pulling a rug from beneath my feet. Debris rained down from the rafters, coating us in pale dust. In the distance, sirens wailed.

"Help!" I screamed, clutching the air for a handhold, but there was nothing. It was foolish; no one could hear. I stepped onto a crate, or something that seemed solid. It lurched beneath me and jerked me off into nothingness. The earth roared in my ears; I had a terrifying sensation of falling through space that seemed to go on forever; then time ceased and there was only blackness.

I don't know when I first realized that it had

stopped. Awareness came gradually as the world around us grew quiet and the rumbling faded away.

Apollo licked my face, as though checking to make sure I was all right. "Boy, that was some shaker," I mumbled, rising unsteadily to my feet. As a native Californian I'd grown accustomed to temblors and looked down my nose at those transplanted Easterners who paled at the slightest movement of earth. But this had been much stronger than anything I'd felt before. It was, I knew, the Big One—at least a seven on the Richter scale. Maybe even an eight. Strong enough to do some heavy-duty damage.

I pictured Dad, passed out drunk on the sofa as usual this time of day, and felt a chill wash through me. What if the ceiling in our run-down apartment had collapsed? He'd never know what hit him. And Mom. She was probably on her way to work when the quake struck. Were the roads damaged? Was the theater where she had a bit part this month intact? Okay, so my parents weren't exactly Ozzie and Harriet. Still, the thought of losing them brought a lump to my throat.

Suddenly I remembered Victoria, alone and half blind in her ancient apartment. What if she was trapped there, or hurt? I had to get out of here, now.

After a cursory examination-by-touch of Apollo to be sure he wasn't injured, I groped my way to the door and turned the knob. It didn't budge. I pushed against it with my full weight

34

and, when that failed, banged my fists and kicked it hard.

"Jammed," I said, feeling cold fear close around my throat. Apollo panted anxiously. "How could that have happened?"

Don't panic, I told myself, ignoring the disturbing thought that no one would miss me for hours—if then. Inch by inch, I moved my hands over the walls, praying for another exit. The one Nathaniel found. Or had it been plastered over during Fenniwick's remodeling?

It was painfully slow going. I've no idea how long in real time; it could have been 30 minutes or three hours. But after what seemed an eternity, I found it—the second door, the entrance to the roof. Pushing it open, I stepped onto a narrow set of stairs leading to the widow's walk on the roof. I took them two at a time. "Thank goodness," I said, realizing how odd I must sound talking to a dog. I inhaled the cool night air, then crossed to the rail and looked down.

It was dark. Pitch dark. I frowned. "Must be a power failure caused by the earthquake," I muttered. Swell. How were we supposed to get down from here? I wasn't exactly Spiderman, and Apollo's squat little legs were hardly built for climbing.

"Hey!" I hollered, waving my hands over my head like a lunatic. "Can anybody down there hear me?"

It was then that the quiet struck me. The sirens had stopped. Why? There wasn't a sound, save for the wind in the trees and a vague clip-clop that reminded me of horses' hooves. Even after an earthquake, there should have been traffic noises. . . . Unless a fallen tree or building had blocked off the street, I thought, somehow reassured that I wasn't in *The Twilight Zone*.

I yelled louder. After ten minutes or so it seemed pointless; besides, it was growing chilly up there. I decided to go back in the attic and huddle inside until morning, when it would be easier to summon help.

I found something heavy and propped open the rooftop door to admit some fresh air. A pale glow of moonlight illuminated the end of the attic nearest the roof entrance. To my surprise, I noticed things piled around on the floor—crates, an old chair, a wicker bird cage, and several large trunks. I was sure they hadn't been there before . . . but of course they must have been. I just couldn't see them without the moonlight. Or perhaps the earthquake had toppled a false wall within the attic. I felt my eyes widen and my mouth turn dry. This was it—the miracle I'd been searching for! If these were what I thought they were—forgotten relics from the Stuart family or, for that matter, later residents from the early part of this century—then there was no way the house could be bulldozed until a thorough search for more historical treasures was completed.

Suddenly the floor beneath me rumbled again. "Just an aftershock . . . The w-worst is over," I tried to assure both myself and Apollo, who was

36

alternately nuzzling my ankles and trying to climb my legs.

The room lurched, hurling me against the interior door. Terror gripped me. I had visions of rafters crashing down, burying Apollo and me up here amid the relics we'd stumbled upon. "Help!" I shrieked, pounding on the door with both fists.

It was hinged. Yet I'd seen that very door come off its hinges when I'd forced my way into the attic just a short time ago . . . unless I was the one coming unhinged, I thought, feeling the hairs rise on the back of my neck.

I pounded harder, my knuckles sore from the force of my blows. Logic told me no one could hear us, but I didn't care. This was getting spookier by the minute, and I wasn't about to take it passively a moment longer.

"We're trapped—get us out of here!" My fear must have been contagious. Apollo began barking. I kept banging. The sounds echoed off the walls in the dark chamber, pounding in my head.

The door burst open. I fell backward, stumbling over a crate. A man's silhouette loomed before me, filling the door frame.

"What in thunderation . . . ?" he bellowed.

I peered out from behind the crate, my heart pounding against my ribs. It was too dark to see his face, but it was evident that he was a tall man, powerfully built. He appeared to be wearing a long shirt of some sort—and nothing else. A shiver ran down my spine. Just what I needed, to be rescued by a half-naked maniac. Probably the local slasher holed up here for the night.

"Who are you? How did you get up here?" he demanded.

"Just let us by," I said gamely. "We won't tell anyone you're here."

He appeared to find my words most amusing. "Why should I care what you tell others? This is my house."

Gooseflesh rose on my arms. This guy was really crazy. "F-fine," I stammered, trying to humor him. "Just let us go, and we won't bother you or your house again."

"It seems to me it is you who owe me an explanation. Who are you, and what the devil are you doing in my attic?"

"I—the door slammed shut during the earthquake."

He scowled, stepping closer. There was something vaguely familiar about him, though I could not make out his features in the dim light. "Earthquake?" he scoffed. "What foolery do you speak of? I was studying the stars on the roof just a short while ago, and there was no one up here. How did you manage to scale three stories to my roof? It's . . . impossible." Bending down, he hauled me to my feet and into a silver beam of moonlight.

I squirmed, loathing the way his gaze swept me from head to toe before hastily focusing on my face. He gasped and released me. I grimaced, wishing I was wearing something less revealing than my metallic zip-up-the-front leotard and hot pink tights. Glancing down, I saw that my clothes, hands, and arms were coated with a pale, powdery dust.

"Are you a ghost, madam?" he asked in an astonished tone, standing as though frozen in time. It was the most ridiculous thing I'd ever heard. Here I was in the attic of an abandoned mansion with a half-dressed crazy man, and he was unnerved by me! I suppressed a laugh, feeling my eyes water at the irony of it. I wanted to shout, "Boo," but restrained myself.

"What if I am?" I heard myself say. Perhaps if I could play on his fears, I could escape in one piece.

"Then I should like to analyze you," he said, studying me beneath furrowed brows. His remark made me shudder; I had visions of being dissected and dumped in a canyon somewhere.

I tried to duck beneath his arms and out the doorway beyond, but he grabbed me around the waist with one strong arm and stopped me. "Prudence believes in spirits, but I always thought it a nonsensical indulgence," he said thoughtfully. "Still, a man of science must always keep an open mind."

I struggled to free myself, thrashing about in his arms, digging my nails through the fabric of his shirt.

He swore and pushed me away from him. "No ghost could draw blood, I daresay," he said with a grimace, rubbing his fingers over the torn fabric covering his arm.

Apollo chose that moment to announce his

presence with a bark. He waddled forward into the moonlight.

The man frowned. "What manner of beast is this?"

I silently thanked Apollo for his cue. "A vicious guard dog." I raised my voice to a tone I hoped sounded forceful. "Trained to rip a man to shreds on my command."

Apollo advanced toward the intruder and promptly licked his hand, then lay down and rested his head on the man's foot.

The man's mouth twitched in amusement. "I daresay he doesn't consider me a threat." To Apollo he said, "Let's get you into the light where I can see you better."

Before I could protest, he picked up Apollo, pushed the attic door open, and stepped into the room through which we'd entered. It was dark, except for a faint strand of moonlight filtered through a window. Light? This guy was really nuts.

"For a dog, you're frightfully shriveled," he said, rubbing Apollo's head reassuringly as he examined him in the moonlight. Turning to me, he asked, "Does it have a wasting disease?"

I marveled at his quaint turns of phrase. "He hasn't had the runs, if that's what you mean," I said, stepping into the room after him. Even if he was a homicidal maniac, which I was beginning to doubt, sharing his presence out here seemed preferable to giving him the opportunity to lock me back up in the attic. "Actually, he's a Shar Pei. A breed from China."

He scratched behind Apollo's ears, eliciting a contented whimper. "I've been to the Orient many a time, but never seen such a creature," he noted, curiosity evident in his tone.

Apollo leapt from his arms and tugged at my shoelace. I scooped him up while our unlikely savior closed the attic door behind me. The man strode several paces and lit a wall sconce.

Wall sconce? I rubbed my eyes. I must have hit my head when I fell; my mind was playing tricks on me. No way could this old house still have a working gas lamp after all these years.

Then I looked around the room. To my shock, I saw that it was fully furnished in turn-of-the-century antiques—except they looked brand-new.

I was dreaming. I had to be—though I'd never dreamed in such vivid detail before. A canopied four-poster bed occupied the center of the room; Oriental rugs covered most of a polished wood floor. A sturdy armoire stood in one corner; a full-length mirror on an ornately carved stand sat in another. Windows were draped in forest-green velvet. Wall-mounted shelves displayed treasures such as a pair of scrimshaw whale teeth carved into pagodas, a wooden mermaid that may have once been a ship's figurehead, and an assortment of whimsical miniature mechanical devices— old-fashioned bicycles, carriages, and an oddly out-of-place model that vaguely resembled an airplane.

It was impossible. The room was empty when we came up—I had to be dreaming. I'd been listening to too many tales of Victoria's childhood here, that was all.

Instinctively I clutched for the locket she'd given me and realized it was gone. The chain must have broken during the quake. . . . Then I looked closely at our benefactor in the lamplight and recognized that haunting face from the photograph staring back at me.

Nathaniel Stuart. Impossible though it seemed, it was he. This dream was weirder than I thought—unless somehow the earth had wrenched beneath me and thrust me back 90 years or so in time. But of course that was preposterous.

"Madam?" He bent toward me, concern evident in those riveting dark eyes of his. His photos certainly didn't do him justice, I thought. I'd imagined him to be stodgy and older. But there wasn't a single stodgy inch that I could see on the man before me now.

He was built like a lumberjack—tall and broad chested, with corded muscles on his forearms visible below the rolled-up sleeves of the shirt he wore. It was, I realized belatedly, a nightshirt. I never would have believed a guy could look masculine in one of those, but somehow he managed it, I thought disjointedly as my gaze fixed on the triangular thatch of dark hair visible beneath the unbuttoned top button of his neckline and the muscular legs bared below the hem of his nightshirt.

"Madam, are you well?" he persisted. "You look as though you've seen a ghost."

This wasn't a dream—it was a nightmare. I must have hit my head harder than I thought. I clutched Apollo tightly against my chest and whispered the first thing that popped into my mind. "Geez, Toto, this beats Dorothy's hallucination hands-down."

"Toto? Is that the dog's name?"

I shook my head to clear it. He was still there. "I meant the dog in *The Wizard Of Oz*."

His eyes flashed like black jade. "Wizardry? Are you a sorceress, then? A witch?"

My limbs felt icy. They burned witches back then, didn't they? I couldn't remember if men were more enlightened on the subject by the turn of the century—if, in fact, the century had yet turned. Apollo did nothing to reassure me when he squirmed free and scampered under the bed. But of course this was just a dream, I reminded myself. I'd wake up before anything bad could happen.

"I'm not a witch. I've never even met one," I said, disarming him with a smile. I might as well have some fun with this.

He lowered his brows, studying me. "Who is this wizard you speak of?"

"He's not a real wizard—it's just a movie."

"Movie?" His expression was puzzled.

"Talking pictures," I clarified, to no avail.

"They sound like something from a carnival," he said, half to himself. He eyed my clothing, disdain evident in his expression. "Have you run off from a carnival, then? No," he corrected himself.

"Your garments are too scanty for public display."

"These are perfectly acceptable where I come from," I defended myself, crossing my arms in front of my chest. Instinct told me not to blurt out that he was a figment of my drowsy imagination—or worse, that I was a time traveler from the future. He'd think I was crazy—and I knew what they did with crazy women back in those days. Better to have him think I was a witch or a carnival freak than to find myself locked up in a madhouse before I could wake up and return to my own time. Besides, for a figment he was incredibly handsome, I thought, mentally tracing the strong jawline and bold chiseled features that looked as though they belonged on one of those bronze statues I'd seen in museums. The idea of staying with him and enjoying this dream while it lasted was starting to seem infinitely preferable to a nightmare ending in a loony bin.

He took a step toward me and brushed the fabric on my shoulder with his fingertips. His touch radiated warmth into my chilled flesh. Warmth? I shivered at the sensation. If this was a dream, why could I feel heat and cold?

"I've never seen fabric like this," he observed. "It isn't cotton, and it has a sheen like silk. Where did you procure it?"

I couldn't very well tell him it came from an aerobics specialty shop down the block. "It was a gift," I replied.

He nodded, a look of scorn crossing his features. "I thought as much." Next he gestured toward the fanny pack around my waist. "That cummerbund, or whatever you're wearing—was it also a gift from one of your many patrons?"

"I don't know what you're talking about," I said, frowning.

He looked at my running shoes. "Curious footwear," he noted, reading the lettering. "*Nike . . .* Why do you wear the name of the goddess of victory on your feet?"

"It's just a brand name," I said, staring at the intent gleam in his eyes.

Sensing my unease, he motioned me to sit down. I did, on his bed. I felt myself sinking in its feathery softness and had an irrational image of losing my innocence here decades before I was even born. Surprisingly, the idea suddenly didn't seem at all undesirable.

"They don't make beds like this anymore," I remarked. Or men like him, I thought. I gave him an inviting smile. This was my dream, after all. I didn't have to behave rationally. I might as well cast myself into a role I'd never act out in real life.

His gaze traveled to the front of my leotard. "Why do you wear that metal device?"

"The zipper?"

"I do not know what this 'zipper' is for."

I shrugged. Heck, this was just a fantasy. Why not live dangerously? I unzipped it several inches.

Beads of perspiration formed on his forehead. "Fascinating," he said, exhaling slowly.

Me? Or the zipper? His next actions answered

45

my unspoken question. With the dispassionate focus of a scientist, he bent forward and tried the zipper—tugging it upward. It caught on my sports bra; I trembled as his hands brushed against my bare skin. The caress of his palm and the warmth of his breath against my exposed cleavage sent a white-hot jolt through me. My pulse quickened; he certainly *felt* real. . . .

Awareness dawned on his face; a muted shade of red spread up his neck as he expelled a ragged breath and fumbled to refasten the zipper.

Humiliated at his less-than-subtle turndown, I slipped my hands under his. "You have to hold the sides together at the top and then pull up, like this." I demonstrated.

He pulled his hands away as though I'd burned him. "Don't ply your wiles on me, woman. I'll not betray the trust of my beloved."

My heart deflated. I'd made a total fool out of myself. Life was the pits. Not even in my dreams . . .

He paced the room, struggling to contain his annoyance. Finally he turned toward me, his features calm. "You needn't be afraid to tell me the truth," he coaxed, standing closer to me. "Despite your wanton behavior, I won't send you back."

"Back where?" I asked, startled. How could he know? I had an irrational thought that maybe this wasn't a dream at all; that I really had fallen into the past—summoned there by some sort of spell.

He flashed a confident smirk that made his mustache quiver. "To the bordello you've run away from. Don't bother to deny it—I should have known it from the first by your clothes, though I confess I've never seen a bodice or corset of such fine cloth."

"Is that what you think?" I said, aghast. Okay, so I'd flirted with the guy—that didn't give him the right to treat me like a prostitute. The nerve! What if he offered me money for my services? Would he become enraged when I refused?

I couldn't help but note the spark of lust in his eyes as his gaze swept downward, over the curves my leotard failed to disguise. "There was a time when I'd have eagerly sampled your wares," he said, raising an eyebrow devilishly. "You're an enchantress, all right," he observed, his lips curling upward in admiration, "though not the sort I first imagined."

"You keep your imagination in check," I warned, crossing my arms over my chest.

Reluctantly he averted his gaze. "I ought to put you out with the cat," he said dryly. "But out of respect for my mother, bless her sainted heart, I won't."

"Your mother?" Great. All I needed was a confrontation with some dowager matron ready to brand a scarlet *A* on my forehead, or whatever the letter was for unmarried wanton women.

"She used to take in fallen women who wanted to reform," he explained. "Soiled doves, she called them. She said it was the Christian thing to do. Papa supported her efforts, despite the scornful treatment she received from some society members."

"She must be a remarkable woman." I relaxed slightly.

"She was. She died when I was just a boy."

"Of course, I should have remembered that," I said, flustered.

He stared at me oddly. "How would you know such a thing?"

I felt a flush rising on my face until I was sure it must match the color of my hair. "I must have heard from someone. . . ."

"One of your clients, no doubt," he said in a clipped tone. "Did they also tell you that my step-mother was a reformed harlot who called herself an actress?"

I inhaled sharply. "I never knew. . . ."

He clenched his hands, his voice raw with emotion. "Papa was smitten with her the moment he saw her onstage, so he endured the snickers of his friends and wedded that Jezebel despite the whispers about her reputation. And what did he get for his efforts?"

"A broken heart," I answered, shifting uncomfortably. This was not, I deduced, the right time to tell him of my theatrical experience, or that I came from a long line of actors and actresses.

"Precisely," he said, staring disapprovingly at my face. "Not long after my sister was born, Jessica ran off to her former life. Papa never recovered from the shock; he died of heart failure not long after. She killed him, sure as if she'd fired a bullet into his heart."

I had an urge to reach out and comfort him, but resisted. With my luck, he'd probably think I

48

was trying to seduce him for a fee. I cringed at the irony of it: This Victorian man was looking down his nose at me—the last known collegiate virgin in the twentieth century—because he believed I was a hooker!

"I'm sorry," I said simply. "I understand why you find it hard to trust me."

He glanced at me warily. "You remind me of her a great deal. Your features, that tangled mass of chestnut hair, even those green cat's eyes resemble hers." He expelled an exasperated sigh. "Still, if you've a mind to change your ways I suppose there's always a faint hope some patient soul might school you for a more suitable profession. Can you sew?"

I shook my head.

"Cook?"

I paused, thinking longingly of the family microwave. "Not much," I confessed.

He looked decidedly unhappy. "Read?" he persisted.

"Yes—I love reading." I smiled, eager to please him even as my mind raced, wondering when I'd wake up.

He gave a grunt of satisfaction. "That's something, I suppose. In the meantime, we shall have to find you a place to stay. It isn't proper for you to remain here."

I felt my stomach fall as he continued. "Naturally something must be done about those clothes," he said, casting a look to melt iron as he glanced at my attire. Seeing my blush, he reached for his robe hanging on a brass wall peg and thrust it into my hands. "Cover yourself with this for now," he ordered.

I obeyed.

"I can't very well send you packing like that," he muttered, shaking his head. At his insistence, I followed him into the darkened hall, Apollo at my heels.

He walked down the third-story hall to a door two rooms down from his own and ushered me inside. Apollo barked obligingly, reminding me of my manners. "Thank you for your hospitality," I said.

He lit a bedside lamp and motioned me to sit. "Don't thank me yet," he cautioned. "This is only for tonight. First thing tomorrow, you'll have to find lodging elsewhere." Picking up a ceramic pitcher, he poured water into a large bowl on the nightstand. "You'd best freshen up," he said, making me wince at the thought of how I must look, plastered with dust and dog fur.

I stepped up to the bowl and splashed cold water on my face, savoring the cool wetness on my grime-coated skin.

"There is a bathroom on this floor, between our rooms, if you require one," he said stiffly.

I smiled, relieved. I'd been wondering whether I'd be forced to use a chamber pot.

He looked down at me, an awkward expression on his face. He was, I realized, a very large man who dwarfed the dainty room in which we stood. Tall, yet more; he had an overpowering presence that was impossible to ignore.

"It seems I've neglected to introduce myself

formally," he said. "Nathaniel Stuart, though I expect you already knew my name before you decided to scale my roof and drop into my attic. Tell me, what do you call yourself?"

"Taylor."

He paused an instant, then accepted my offered right hand. His grip was strong, yet surprisingly gentle. "A solid surname," he acknowledged. "And your given name?"

"Taylor is my first name," I explained. "James is my last. After the singer . . . I mean, an artist my mother admired."

"Never heard of him."

"Next to Jim Croce, he was her favorite," I rambled, wondering why I was speaking in past tense about someone who theoretically hadn't been born yet. This dream was certainly taking a long time to get over with. The lyrics of Croce's "Time in a Bottle" floated through my head: "If I could save time in a bottle, the first thing that I'd like to do . . ." Was that what I was doing—saving time? Or, perhaps, saving lives. Was it possible that this wasn't a dream—that I really was in the past, and could change the course of events? My mind reeled. But of course that was absurd.

A corner of Nathaniel's mouth tilted downward as he gazed at me in puzzlement. "Taylor. Odd name for a female, especially one as . . . becoming as yourself." I could see him mentally pondering the origin of my name, not the sort one would acquire in my supposed profession. I imagined him wondering why I wasn't calling myself Belle or Brandy or Flame, and found myself irrationally annoyed at the prospect. Why should it matter to me what he thought? Just as long as he didn't think me crazy enough to boot me out on the street.

A voice from the hall interrupted my thoughts. "Nathaniel? Are you in here? I heard someone talking. . . ."

A beautiful child burst into the room, reminding me of a porcelain doll with her smooth ivory skin and long dark ringlets that fell to below the waist of the prim nightgown she wore.

"Victoria!" Nathaniel scolded. "Haven't I taught you to knock before barging into a room?"

My mouth dropped open. This was the little girl who was to become the scarred old spinster I had interviewed just this morning, yet she seemed more unlike that ancient Victoria than I would have believed possible. I was astonished by the contrast between the faded photographs I'd seen and the vibrance of the youthful Victoria who had just burst into the room, exuding more color and vitality than a Renoir painting. She looked to be around 11 or 12 years old, which meant my dream must be set sometime in the early 1900s. Post-Victorian era, but just barely.

"I'm sorry," she said, looking up at him through long silky lashes. Her eyes darted from Nathaniel to me, then back again. "I didn't know you had company."

Suddenly my gaze fastened upon the gold chain around her neck. As though reading my mind, she slipped the locket that had been tucked inside her gown free and fingered it idly. It was,

I saw instantly, the identical locket that the elderly Victoria had given me—the one I'd lost during the earthquake. My tongue felt frozen in my mouth. This was too much of a coincidence. . . .

The truth hit me with the force of a 9.0 quake. I'd "lost" the locket because it couldn't be in two places at one time. If this really was the early 1900s, then Victoria wouldn't give me that locket for another 85 or 90 years! Could time shifts occur simultaneously with the disruption caused by shifting geologic plates colliding here? Geomagnetic forces out of whack . . . the reason why compasses failed to work in this house, as Victoria had once told me. . . .

I tugged free the odometer with built-in compass clipped to my fanny pack and held it up before me. The hand was pointing in the wrong direction. I spun it about and stared at it, dumbstruck, as it wobbled to a stop—pointing due south.

Chapter Three

My heart felt like a freight train thundering against my ribs. My parents' faces flashed through my mind; I felt terrified to realize I might never see them again. Incredible though it seemed, I knew then that I'd somehow been thrust back in time to post-Victorian San Francisco. The Edwardian era, to be technical about it. My head spun at the awesome prospect.

Apollo, who had enthroned himself comfortably on a ruffled pillow at the head of the bed, roused upon hearing the girl's voice. He cocked his head to one side, then bounded across the room and leaped into her arms as though greeting a long-lost friend. Could he somehow sense that this was the same Victoria who in another lifetime had pampered him with chamomile tea? He licked her face, wagging his tail shamelessly.

A grin spread across her face. "Isn't he marvelous?" She glanced at me out of the corners of her eyes. "What do you call him?"

"Apollo," I answered, still in shock.

She studied him nose to nose. "Yes," she said. "It suits him. He is a handsome beast, in a funny sort of way."

Turning to her brother, she asked in a pert tone, "Nathaniel, aren't you going to introduce me to your guest?"

Nathaniel's discomfort was tangible, cast toward me like a lifeline thrown to a drowning person. I detected a scarlet flush creeping up his neck. What must Victoria think, finding me alone with her older brother here at night, dressed only in his robe and my skimpy aerobics outfit underneath?

"I'm a cousin of yours," I improvised, ignoring the warning glance hurled my way from Nathaniel. "My name is Taylor."

Victoria's face lit up. "A cousin! On my mother's side?"

"Our father's," Nathaniel said sternly. "A distant cousin, I should say."

If Victoria was disappointed, it scarcely showed. "I never knew I had any girl cousins," she said, covering her mouth with the back of her hand to stifle a giggle. "You must be here for the wedding. We shall have such a time together, you and I! Did you know my mother well? You shall have to tell me all about her."

"I never met her," I said, feeling guilty over my deception. Was she referring to Nathaniel's wedding to Prudence? If so, the event must be close at hand, which meant that . . . I felt the hairs on the back of my neck stiffen over that chilling prospect.

"Oh." Victoria looked crestfallen. "Well, it doesn't matter. Will you be staying long?"

"I'm afraid Miss James can't—"

"I've come a long way to see you," I interrupted, daring a glance at Nathaniel, who was glowering at me over the child's head. "Believe me, I wouldn't miss this wedding for the world."

Her brother looked as if he were about to blow a gasket, but I knew he wouldn't contradict me. How else could he explain my presence, save to admit that he'd invited a woman he believed was a whore into his home for the night?

"Hooray!" The child flung herself at me, wrapping her arms around my legs, squeezing Apollo in between us. She glanced up at me, a mischievous twinkle in her eyes, and I had the unsettling feeling that she knew exactly what she'd just accomplished.

Nathaniel pried her loose and freed her hold on Apollo as well. "After the wedding Saturday, Miss James has other matters to attend to," he said, his mouth a firm line. "First thing Sunday morning, she must be on the road."

Sunday—what day was this, anyway? The wedding, assuming it was Nathaniel's, must be no more than a few days away. But perhaps it was another wedding, a friend or relative. "In my travels I'm afraid I've quite lost track of time," I fished. "Nathaniel, could you be so kind as to tell me today's date?"

"April 11th. Wednesday."

I felt as if the ground were giving way again beneath my feet. "1906?" I whispered, scarcely daring to breathe.

He looked at me as though I'd lost my mind. "Of course."

One week before the earthquake. Was that why I'd been brought here—to alter Victoria's fate? Or Nathaniel's, for that matter. Maybe even the whole Stuart family. I staggered a step backward and gripped the bedpost behind me, speechless.

"Come, Victoria." Nathaniel hooked his arm through his little sister's and led her out the door. He glanced at my face, which must have been white as a bridal gown, and observed, "I'm sure Miss James is quite exhausted from her trip."

She looked back at me triumphantly. "Yes, dear brother. I'm sure you're quite right. But tell me, where are all of her bags?"

"Lost in transit," I answered for him. He didn't show me any gratitude, but at least he didn't look furious enough to lock me back up in the attic, for now.

"Oh. Well, I'm sure they shall turn up. Good night, Miss James," Victoria offered.

"Please call me Taylor," I insisted.

"Taylor. I like that. It sounds like a person who can create wonderful things from whatever materials are at hand. Someone who can alter things. Sweet dreams." She smiled, then vanished into the hall.

I'd never thought of my name quite that way. "Good night," I said, intrigued.

Nathaniel gave me a drop-dead look before closing the door behind him. "Don't let the bed-bugs bite you," he said through gritted teeth, "*cousin*."

I slept fitfully and awoke when the first rays of dawn streamed through the wooden blinds, bathing my face in warmth. Opening my eyes, I experienced a momentary shock at my surroundings until the night's events came flooding back to me. I blinked, but nothing changed. I really was living in the past—Victoria's past.

I mulled over the events of the night before and found my thoughts dwelling on Victoria's strange comment about my name. Taylor . . . someone who can alter things. Like the past, perhaps. Could I really change history? Should I? If I did, would I be stuck here forever? The prospect chilled me to the bone.

One step at a time, Taylor, I told myself. I rose stiffly, discovering sore muscles from the tumbles I'd taken during the quake. Would the big one due to hit in six days be even worse? I shuddered, aching for a hot bath and a hot cup of coffee.

Then I saw the clothes laid out at the foot of the bed—a bustled dress in muted shades of gray trimmed with pearl buttons, a matching bonnet, heavy stockings, and a pile of awkward-looking underwear. "Suitable for a missionary," I mumbled, wondering how on earth I was supposed to fasten all those tiny buttons on the back of the dress by myself. I picked up a pair of high-topped shoes and found the answer—a buttonhook tucked inside.

Stealing a glance at Apollo, who had burrowed under the bedcovers and was snoring contentedly, I decided now was a good time to check out the facilities next door. So I bunched the clothes up into my arms, slipped down the hall and into the bathroom between my room and Nathaniel's without so much as a second thought about my sleepyheaded pup.

Eagerly I stripped off my leotard and tights, ran piping hot water in the claw-footed porcelain bathtub, and dumped in a capful of lavender water from a bottle on a shelf. Victoria's, no doubt.

After relieving myself in a pull-chain toilet that looked as though it belonged in an antique store, I turned off the water, climbed into the tub, and sank back, savoring the fragrant hot water that rose almost to my neck.

I lay with my eyes closed for a long while, unwilling to face the complications that lay ahead just yet. Somehow I had to find a way back before the April eighteenth earthquake struck. But how?

It hit me like a seismic wave. I'd come here during an earthquake, so it stood to reason that if I could arrange to be in the attic at the critical moment, I could return the same way. The way, perhaps, that Nathaniel had disappeared.

Would disappear, I corrected myself.

I pondered the consequences as I began washing up. Could I stop him? Should I? Was Nathaniel's body buried beneath the rubble during the earthquake, or did he truly disappear, as Victoria suggested? Perhaps he too wound up as a traveler in time. But if so, where did he emerge—in the future? Or was he thrust further into the past, as I was? The prospects were mind-boggling.

My relaxation broken, I concluded it was time to face the day. I stood up, soap bubbles clinging to my damp skin, and reached for a towel hanging on a wall hook beside the tub.

I was so caught up in my thoughts that I didn't even hear the door open. But I did hear Nathaniel's startled intake of breath as he saw me standing there, stark naked except for a few strategically placed bubbles.

He looked away hastily. "Excuse me, Miss James," he said, backing out the door.

I grabbed for the towel, splashing water onto the floor. My foot slipped on the soapy tub and I felt myself falling.

Nathaniel dashed forward, catching me just as I stopped myself from bashing my head on the edge of the tub.

"Are you all right?"

"F-fine, thanks. I think," I sputtered, pulling myself out of the water. The towel was sopping wet.

His face reddened as he realized where his hands rested—on the waist and rump of a dripping wet nude woman. He yanked his hands off me as if he'd been burned; I too felt scorched from his touch, which seared me like a brand.

"Here, allow me to help," he insisted, offering me a dry towel monogrammed with his initials as he assumed a more proper distance, if there were such a thing under the circumstances.

I snatched the towel and pulled it around me, my skin still scorched from the imprint of his hands as a rush of heat flooded through me.

"I was out in my workshop," he tried to explain. "I didn't mean . . ." He paused, wrestling for the right words. "I passed by your room when I came back in and heard—"

"Snoring?"

"Precisely," he said, clearing his throat. "I assumed you were still abed."

I clutched the towel against my breasts. "It was the dog. I'm quite awake, I assure you."

"Yes," he said, a rakish grin playing at the corners of his mouth. "That much is obvious now." His hand brushed the dark stubble on his chin. "I intended merely to shave, not indulge myself in a more entertaining diversion, though I'll confess the notion is tempting. You're quite captivating—nearly enough to make me forget I'm an engaged man. . . ."

My skin prickled at the turn his thoughts were taking. I glanced toward the garments hanging on a second hook, anxious to change the subject. "Thanks for the clothes." For some perverse reason I asked, "Do they belong to Prudence?"

The lust in his eyes turned to stone at the mention of his fiancee. "Of course not."

"Oh," I said, feeling like an idiot as he turned away and stepped into the hall without another word, pulling the door closed behind him.

I stood there wrapped in his bath towel, feeling the heat of his gaze—and hands—on my bare flesh long after he left the room. I recalled the seductive feel of him touching me the night before, when I'd given him a crash course in Zippers 101, and found myself imagining what a worldly man like Nathaniel Stuart might teach me in return.

Unnerved, I turned my attention to the chore of dressing. I fingered the undergarments: a corsetlike device with a built-in brassiere, a thin cotton garment similar to a teddy, petticoats, drawers, stockings, and a collapsible bustle. In what order was I supposed to put them on?

I was stumped. During my time as a theatrical costume assistant during my father's heyday, the actresses had only needed to appear authentically clothed on the outside—never underneath.

After struggling with the bulky underwear for half an hour, trying to figure out how to lace a corset on myself, I was ready to chuck the whole pile and flout convention by wearing my leotard and tights beneath the dress. Then someone knocked on the door.

"Miss James? Are ye in there? Mr. Stuart told me o' yer arrival and said ye might could use a hand dressin'. May I come in?"

I flung open the door and found a short, plump, white-haired woman wearing a housekeeper's uniform, a sparkle in her blue eyes and a grin that spanned her rosy cheeks.

"Thank heavens," I said, relieved. "I'm afraid I'm not used to—"

"T' dressin' yourself. O' course not. What lady o' means is?" chuckled the woman. "I'm Mrs. O'Hara, by the way. Turn around, now,'n' let me take care o' that for ye."

O'Hara, I registered the name mentally. The housekeeper who doused the flames that burned Victoria. She could be a good ally, I sensed. At least she thought I was a lady—not a slut.

"Thank you," I said, obliging her request.

Fifteen minutes later I was properly decked out in what I assumed was the fashionable vogue of the era. I surveyed myself in the mirror. The bodice fit too snugly and the hem was too short, stopping just above my ankles. Overall, though, the outfit was conservative to say the least. Give me a lunch satchel and I could pass for a character from "Little House on the Prairie." But at least Nathaniel would be able to pass me off as a relative rather than some hussy straight out of a whorehouse—or a stranger from another time.

"Pity about your trunks bein' lost durin' a train robbery," Mrs. O'Hara sympathized.

"Robbery . . . ?" I started to question, then realized Nathaniel would have had to come up with some logical explanation to explain my lack of attire. "Yes, it was."

"Now, if ye'll tell me where yer travelin' clothes are, I'll see to launderin' them for ye," she said, frowning as she adjusted the train attached to the bustle on my behind.

"I don't have any. That is," I corrected hastily,

63

"they were ruined during the, uh, robbery. So I threw them away." I used my toe to nudge the spandex beneath a crumpled towel on the floor, flushing at the memory of Nathaniel's hands on the towel—and on me.

Mrs. O'Hara shook her head. "The law ought t' do something t' stop those ruffians. It isn't right. . . ."

A doorbell chimed downstairs. "Oh my, company so early." She fluffed her cap and smoothed down the pinafore over her uniform. "If ye'll excuse me, ma'am—"

"Of course," I said.

"I'll see there's some breakfast downstairs for ye when ye're ready." She bobbed her head and departed.

After she left I attempted to stuff my feet into the high-topped shoes, but it was hopeless. They were two sizes too small. I was no Cinderella. My size-nine running shoes would have to do, for the moment.

I ducked into the hall and stopped in the guest bedroom to check on Apollo. He was, I saw to my dismay, awake and making himself very much at home.

"Bad dog!" I yelled as I lunged toward him, ready to wring his wrinkled neck. But the damage was done.

Two columns of teeth marks lined the mahogany bedpost and the sheets were stained with dog slobber. Worse, Apollo had succeeded in shredding the hand-embroidered comforter and strewing goose down all over the room. Now he

64

was perched on the remains of a bed pillow in the midst of the destruction, flashing a lopsided grin, hanging his tongue out like a proud banner.

I pressed a hand to my forehead to steady myself. Dorothy never had to put up with hassles like this, I thought, groaning. At that moment I'd gladly have coped with witches and flying monkeys instead of the four-footed cyclone on my bed.

A hand closed on my shoulder from behind. I nearly jumped out of my skin at the sound of Nathaniel's steel-edged voice.

"What manner of demon have you brought into my home, woman?" he demanded.

"I'm sorry," I said unsteadily. "I can't believe what a mess he made. . . ."

"I'll make sure the little hellion doesn't get a second chance," he bellowed, advancing on Apollo with a murderous glare.

I stepped between them, facing him head-on. "Please don't hurt him. . . . I'll make it up to you." Dumb move, I thought the moment the words left my lips. I didn't have any money to pay for the damage—at least, none that had been minted yet. Recalling my supposed profession, I was afraid he would demand payment in trade.

"Don't tempt me," he growled. He pushed me aside with no more thought than if I were a gnat and hoisted Apollo by the scruff of the neck. "Wretched animal," he cursed, glaring at the dog nose to nose. "I ought to tan that wrinkled hide of yours."

Stuffing the dog under his arm, he turned back

toward the door—and me. To my shock, the angry expression melted from his face as he took in the new me. A subtle light of approval shone in his eyes and he nodded, stroking his chin thoughtfully with his free hand. "An amazing difference," he said. "If I didn't know better, I'd almost believe you were a proper lady."

I wasn't sure what to say to that backhanded compliment, so I kept my mouth shut. Uncomfortably I wondered if he was remembering what I looked like naked and found myself recalling against my will the heat of his hands radiating against my bare, damp flesh—a far from unpleasant sensation, to be honest.

He raised one hand to the nape of my neck and lifted my hair from underneath. "Do something about those tresses, however," he muttered. "Your hair is wild as the March winds. Reminds me of Victoria's—the way the child has run about like a ragamuffin after her mother ran off. . . ."

"Okay, I'll fix it. But wait for me," I pleaded, relieved that he'd distracted himself from murdering Apollo, at least for the moment. Grudgingly, he nodded.

I snatched up my fanny pack from the bedside table and fished in it for my scrunchy ponytail holder. Hastily I stuffed my hair through the holder and did my best to tie the whole mess up in a knot. I studied his face—handsomer in daylight than by lamplight, dusted now by a faint stubble of beard—in the mirror above the white vanity in front of me as I worked. "You love your sister very much, don't you?" I asked, tucking the rebellious ends of my hair back up under the elastic holder.

He paced restlessly, Apollo squirming under his arm. Finally he plunked the dog down on the floor at his feet. "Stay," he commanded gruffly. To my amazement, Apollo obeyed.

"The child needed a firm hand to guide her," he replied at last. "I've been more a father to her than a brother, though lately I've wondered if that's enough." A nostalgic look clouded his hauntingly dark eyes. "It's hard on a child, losing a parent."

"You still miss her, don't you?" I asked quietly.

"Jessica?" His voice sounded startled.

I shook my head, suddenly feeling the pain of a small boy losing his mother to death. "Your mother."

A shadow fell across the craggy features on his face. "I was young; I scarcely remember her." After an awkward pause, he changed the subject. "You realize you can't possibly attend my wedding, despite your rash promise to Victoria."

Startled, I dropped the brush. "What?"

"It's out of the question, of course," he said, his bass voice resonating in the small room. "Not all the wedding guests are saints. What if one of the upstanding gentlemen of the community there should recognize you?"

I let out the breath I'd been holding. "They won't. I'm absolutely sure of that."

He stroked his mustache thoughtfully. "You told Victoria you'd come a long distance. . . . Is that true?"

I nodded, not daring to say more.

"So you ran off from a brothel in some one-horse town and came to the big city," he concluded, apparently satisfied. "And the men in San Francisco haven't yet sampled your, er, charms?"

I vented my resentment by cinching the scrunchy up tighter. "No! That is . . ."

The scrunchy distracted his attention. "Odd, but practical," he pronounced after inspecting it up close. "I fancy Victoria would enjoy one of those."

"I have an extra. She can have it," I said quickly, to stop him from asking where he might buy something that wouldn't be invented for years.

"That won't be necessary," he said, frowning.

My heart sank. Naturally, I realized, Nathaniel would never deem it suitable for his precious baby sister to sport a hair ornament worn by a whore.

For an instant I wanted to blurt out the truth—to tell him I wasn't what he thought. But pride stopped me. I couldn't bear the thought of having him look at me thinking I was crazy, as he surely would if I told him where I'd really come from.

He glanced at Apollo, who waited obediently at his feet, then turned to me. "There's a wire pen out back; my mother used to keep geese there for her comforters."

"Like that one?" I glanced toward the shredded bed, feeling the pit of my stomach cave in.

"It was one of her better creations," he said

gruffly. "In the future, that monster of yours must stay in its pen."

"Of course," I agreed quickly. "Then . . . I can stay for the wedding?"

"Only because Victoria has her heart set on the idea." He stooped down, making eye contact with Apollo. "As for you, young scamp, it's high time you learn who's in charge."

Apollo arose, studying Nathaniel through narrowed eyes as though he'd understood every word. To my amazement, Nathaniel scratched the ingrate under his chin and spoke to him in a low, soothing tone.

"You really ought to show some self-restraint," he admonished. Showing no sign of adhering to the Victorian creed, Apollo lolled onto his side, inviting Nathaniel to scratch his belly. "Your mistress tells me you're from China," Nathaniel observed, stroking the wrinkled, silky skin. "I'll wager you must come from a line of emperors' pets, judging from your behavior."

I rolled my eyes. Apollo certainly managed to turn on the charm when it counted.

"Dogs are no different than women," Nathaniel proclaimed. "Both must be taught their proper place."

I couldn't believe my ears. Of all the male chauvinistic, pigheaded things I'd ever heard, this took the cake. I opened my mouth to protest, but before I could get the words out Nathaniel had scooped up the dog and motioned me to follow. "Come," he ordered as we stepped into the hall.

"You must be hungry. I'll take Adonis to his pen—"

"Apollo."

"Whichever. Let me show you to the kitchen. Breakfast should be ready. Perhaps our cook can find a juicy ox bone for the dog."

I grimaced. "Apollo doesn't like bones."

He stared at me as though I'd lost my mind. "Doesn't like . . ." he grumbled, visibly checking his temper at the top of the stairs. "Well then, what the devil do you feed him?"

"Pampered Pooch gourmet doggie delights," I answered uneasily.

He looked like a volcano ready to erupt.

"Of course, a nice hamburger patty will do," I added hastily. "Medium rare, heavy on the steak sauce. Or some eggs on toast, over easy with just a touch of salt."

Before he could comment on Apollo's dietary requirements, Mrs. O'Hara ascended the stairs and met us. "So there ye are." She bobbed her head to Nathaniel. "Miss Pratwell and her mother are downstairs, sir. They wish t' see ye."

"Prudence?" Nathaniel's face lit up before he glanced at me. To Mrs. O'Hara he replied, "Tell her I shall be with her just as soon as I take care of some . . . bothersome matters."

The housekeeper bobbed her white head and walked briskly down the stairs. I was unaccountably irritated. Bothersome matter? Was that how he thought of me—as a problem to be rid of so he could run off to the woman waiting for him downstairs? Perversely, I found myself hoping

Prudence was every bit the airhead that Victoria had made her out to be.

Apollo whimpered as Nathaniel stuffed him under one arm and clenched my elbow with the other. "He's really not such a bad pet," I defended my dog as Nathaniel steered me down the stairs. We passed beneath the dazzling Tiffany chandelier that would soon be dashed to smithereens—the last thing Victoria would see before her accident. "Actually, he's a very good judge of character," I rambled on, pushing darker thoughts aside for the time being. "He adores children, and he only growls at people he doesn't trust. You should see what he did once to this guy who tried to . . ."

Just then, Apollo squirmed free and bounded down the last flight. He bolted across the ballroom below and through a wide door frame with Nathaniel and me in hot pursuit, emerging into a room that I recognized as the parlor from the old photos I'd seen. The dog made a beeline toward an elegantly dressed young woman wearing a rosebud-pink Gibson Girl ensemble. Prudence, I presumed, drawing in my breath sharply.

"Apollo," I scolded, lunging forward in a botched attempt to snatch him up before he could cause more mischief. I missed, tripped over my shoelace, and fell face-first onto an Aubusson rug smack-dab in the middle of the floor.

I rolled over and found myself staring at the toes of Prudence Pratwell's pointed and perfectly polished shoes.

Chapter Four

"Eeeeeek!" Prudence shrieked. "Get that wretched beast away from me!"

I pulled myself up in time to see her frantically trying to shoo Apollo away from the hem of her skirt. "What sort of monster have you taken into your home, Natty? It looks like a—a gargoyle!"

I was so humiliated I wanted to sink through the floor. Then the realization of what Apollo was up to hit me. "Stop it!" I commanded. "Apollo, don't you dare—"

Ignoring me, Apollo sniffed the woman's hemline, pawed at the fabric, and promptly lifted his leg to piddle on Prudence.

"Nathaniel—get rid of it!" she screeched, whacking Apollo on the head with a parasol as a damp stain spread across the front of her gown. "Kill it!"

Afraid he might do just that, I snatched Apollo out of harm's way, scrambled to my feet, and turned to face Nathaniel's fiancee.

So this was the woman who would barely wait until her one-year mourning period was up to marry another man after Nathaniel's supposed death; the woman whose bad judgment was destined to ruin this house and the Stuart family fortune. Prudence—the woman whose name couldn't be farther from the truth.

Put a lid on it, I told myself. You've got to keep an open mind. After all, you only know what Victoria's told you.

I forced myself to study Prudence objectively. She wasn't the soft spoken bit of fluff I'd imagined—though she was more beautiful than her photo implied. In fact, she could have given Miss America a run for her money with her delicate features, creamy complexion, and dark hair swooped up under a hat trimmed with enough pink ostrich feathers to make a good-size duster. Instinctively I touched my hair; tufts stuck out every which way above the ponytail holder hanging lopsidedly at the base of my neck. In the frumpy gray dress, I felt like a park pigeon displayed beside an exotically plumed bird.

Even if she was screeching like a plucked cockatiel.

Look, I chided myself. Give her a chance. You'd be ticked off too if someone's pet had just christened your petticoat.

"I'm sorry," I apologized. "I really don't know what came over him."

Prudence calmed down finally and raised a properly powdered nose in the air. "Nathaniel"—she sniffed—"do have your servant remove that creature at once."

I cleared my throat. "I'm not a servant."

Nathaniel stepped between us. "Must your every step be a misstep?" he demanded of me under his breath as he pried Apollo from my arms. "You haven't been imbibing, I hope."

"Of course not!" I whispered indignantly, thinking of my father. "I'm no alcoholic. I—"

Ignoring my protests, he turned to his fiancee, grasping Apollo by the scruff of his neck. "Prudence, my dear. I'd no idea you were coming this morning. . . ."

A portly woman rose from the depths of a crushed velvet loveseat behind Prudence. "Really, Nathaniel." She looked down her nose at our host. "After you wed my daughter you simply must maintain a more respectable decorum in this . . . this menagerie of yours."

He swallowed hard and flashed me a frosty stare as he addressed his future mother-in-law. "I assure you, Mrs. Pratwell, this won't happen again." Glancing at the puddle beside Prudence's gown, he yanked on a tasseled bellpull. Instantly a maid appeared.

"Clean up this mess and see if there's a clean frock somewhere for Miss Pratwell," he ordered.

"Yes, sir," she said, scurrying to the first task.

"Borrow a gown from a maid? Nathaniel, I shall do no such thing," Prudence fussed, crossing her arms as her lower lip poked out in a pout. "My favorite dress—it's ruined, I'm certain of it!"

The maid sponged and dabbed while Prudence sulked some more. "You needn't carry on so," Nathaniel told her, the corners of his mouth curving downward in disapproval. "It's only a frock, after all."

Prudence managed a faint smile and batted her eyelashes at Nathaniel. "You're right, of course," she said in a sugary tone. "How foolish of me to forget. Once we're married, I'm sure you'll buy me all the gowns I need."

I felt sick. How could Nathaniel be taken in by a woman like that? She was as shallow as a tide pool on a rock, and even more transparent. But Nathaniel loved her—didn't he? Maybe she had some redeeming qualities I hadn't seen. I owed it to Nathaniel to find out.

Apollo squirmed in Nathaniel's grasp, forcing him to resume his mission. Halfway to the door he tightened his grip on the dog and turned to Prudence, who was smoothing down every dark hair on her head.

"Forgive my lapse of manners." He gestured toward me. "Prudence, allow me to introduce my cousin, Taylor James. She's come for the wedding. Miss James, I'd like you to meet my betrothed, Miss Pratwell, and her mother, Grace."

Grace? I fought down a giggle. The woman had about as much grace as a Roller Derby queen.

Prudence appraised me head to toe with all the affection she might display toward a rat in the pantry. "That's odd," she said, her ice blue eyes puncturing me with a pointed stare. "Nathaniel never mentioned any cousins."

"I can certainly see why not," her mother hissed under her breath, giving me an equally scalding once-over.

Nathaniel spread a broad hand to muzzle Apollo, who was glaring at Prudence and emitting a low growl.

"I'd best show this troublemaker to his new quarters," Nathaniel said, catching my eye. "Ladies"—he emphasized the word, silently warning me to behave—"do make yourselves comfortable."

The maid finished the cleanup, leaving Prudence with only a small irregular damp spot as a souvenir of the occasion. Two other servants appeared, carrying a silver tea set and a platter of scones just as Nathaniel left with Apollo.

For Nathaniel's sake, I settled myself into a tapestry chair opposite Prudence and her mother, determined to make the right impression. "So," I began awkwardly, "how are the wedding plans coming along?"

"Well enough," Grace Pratwell replied in a clipped tone.

Without thinking, I crossed my legs, exposing my white-and-neon-green sneakers. Not exactly high fashion for the day, I was sure. I uncrossed my feet and bent forward, tugging the hemline down.

Prudence's mouth formed a bow. "My, what unusual footwear," she commented dryly. "Though I suppose it's no more surprising than that quaint costume you have on."

I was startled as much by her criticism of Nathaniel's clothing choice as by her rudeness. "What's wrong with my clothes?" I asked.

Her lips curled up at the edges. "Why, nothing," she said, assuming an innocent air. "It's just that I haven't seen anyone wear a bustle since I was a child. Wherever did you find one?"

Men—I guess they never have had any fashion sense. Nathaniel must have dredged up some old dress from one of the maids' trunks. Still, I felt grateful to him for taking me in; at least he hadn't left me to face his fiancee in my leotard and spandex.

"My other clothes were stolen by train robbers." I used the lie to protect Nathaniel. "My cousin loaned me these."

She looked mildly disappointed in my answer, as though she'd hoped my taste was really the pits. Or perhaps she was simply wondering what her fiance was doing with another woman's clothes in his house. Or with another woman, for that matter. I smoothed down the wrinkles in my dress, feeling more uncomfortable by the minute. How much longer until Nathaniel would return?

Mrs. Pratwell poured tea. I sampled mine, resisting the urge to wolf down the whole plateful of scones. After all, I hadn't eaten since lunch yesterday afternoon—a lifetime ago.

"Tell me, Miss James"—the older woman probed, lowering her teacup—"where are you from?"

I swallowed hard, scalding my throat on the hot tea. "I, uh, grew up in the Mission District," I stalled, hoping there was a Mission District back then. Of course there was, I recalled, relaxing. The Mission itself was old, even in 1906. "Since then I've . . . traveled quite a distance."

I was spared any more of the inquisition by Nathaniel's return. "So," he said, settling down beside Prudence. He gave his bride-to-be an affectionate smile and asked, "What brings me the pleasure of your company this morning?"

Pleasure of her company . . . I clenched my teeth. Prudence was proving to be about as pleasant as a cold sore.

"Why Nathaniel, dearest, don't you know I can hardly stand to go through a day without you?" she crooned, smiling seductively.

For a woman raised in the Victorian era, she certainly had a well-perfected pair of bedroom eyes. I felt a pang of jealousy shoot through me. Jealousy? The thought jarred me. The guy was almost a century older than me and engaged to be married on Saturday. Why should I care if he'd slept with a bimbo like Prudence or not? But to my surprise I did.

Mrs. Pratwell cleared her throat, giving her daughter a glare that would wither a giant sequoia. "We've come to go over some final details regarding your upcoming nuptials, not to mention the wedding supper," she informed Nathaniel. "Now, if you'll be so kind as to . . ."

I took this as a convenient cue to exit. "If you'll

excuse me," I said, rising, "I really ought to check on my dog."

"Your dog?" Mrs. Pratwell raised her silver eyebrows. "I might have known," she sniffed, dismissing me without so much as a good-bye.

To his credit, Nathaniel saw me to the back door. "Are you all right?" he asked, a concerned expression on his face.

"Hunky-dory."

He furrowed his brow in confusion. "I know that must have been awkward for you," he said quietly. "You didn't . . . ?"

"Tell them I was a whore?" Seeing the look in his eyes I knew I'd struck a bull's-eye, and it hurt. "No, of course not."

He relaxed visibly. "I'm sorry. I didn't mean for you to meet Prudence this way."

"Were you so afraid that I'd embarrass you?"

His silence told me the truth of my statement. I felt my eyes start to water and closed my eyes to force back the tears. I wasn't good enough for him—or anyone else. I'd lost everyone and everything I'd ever known when I fell back nearly a century, but I still had my pride. I wasn't about to let him see me fall apart.

He gaped at me awkwardly. "There, don't do that." He reached out to dab at my tears with a handkerchief. "It can't have been all that bad."

I blinked, sniffling. "E-even my d-dress wasn't good enough for them." I clasped his handkerchief in my hand and wadded it into a ball. "I'll n-never fit in here, never."

A disturbed look crossed his face. "That's a perfectly fine gown," he said. "Though no doubt a trifle more . . . subdued than you're used to. It was my mother's."

"Your mother's? Nathaniel, I'm sorry," I said, but the damage was done.

A mournful howl emanated from the make-shift kennel outside. Nathaniel stiffened. "Go tend to your dog," he ordered. Pivoting abruptly, he left me standing in the door frame.

I had the uncanny sensation that I'd just been put to a test of some sort—and failed. I clenched my fists in frustration.

Somehow I had to find a way to break through that stone wall he'd built around himself and make him believe in me.

I couldn't just walk back into his attic and disappear out of his life—at least, not without making him see that his marriage to Prudence had to be stopped—for his sake, as well as Victoria's.

A chilling thought sent a ripple down my spine. If I could stop him from marrying Prudence, I'd be changing history. Even if changing the past—make that the future—proved possible, it could be risky. What if I made things worse?

C'mon, I chided myself. Things can't get a heck of a lot worse than disappearing during an earthquake and having your kid sister torched. I pushed my doubts over tinkering with fate to the back of my mind and concentrated on the more ominous problem at hand: What could I possibly do or say to convince Nathaniel that I could foretell the future?

* * *

I found Apollo sulking in his kennel, sprawled on his belly with his nose resting on his paws, an untouched stew bone on the ground just inches from his snout. "I know exactly how you feel," I informed him. I tried to sit down, but the bustle kept getting in the way. Finally I subsided awkwardly on one hip, spreading the gray skirt out carefully so it wouldn't become soiled. Apollo crawled to the chicken-wire fence and pressed his nose against my hand, whimpering pathetically. If misery loved company, we were a perfect match.

"There, sure 'n' it can't be as bad as all that," came Mrs. O'Hara's kindly voice. I raised my head; she was staring at me curiously. "Meself, I don't favor coddlin' animals. But the little mite looked so forlorn, Victoria convinced me he might could use some pamperin', just this once."

I grinned broadly as I spotted the plates she held. On each were two fried eggs and a side of crisped bacon. "Bless you," I said, accepting my plate. I watched as she opened the cage door to place the offering before Apollo. His limp ears perked up and he nuzzled his head against Mrs. O'Hara's ankles. To my amazement, she reached down and scratched his ears. "Sure 'n' he's not such a bad breed after all," she conceded as Apollo proceeded to attack his food with all the grace of a lion devouring a zebra.

My stomach was growling louder than Apollo in a bad mood as I sampled my eggs. "Where's Victoria this morning?" I asked in between bites. "At school?"

The housekeeper shook her head. "The dear child's feelin' poorly this mornin', so she said. Asked for her breakfast in her room, she did."

"Oh." I made a mental note to look in on Victoria later and thank her for making the changes to Apollo's menu.

Time weighed heavy on my hands. I paced the garden near Apollo's cage, anxious for a chance to speak alone with Nathaniel. I wandered among fruit trees and vegetables planted nearby, trying in vain to distract my mind by guessing what was inside each of the various outbuildings. Not even a stroll through the English-style flower garden, spilling over with fragrant blooms and half-wild flowering vines, could calm my frazzled nerves.

But the sight of Nathaniel sent my blood pressure soaring. Without noticing me, he stepped into a large, whitewashed outbuilding and closed the door.

After a few minutes, my curiosity got the better of me. Pushing open the wooden door, I stepped inside.

Nathaniel was seated at a large table on the far side of the room, his back to me. He'd removed his jacket; his cuffs were rolled back and the back of his writing hand was stained with ink. He was studying some plans or blueprints spread out before him, so intent on his work that he didn't hear me enter. On the wall near him were tools of every sort arranged above what was obviously a workbench. Nathaniel's workshop . . . my heart quickened as my eyes adjusted to the dimness.

One wall of the room was covered with detailed drawings and blueprints, all of the same thing. A shelf held a three-foot-high three-dimensional model of the object—a wooden skeleton with two sets of broad canvas-covered wings, a motor, and a rear propeller. Clearly I was looking at plans for Nathaniel's latest invention—a flying machine.

When were airplanes invented? I searched my memory trying to recall what Alex, my brother, had taught me. A lump formed in my throat at the thought of him; sometimes I still couldn't believe he was gone. But the stories he'd told me were alive and kicking. The Wright brothers made their historic flight in 1903, I recalled, though few believed them at the time and only two newspapers in the nation bothered to print the story. The next significant advance, the Curtiss biplane, wasn't developed until several years later, which meant Nathaniel's flying machine predated it—and should rightfully be the first to break the Wright brothers' record. I felt my adrenaline pumping full speed ahead at the prospect.

I took a step toward him. He looked up then and turned slowly toward me. A defensive look flashed across his face, the look of an animal protecting its den from a predator. Hastily he scooped some official-looking papers off the table next to the blueprints and slid the folder under a blotter. Vaguely I remembered Nathaniel's secretive business deal that Victoria—the old

Victoria—had once alluded to, but quickly dismissed the thought as a product of my overactive imagination.

"Who told you you could come in here?" he demanded, leaping to his feet.

I walked toward him, ignoring the wobbly feeling in my knees. "It wasn't locked. If you meant this to be off-limits, you should have said so."

"Can't a man have any privacy in this house? Damned interfering woman." He grasped my shoulders; his touch sent an electric shock up my arm, even through the sleeves of the wool gown. "First you invade my bedroom, and now this!"

"Do you hate me so very much?" I asked softly.

He recoiled as if I'd fired a gun. "Hate you . . . No, that isn't it at all." The air between us crackled with electricity. "A woman needs to know her place, that's all."

"Is it?" I asked, suspecting there was more than macho blustering beneath his gruffness.

"Of course." His cheek muscle twitched. "Now, are you going to leave voluntarily, or do I have to throw you out?"

"What are you so afraid of?" I asked quietly.

"I'm not afraid—certainly not of a meddlesome female."

"Maybe not," I persisted, summoning my courage. "But at the very least, you don't trust me. Or maybe you don't trust any woman."

"I'm engaged to be married to one!" he protested.

"To one who's safe—a society debutante who wouldn't dare leave you." There was so little time left to make him wake up and smell the coffee before it burned him. Victoria's words haunted me: "I've often thought how different things would have been if only that marriage had never taken place."

He released me as if I were unclean. "Prudence is a good, decent woman," he said. "I owe it to Victoria to marry a suitable wife."

"Someone to mother her?" I asked gently.

"Yes. A child needs that."

"Is duty to your sister really a good enough reason to marry?"

He looked uncomfortable. "Of course it is. What could be more important than the welfare of a child?"

"What about love?" I asked, suppressing the urge to reach out and stroke the fine lines of pain etched around his eyes.

"Love? For a woman in your profession, you certainly entertain some romantic notions."

His words stung. "Maybe I do," I admitted, looking down. "Then again, I'm not so sure love is all it's cracked up to be, either. I've had men say they loved me, but . . . I just couldn't feel anything in return."

"Cynicism doesn't become you," he said. "Though I suppose it must come with your trade."

I shook my head, feeling a warm flush spread over my face as I realized what he'd been thinking. "That's not it. . . . I think it has something to do with how I was brought up." Always insecure, never knowing what it felt like to feel loved, I

85

added silently. "My family wasn't exactly the Brady Bunch, so I've got some idea how you must feel."

"I don't know any Bradys and I can't imagine any similarity between your family and mine."

"Your stepmother abandoned you when you were what, nineteen?"

"Seventeen. What of it?"

"And I'll bet you still resent your mother too, for abandoning you through death." I had to make him understand himself before I could expect him to see why marrying Prudence would be a big mistake.

"That's not true," he protested. He turned away, but not before I saw the wounded look in his eyes.

I stepped toward him and placed a hand on his shoulder. He stiffened at my touch.

"I know what it's like to lose someone you love," I said softly, picturing Alex briefly before sealing those awful memories into a darkened recess of my mind. "For what it's worth, according to Al-Anon it's normal for kids from dysfunctional families to have trouble forming lasting bonds."

Nathaniel stepped in front of the model airplane and blocked my view. "I don't understand this nonsense you're babbling. A1 someone-or-other and defunct . . . whatever you called it. You've seen my deep dark secret. Now leave me be."

I moved beside him and studied the model. "It's a fine plane. I've seen plenty of them before, though none quite like this."

"You have?"

"Are you building a real plane somewhere?"

Silence.

My heart thumped with excitement. "You are, aren't you? Does it fly? I'd love to try it before I leave."

He dropped his jaw in amazement. "You would? You don't think it's . . . foolish?"

"No," I said, moved by the vulnerability written across his face. I gathered Prudence wasn't exactly the next Amelia Earhart. "I don't."

To my surprise, he clasped my hand and led me to his drawing table; a bolt of heat shot up my arm at his touch. Releasing my hand, he stood behind me, his breath warming the back of my neck as he spoke. "It's a variation on the model conceived by Orville and Wilbur Wright back in 1903," he explained, his voice filled with suppressed excitement. "Actually, I was working on my version long before their Kitty Hawk flight, which lasted less than a minute. I've been fascinated with the concept ever since I read Jules Verne's fanciful tale of flying machines."

"Didn't he also write *Time Machine*?" I fished.

"A dreadful book." He dismissed it with a condescending gesture. "Traveling through time— preposterous."

My stomach sank. This wasn't going to be easy.

"Anyhow," he continued, "I've made a few aerodynamic changes over the Wrights' version. Designed mine as a two-seater with a thirty-five-horsepower, eight-cylinder engine driving a geared pusher propeller." His arm brushed my shoulder in a casually intimate gesture as he pointed to various features on the drawings. "Changed the wing angles and reconfigured the propellers to maximize velocity, among other things."

"Good," I said, my enthusiasm mounting even as I forced myself to ignore the prickles of fire his touch ignited. "So have you taken it for a test drive yet?"

"I have. Got it off the ground, barely, but the blasted thing keeps pulling off the field when I throttle down."

I peered at the blueprints intently. "The propeller doesn't look right, somehow." I squinted, envisioning Alex in the biplanes he used to fly. "The angle's wrong—you need to change it, like so." I picked up a pencil and illustrated my point. "You might also try tying a rag or something on the elevator in front so you can keep an eye on shifts in wind direction."

He looked at me as if I'd just told him I was from Mars. "Where the devil did you learn so much about flying machines?"

"From my brother. He used to be a stunt pilot for Hollywood."

"Hollywood? Never heard of him. I didn't realize anyone other than the Wrights had developed a successful flying machine."

"They haven't. Well, not exactly." I quickly changed the subject. "Who's your flying partner?"

His enthusiasm deflated. "Unfortunately, my

attempts to date have been solo. I'd hoped Prudence would join me, but she doesn't approve of my 'folly,' as she calls it. Wants me to give it up once we're married. She's afraid I'll break my fool neck and leave her a rich widow, I suppose."

"You can't just give up on your dreams."

A shadow fell across his face. "That's my concern."

"It isn't right. Besides, you could set a new record."

He stared at me as though seeing me for the first time, then smiled wistfully. "You're not at all like the other women I've known."

How many other women had there been? I wondered. "You're not like other men I've known, either," I replied honestly. The more I learned about Nathaniel Stuart, the more he intrigued me. Like his sister—only more so.

I recalled what Mrs. O'Hara had told me about Victoria's illness, and mentioned it to Nathaniel.

He frowned. "That's odd. Victoria didn't say anything to me, though she did look a bit pale when she came downstairs after you left. She asked for a word alone with Prudence. I suppose it's a good thing the child is warming to her new stepmother."

Like warming up to frostbite, I thought. Fire and ice.

Fire. I shuddered as the gruesome image of Victoria engulfed in flames flashed in my mind. I couldn't stand by and let that innocent little girl be burned in the earthquake. . . .

"Nathaniel." I drew in my breath sharply.

He cocked his head. "You look pale. Are you ill?"

"I'm not sick. But I'm not what you think I am," I blurted out. "The truth is—"

The workshop door flew open and a blurred mass of fur burst inside, propelling itself against me like a cannonball.

"The little imp must have dug a hole under the fence," Nathaniel observed. His irritation was evident as I scooped Apollo up and brushed the dirt off his nose and paws.

I stroked the dog's suedelike fur and crooned some reassuring words, silently cursing his interference before Nathaniel relieved me of my burden. "I'll put some rocks along the fence line this time. That ought to keep you out of mischief," he informed the hyperactive pup. To me he added, "Would you mind looking in on Victoria for me while I deal with this troublemaker? Tell her I'll be along shortly."

"Yes, of course," I murmured, knowing a dismissal when I heard one. He was beginning to trust me, I sensed, even if he did still think I used to sleep with men for money.

I'd just have to find another chance to tell Nathaniel the truth, I told myself as I walked toward the house. But what if he didn't believe me?

I shivered, unwilling to consider the prospect.

Chapter Five

"Victoria? It's Taylor. May I come in?" Muffled sobs came from inside her room. Had Prudence done something to get the girl so upset?

The door opened. Victoria's eyes were puffy and red rimmed; her face was bloated and tear streaked. I stepped inside and pulled her into my arms. "Mrs. O'Hara told me you weren't feeling well," I said cautiously. "Would you like to tell me about it?"

She looked up at me with fear in her eyes. Why was she afraid? Was she really sick?

"Prudence said I shouldn't talk about it," she said, her lower lip quivering.

I led her to the canopied bed and sat down beside her. "Why not?" I probed.

She sniffled into an embroidered handkerchief. "S-she said it was dirty. A woman's curse, she called it. That's why I'm bleeding."

Suddenly I understood. "Victoria," I began, "you're not dirty, and you're certainly not cursed. You're just becoming a woman."

Her eyes widened. "I am?" she asked, suspicion tinging her voice. "How do you know?"

I gave her a reassuring smile. "Because I went through the same thing at around your age—we all do. It's normal—and certainly nothing to be ashamed of."

Her face relaxed as her eyes met mine, questioning. "But then why did Prudence say it was shameful?"

I reminded myself I had no right to be upset with Prudence for scaring the kid; after all, women were far from enlightened in this day and age. "Some people believe that," I answered, keeping my tone level. "But I don't, and you don't need to, either. What you're experiencing is perfectly natural. It will last for several days every month, but there's no reason to let it upset you, or interfere with anything you want to do."

She looked out the curved turret window to the gardens below. "I thought I was dying—my insides have been cramping all night, and this morning there was so much blood. . . ."

I thought a moment. "Did Prudence show you what to do?"

Victoria frowned. "She gave me some clean linen rags, and told me how to use them."

I nodded. "Good." At least Prudence had accomplished something. I wouldn't have known what to offer Victoria with no tampons or sanitary pads available. "What else?"

"She said I should take two tablespoonful of that foul-tasting tonic." She motioned to a bottle of liquid on a bedside table and made a sour face. "But I can't stomach it."

I picked it up and read the label: " *'Lydia Pinkham's tonic for the vapors and women's complaints.'* " Opening the bottle, I smelled the contents. "Whew," I said as the vapor cleared my sinuses. The stuff had enough alcohol to keep Dad snockered for a week.

"Hang on," I told Victoria. "I'll be right back with something that should help."

Returning a couple of minutes later with my fanny pack, I fished inside and pulled out a bottle of ibuprofen. "These pills should stop the cramps," I advised her. "Take one every four to six hours. What else did Prudence tell you?"

"That I musn't exert myself, or bathe, or do anything to tire myself. S-she warned me to stay in bed until the curse is over. Oh, but Taylor— the wedding's the day after tomorrow and I can't miss it, I just can't!" She dissolved into tears again.

I dried her tears and smoothed her hair, fighting my rising annoyance at Prudence. Telling a girl to miss her brother's wedding because she was having her period went beyond the normal Victorian prudery, I was sure.

"That's nonsense," I said. "Why, I work out at the gym and jog two miles with Apollo every day, even when it's my time of the month."

"Jog?"

"Like running, only slower," I explained. "You can exercise and bathe all you want. As for your brother's wedding, you won't have to miss it. I promise."

She flashed me a grateful smile, then threw her arms around me and hugged me tight.

"Taylor," she whispered as I returned her embrace.

"What?" I asked.

She looked up and blinked away a film of tears. "I wish you were the one marrying Nathaniel."

"Victoria! You know that's impossible," I said, but I couldn't keep from trembling. He's a man raised in the Victorian era, I told myself. Self-confident, domineering, scornful of women . . . An idealist, a dreamer, a man who loves his sister and is altogether too handsome for his own good, my desires argued back.

And he's over a hundred years older than you, my rational self prevailed.

Still, I hoped Victoria didn't detect the tremor in my step as I mumbled some excuse to leave.

I stepped into the hall and was so distracted that I plowed right into Nathaniel, who was standing just outside the door. His arms closed about my waist to steady me and I found myself pressed against his granite-hard chest. He stared into my eyes; in his gaze I saw a new esteem, and something more.

"Thank you," he said softly. "It was kind of you to see to Victoria's troubles. I should have realized she needed . . ." A red glow spread up to his neck to the tops of his ears. "That is, I hadn't noticed my little sister was growing up so quickly."

"You were listening?" I wondered uncomfortably what he'd thought of Victoria's last suggestion.

"The door was open. I didn't mean to eavesdrop. But when I heard Victoria crying, I was concerned."

I nodded, intensely aware of the heat radiating from his arms, still holding me captive. His concern for his sister was so great I found it impossible to be angry with him for eavesdropping.

"She'll be fine," I reassured him. "It's really no big deal."

His face darkened. "Prudence certainly seemed to think it is. She'd no right to upset that child."

I said nothing, silently glad that he'd seen the light about Prudence.

A look of realization came over his face and he released me abruptly. "This whole incident just goes to show how much the girl needs a woman in the house. Someone to make sure she knows all those . . . female things."

"Like staying in bed and missing her brother's wedding just because she's—"

"I shall speak with Prudence about that. You're right; she was out of line to suggest that my sister miss the ceremony. Still"—he frowned—"the child needs a suitable paragon to guide her in what a proper young lady must know to marry well. Prudence is well bred; she comes from good stock. Surely you can understand the importance of that."

"Not really," I said, hoping my hurt feelings didn't show.

He cocked an eyebrow, studying me in a way that made me feel like a bug under a microscope. "Your jest is not amusing."

"I wasn't joking."

He frowned in disapproval. "I take it your family tree has more blackguards than most. I suppose that's to be expected, given your choice of profession."

"If you must know, I come from a long line of bastards," I said, miffed by his condescending tone. "I was a first in my family. My parents actually made it to the altar before I was born—barely."

He gave me an intense stare, as though seeing past my sarcasm to peel away the layers protecting my inner self. I kicked myself mentally for allowing my temper to undo what little progress I'd made toward gaining his trust earlier.

"A misbegotten child," he mused. "Is that why you . . . ?" he started to ask, but stopped. For an instant I saw a flash of empathy in his eyes, a look of understanding that passed between kindred spirits from one neglected child to another, before the veil of formality closed once again.

"I've no interest in hearing about the skeletons in your family closet," he concluded firmly. "Prudence meant well. She has a good heart. Once we're married I'm sure Victoria will come around."

He strode away, leaving me to wonder whether he was trying to convince me—or himself.

Alone in my room, I rifled through the contents of my fanny pack, hoping desperately to find something I could present to Nathaniel to prove to him that I was from the future. But no luck. I never carry a wallet when I'm exercising, and the date on my emergency quarter-for-a-phone-call was illegible. A tube of strawberry-flavored lipstick, hairbrush, keys, chewing gum, Apollo's leash, and a container of Mace were hardly irrefutable evidence of time travel. I'd just have to find some other approach to save Nathaniel and his sister.

Needing something to settle my stomach, I went downstairs and coaxed the cook to warm me a cup of chamomile tea on the cast-iron Sears Roebuck stove. While the water was heating I opened the pantry, hoping to find some honey for my tea. "Did you know something's spilled down here?" I said. "Here, I'll clean it up—"

The cook rushed forward, shooing me away. "Sit down and I'll serve whatever you wish, but mind you stay out of the pantry. That powder you nearly put your hands in is arsenic—keeps the rats out of the dry goods."

"Arsenic!" I jerked my hands away.

"If Muffin there would do her job as a mouser, we wouldn't need it, now would we?" She motioned to a fluffy white cat licking its paws by the back door.

Obediently I sat down at the kitchen table; the cook raised a questioning eyebrow as she served me my tea with honey.

I sipped my tea, toying with the idea of taking

Victoria back to the future with me. Plucking someone out of the past could be dangerous—not to mention pretty darned tough to explain, even if it worked. I could just picture the awkward scene: "Hi Mom, Dad. I'd like you to meet Victoria. Oh no, that's not a costume. She always dresses that way—she's from 1906. I brought her back to save her from the earthquake. You don't mind if she comes to live with us, do you?"

No doubt about it, the idea was out of the question. I must be going nuts even to think of such a thing.

I considered reasoning with Victoria, but having glimpsed her rebellious nature, I wasn't at all sure she'd cooperate. Still, she was a child. There were ways to protect her; I could hide her candles or lock her in my room as a last resort.

Her brother, however, was another story. Sure, I could blurt out the truth to Nathaniel and hope for the best, but given his stubborn streak the chances of him believing me were probably slim. I could wait and hope I'd figure out a way to keep him out of the attic when the earthquake hit, but I doubted if I'd succeed in getting his attention once Prudence was sharing his marriage bed. The mere thought made me nauseated.

There was just one option left. Somehow I had to stop Nathaniel from marrying Prudence.

But telling the truth was too risky—and too farfetched. Nathaniel would probably just drop me off at the nearest mental hospital. After all, I thought as I set my teacup down decisively, there was more than one way to convince the guy that

I could foretell the future.

Mrs. O'Hara found me mumbling to myself and gave me a curious glance. "Is somethin' amiss in the dining room?" she asked.

"Not that I know of," I answered, wondering why she'd ask a question from left field.

"Ye're the master's cousin; ye're a guest in his house. It isn't fittin' for you to be takin' tea in the kitchen with the servants."

"Oh," I said sheepishly. "Sorry. I just didn't want to put anybody to any extra trouble." Protocol had been the farthest thing from my mind when I'd sat down and asked for tea, which the cook dutifully prepared.

"Mr. Stuart requests ye make yerself ready for an excursion," Mrs. O'Hara informed me next.

"Oh? Where to?" Goosebumps rose on my arms. Had I annoyed him so much that he was sending me away? I couldn't leave yet; I hadn't accomplished what I'd set out to do.

"Be ready promptly at eleven o'clock," she informed me. "Ye're t' meet him in the carriage house."

My stomach flopped. So this is it, I thought, certain that I'd managed to offend Nathaniel sufficiently that he was ready to plop me into a carriage bound for the nearest train station—or brothel. Depressed, I glanced at my inappropriate footwear. *You've really done it this time, Taylor. Expelled from Oz without so much as a pair of ruby slippers.*

Somehow, I'd have to find a way back home on my own. But how could I save the Stuart family and their house while Nathaniel was more stubborn than a mule with blinders on when it came to his bride-to-be?

Maybe I couldn't change history. But I sure as hell wasn't going to let myself get thrown out without giving it the old college try.

It was, I concluded, time to tell Nathaniel a story. Just one little white lie. Or maybe not so little.

Okay, okay, I thought, suddenly grateful for my acting experience. So it would have to be a whopper.

Nathaniel met me in front of the carriage house, tweed jacket slung over one shoulder. I stopped in midstep at the sight of him; my heart skipped a beat. I'd thought he looked like a hunk-of-the-month in his nightshirt; even better in the suit he'd worn during Prudence's visit. But now he was . . . devastating. Like Robert Redford with dark hair and a mustache, only better.

His shirtsleeves were rolled up to his elbows, exposing bronze hairs that rippled in the morning breeze on his tanned, muscular forearms. He wore a tweed vest, brown wool pants, burgundy-colored bow tie, and brown leather gloves; a wool scarf was wrapped around his neck, and a tweed cap perched jauntily on his head. A playful glint danced in his eyes, which in the sunlight I saw had flecks of gold. It was a side of Nathaniel Stuart I hadn't glimpsed before, and one that I found incredibly appealing.

"You need new clothes," he informed me. "I

100

can't have you passing yourself off as my relation without at least providing you more suitable attire, so I've decided to take you shopping."

New clothes? So he wasn't sending me away after all. He'd seen how embarrassed I was after Prudence's snide remarks about the hand-me-downs I wore—he actually cared about my feelings.

Best of all, it meant I had a little more time to gain his confidence before hitting him with my grand finale.

My elation faded at the prospect of how we would get to the mall. Horses and I had never gotten along ever since one kicked me backstage during a summer theater performance.

"Close your eyes," he instructed. I obeyed, wondering why.

I heard the carriage house doors open, followed by the unmistakable sputter of an engine turning over. Opening my eyes, I stared in amazement at the sight of Nathaniel driving toward me in a gleaming silver automobile. I rubbed my eyes. Automobile?

Leaving the engine running, he leapt out, raced around the car, and opened the passenger door for me. "Have you ridden in a horseless carriage before?" he asked as he helped me over the running board and up into the rich leather seat.

"Not like this," I answered, breathless. I'd forgotten that cars were around this early in the century, and was doubly surprised by the elegance of Nathaniel's vehicle—not at all the way I'd pictured the forerunners of Henry Ford's

101

clunky, mass-produced Model T.

He beamed. "It's a Silver Shadow, billed as the finest motorcar in the world. I brought it back aboard one of my ships from England last month. Made by a new company, Rolls Royce."

I was stunned. I'd known Nathaniel was wealthy, but . . . a Rolls Royce? It must have cost a fortune, even in his day. No doubt about it, this guy was a class act.

Seeing my dazed expression, he said, "If you're worried about proprieties, you needn't be. As far as anyone in this town knows you are my cousin, and it's perfectly acceptable for a gentleman to escort his cousin about town."

"Oh," I said. "That's good."

He shut my door and reclaimed his seat at the wheel, which was on the right side. Stepping on the accelerator, he propelled us down the driveway and onto Van Ness Avenue.

I raised a hand to shield my eyes from the sun, blinking at the unfamiliar sights. This street looked nothing like the one I'd jogged down with Apollo just yesterday—in 1989. I resisted the impulse to let my jaw hang open, fishlike, as we drove past rows of stately formal mansions, freshly painted, their colors vibrant, bursting with life. I couldn't decide which thrilled me the most—the sight of all those historical landmarks I'd studied and written about, or being out alone with Nathaniel, the man I'd dreamed of waltzing with when I'd seen only his picture—which was nothing compared to the real-life man beside me now.

I dug my nails into my palms, reminding myself that this was reality, not a dream. In less than a week, I had to find a way back to my own time. It was crazy to have the sort of feelings I was having for a man I'd never see again, a man who thought I was a whore—and was planning to marry another woman.

A woman he as much as admitted he doesn't love.

Stop it, I told myself. You've got to concentrate on fixing things and getting home in one piece instead of mooning over Nathaniel Stuart. Start by winning his confidence; ask him something about himself.

I glanced at him out of the corners of my eyes. The commanding way he gripped the wheel reminded me of a captain at the helm. Of course, I recalled, Nathaniel had sailed around the world as a young man aboard his father's ships. Victoria, the old-timer, used to captivate me with endless tales of his adventures and the exotic gifts he'd brought back for her from distant corners of the globe. I'd envied his freedom, until Victoria told me how after Nathaniel was left with the responsibility of raising his baby sister, his globe-trotting days came to an end, with only an occasional trip.

"Do you miss it?" I wondered aloud.

"What?" he glanced at me, puzzled.

"Traveling. Seeing the world, the way you used to."

His grip tightened on the wheel. "That's a preposterous question. Of course I miss it." A nostalgic look came over him. "The jungles of Africa, the gilded court of the Chinese emperor, the Turkish bazaars where one could buy or sell most anything . . ."

I was captivated. "What did you like best?"

He pondered the question. "Tiger hunting in India with the maharaja was certainly enthralling, and fighting off pirates in the South Seas had its dramatic moments." A teasing note crept into his voice. "Though I suppose it's the women who are the most memorable. The Chinese courtesans, the geishas of Japan, and those ravishing women in the South Pacific." He glanced at me, cocking a rakish eyebrow. "Why, I once knew a French cancan dancer who—"

"I get the picture," I cut him off. Why should I care how many other women he'd known? But for some reason I did.

The corner of his mouth twitched in amusement. "For a woman in your profession, you can be rather prudish."

I bristled. "I am not a prude. I happen to be a perfectly broad-minded, modern woman on the subject of sex. Why, I read MS. and COSMO every month!"

"Cosmo? Must be a new author; I've never heard of him. Do calm down—you're distracting my driving. I wasn't criticizing you. Actually, I find your modesty oddly charming—if misplaced."

"You've led a colorful life yourself, I'd say."

"I'm a man. That's different."

"Typical male chauvinistic attitude! What's

sauce for the goose is sauce for the gander, my grandma always says."

"Wanton ways must run in your family," he said dryly.

It was time to give this guy an education. "A woman can do anything a man can do," I argued. "Climb mountains, drive a forklift, even run for president!"

He snorted derisively. "That's absurd. I consider myself enlightened on the topic of women's rights—I happen to believe the suffragettes have a point—though of course they'll never win. But women running for political office? It will never happen."

"It will. Women will get the vote in the 1920s, under President Woodrow Wilson. Within a few decades, we'll have women in the House—and the Senate."

He shrugged. "If it pleases you to believe such nonsense, so be it."

I took a deep breath. "I'm not just guessing. I know those things will happen. I've seen the future—you see, my friends say I'm psychic."

A laugh exploded from his lips. "Don't tell me you believe that rubbish!"

I crossed my arms in annoyance. "I'd have expected you of all people to be more open-minded. Surely you've been exposed to new ideas, new ways of thinking on your extensive travels?"

"My traveling days are all in the past and those tales of adventure aren't important anymore."

"Why not?"

"I have responsibilities," Nathaniel said in a

tone that brooked no argument. "It's the future that's important now."

"At least we agree on something," I groused, shoving my hands into the folds of my skirt for warmth.

We jolted over a pothole; mud splattered up onto my wind-whipped hair. Glancing at my bedraggled appearance, Nathaniel tugged the scarf free from around his neck. "Here." He tossed it in my lap. "Tie that around your hair."

"Thanks." I looped his scarf over my head and wrapped the ends around my neck, savoring the warmth as well as the masculine scents of leather and tobacco that clung to the wool plaid.

He braked to a stop in front of an enormous house. I stared, wide eyed. "Isn't that the Spreckels mansion?" I'd seen pictures of it, but none that did it justice. A chill shot up my spine as I recalled the magnificent home's fate—gutted by fire after the earthquake.

"The same," he answered. He tipped the brim of his cap back with his thumb and cast me a quizzical look. "Surely you've seen it before?"

"I haven't, er, been here in a while."

"Oh." He nodded in comprehension. "I suppose they didn't let you out much." His voice grew gentle. "Did the madam or some customer mistreat you—is that why you ran away?"

My cheeks felt scalded. "Will you quit jumping to conclusions about me?"

"Never mind." He shook his head. "I shouldn't pry. Now I have to drop some papers off inside."

"What kind of papers?" I asked.

"It's safer for you not to know. My enemies have already sent a warning, sabotaging one of my ships. No point involving you."

Warnings . . . Sabotage? What sort of business dealings was Nathaniel involved in? I wondered.

"Wait here," he said, before I could ask more. "This will just take a moment."

So I was too much of an embarrassment to take inside the Spreckels home, was I? Swallowing my disappointment, I pretended not to care. "It's okay; I'll wait here and enjoy the scenery."

He emerged a few minutes later and started up the car. I was silent, my thoughts filled with nightmare images of all those beautiful homes destroyed. I couldn't do anything to stop the earthquake or fire, but I sure as heck ought to be able to save Nathaniel's home from being ruined by Fenniwick's greed. I gritted my teeth, determined not to let my frustration show.

The corners of Nathaniel's eyes crinkled with concern. "Is something wrong?"

"Yes." I placed my hands at my temples, assuming what I hoped sounded like a mystical tone. "Something is terribly wrong. I've seen a vision." I closed my eyes tightly. "Buildings falling, the very earth trembling! And fire—I see flames sweeping the city." Swaying in my seat, I raised my voice ominously. "This house will burn. . . ."

A moment later, I opened my eyes and rubbed them. "What happened? My head hurts."

"You ranted something about a fire."

"I did?" I made my eyes widen. "Oh, dear. I

suppose it was another trance. They say I've inherited Grandma's gift. She was a gypsy fortune-teller. From Romania."

"You don't look like any gypsy fortune-teller I've ever seen," he said, cocking his eyebrow in annoyance as he studied me. "Next I suppose you'll be asking me to cross your palm with silver."

"It's the truth! I'm telling you—"

"Will you stop with that nonsense? I've promised to help you rise above your past. You needn't try to con me as well with this preposterous gypsy hoax."

I didn't dare push him farther for fear he'd toss me right out of the car. So much for Plan A.

Thoughtfully, he ran a gloved hand through the windblown hair protruding beneath his cap. "I've upset you with my intrusive questions about your past—so you've decided to make up a better one."

"I did not—"

"You needn't protest." He cut me off short. "I pushed you to it. Please allow me to make up for my rudeness by giving you a proper tour."

Before I could reply, he veered and sent us thundering down Market Street, past horsecars and pedestrians. A bell clanged; I looked up in time to see a cable car coming toward us. Nathaniel dropped his elbow over the driver's door to honk the horn as he swung the car wide, deftly avoiding a collision, then continued onward, unruffled.

"Can you imagine Ruef and his cohorts wanting to build a network of trolleys connected to overhead wires—a damnable blight on the city, if you ask me," he grumbled.

"Ruef—Boss Ruef?" I started at the mention of the notorious boss who'd ruled San Francisco's corrupt political machine in the early years of this century.

"Spreckels has a plan up his sleeve to stop Ruef's madness. With my help and God's will, it has a good chance of success."

"Is that what those papers were about?"

He glanced at me sideways. "Never mind. It's safer for you if you don't know."

"Safer? How come?" What was Nathaniel involved in that might be dangerous?

"Look." He changed the subject without answering my question. "Over there is the Palace Hotel, finest in the world." He gestured proudly toward the landmark.

It was a historian's dream come true to see the glitter and glory of old San Francisco—a whole city wiped out by one of the worst natural disasters in U.S. history. I felt like a kid on Christmas morning as he pointed out other buildings named for the movers and shakers of the day: the James Flood building, Crocker Bank, the Claus Spreckels building. I didn't have the heart to tell him that most would soon be reduced to rubble. He wouldn't have believed me anyhow.

For the next half hour we swooped over hills and darted down side streets as Nathaniel told me tales of the city's history that I hadn't heard before. Though clearly a man with an eye toward the future—a man ahead of his time in many ways—to my delight I discovered that Nathaniel also shared my love of the past. If only he'd be half as concerned when it came to his own future, I thought. In less than a week, all hell would break loose. I was running out of time—I had to think of a new plan, and fast.

At the harbor, Nathaniel pointed out several of his ships and told me of his father's foresight in building a wharf back in the gold rush days, patiently enduring my endless questions. I heard the pride in his resonant voice and felt a surge of frustration over my inability to stop the chain of events that would ruin the shipping company Nathaniel loved so much. I had to stop it from happening. But how?

We passed City Hall, where Nathaniel detailed more of Ruef's infamous exploits. We drove through the ethnic neighborhoods in Chinatown, Telegraph Hill, and Russian Hill, then passed by the opera house, where the marquee advertised Enrico Caruso's upcoming performance in Carmen. Later, as we passed the Orpheum and Columbus theaters, Nathaniel delivered a tirade on the immorality of actresses; I tried not to visibly cringe.

Tactfully, Nathaniel avoided the Barbary Coast, home of the city's most notorious brothels. But we saw almost everything else. It was disorienting at times; I kept expecting to see the TransAmerica pyramid or Golden Gate Bridge.

"There, now you've seen it," he concluded, a smile tugging at the corners of his mouth. "If we're to outfit you with new clothes, we'd best see to it."

"Can you show me Nob Hill?" Seeing his doubtful expression, I added, "Please? I won't need much time to pick out clothes. I'm a speedy shopper, honest."

He weighed the question visibly before nodding. I practically shouted "Eureka" as we rode up the steep hill that was home to the richest families in San Francisco. I saw the opulent Fairmont Hotel and the ostentatious mansions lining the West Coast's most prestigious street, knowing that not a single one of them would survive the events of the next week. What I wouldn't have given for a camcorder . . .

"Who's house is that?" I asked as we crested the hill and an enormous white Greek revival–style mansion caught my eye.

He shifted uncomfortably. "It's owned by Mortimer Pratwell, president of Pratwell Bank of Commerce."

"Prudence's father?"

"Yes."

So her family was loaded. Prudence might be a lot of things, but gold digger must not be one of them.

Still, she was dead wrong for Nathaniel. I had to stop him from marrying her. He'd left me no choice, I realized as we pulled up into the shopping district and he helped me out of the car. The minute I got him alone again, I'd have to tell Nathaniel the truth.

Chapter Six

"*Oui*, Monsieur Stuart. Your cousin has a most attractive face, and her figure, *c'est magnifique*! It will be my pleasure to assist her in choosing a wardrobe," Mme Riviere, the department store saleswoman, gushed.

Nathaniel nodded approval, his massive frame oddly out of place against the racks of women's clothes. I'd expected a prolonged fitting with a seamstress, forgetting that ready-to-wear clothes were easily available by 1906 due to the proliferation of garment factories following the invention of the sewing machine.

"See to it that my cousin receives everything she will need for the next three days," Nathaniel instructed. "Shoes, hats, whatever you think appropriate. Top to bottom and outside to, er, inside." His gaze appraised me from head to toe and I had the unsettling feeling that his imagination was at work again picturing me in—or out of—my new underwear.

"As you wish," Mme Riviere replied. "Is there anything specific—styles, colors?"

"Nothing too flamboyant." No doubt he was recalling my leotard and hot pink tights. "Something simple. Conservative."

His words grated on my nerves. Prudence could parade around wearing enough frou frou and feathers to drive several species into extinction and he'd hang on her every word, but when it came to me Nathaniel wanted only drab, practical clothes. Okay, so I wasn't exactly a saint in his eyes. But did he have to insist on dressing me like a missionary?

Madame raised an eyebrow. "As you wish, monsieur. Let's see. Your cousin will need at least two tea dresses for daytime wear, an evening gown, and of course a fabulous ensemble for the wedding. I have a Worth original, from Paris, that should be just the thing."

His lips tightened as she ticked off a litany of accessories. "Don't forget a traveling outfit," he added. "For Sunday."

I bit my tongue to keep from objecting. So he was serious about sending me away right after the wedding—and before the earthquake. I was running out of time.

Nathaniel sat down in a chair, planted his feet firmly on the floor, and crossed his arms decisively. Nodding to Madame, he said, "You may proceed."

113

Madame ushered me behind a dressing screen and fitted me with the proper underwear: two chemises—one silk, one cotton—drawers shaped like boxer shorts, garters and silk stockings, a brassiere stiffened with whalebone, the new-style full corset, which Madame assured me was designed to give an S-shaped figure by lifting the bosom and padding the posterior, a corset cover with ribbon insets, and two of the new "silent" petticoats. "No more gauche rustling when you walk," Mme Riviere explained, staring pointedly at Nathaniel's mother's outdated horsehair petticoats.

I felt like a trussed turkey. But when I stared at my transformed image in the mirror, a rush of pleasure hit me. The woman in the mirror looked nothing like the old me. She was prettier, more feminine somehow. I never knew wearing nothing but underwear could be such a kick. . . . Maybe Madonna was on to something after all.

"Don't worry," Madame whispered in my ear. "We will change your cousin's mind about his conservative tastes. An attractive woman should display her beauty, not hide it, *oui*?"

I wasn't at all sure Nathaniel would agree. But at Madame's urging, I tried on a simple brown dress.

Hesitantly I stepped out from around the screen, hoping Madame knew what she was doing.

Nathaniel looked at me and scowled. "She looks like a washer woman. Can't you do better than that?"

114

I forced myself not to show my smile. So Cinderella wouldn't be going to the ball in rags, after all.

Next I tried on a mint-green tea gown with a scooped neckline, nipped in at the waist with a circular skirt. To my dismay, I discovered it had weights sewn into the hem. "To keep it from lifting in the breeze," Madame informed me. "You would not want to entice any rogues by baring your lovely ankles."

I came out feeling like an upside-down parachute.

Nathaniel raised his eyebrows, nodding approval. "Much better. The color suits you—it brings out the green in your eyes."

After gaining his approval on a second tea dress with a starched whalebone collar, a modest evening gown, and a bolero-style traveling suit, I tried on the grand finale—a Worth original satin gown in a soft-peach color. The neckline was cut so low that I was afraid to breathe for fear I'd pop out; the back was shaped into what Madame described as a "waterfall"—tucked at the hips, pleated at the waist behind, with a cascade of creamy fabric falling freely to swirl around my ankles.

"It's gorgeous," I whispered. "But it must cost a fortune. I don't feel right—"

"Nonsense," Madame scoffed. "Besides, Mademoiselle Pratwell spends several times this amount every time she comes in. Your cousin had best get used to loosening his purse strings if he means to marry that one."

Not a gold digger, but merely a clotheshorse, I noted. Though Nathaniel could afford to indulge Prudence's hobby, I supposed.

"What the devil is taking so long?" Nathaniel groused from the opposite side of the screen.

"Patience, monsieur," Mme Riviere answered, winking at me. "All works of art take time, *oui*?" She brushed and teased my hair up into a pompadour style and, for good measure, added a matching hat trimmed in seed pearls with a delicate half-veil.

I held my breath as I walked out, anxious for Nathaniel's approval. At the sight of me his eyes widened and he stood up, taking a step closer. It was, I supposed, a fairly dramatic transformation from the dust-covered banshee he'd found screaming in his attic the night before.

"Remarkable," he said, examining me from head to toe, his gaze lingering a shade longer than proper on my corseted wasp-waist and the lacy edge of fabric that brushed just below the tan line from my bikini top, baring a more than generous amount of me.

"Turn around," Madame instructed. I obeyed. Finishing, I stepped toward Nathaniel, anxious for his decision.

"Well?" I asked. "What do you think?"

He ran a finger around the inside of his collar, loosening it. "I think," he said, swallowing hard, "that's it gotten quite warm in here."

Turning to Madame, he said, "It will do. Wrap it up . . . but first, sew some lace or something across the top."

Madame puckered her face. "But Monsieur Stuart, that would ruin the line of the dress. This is the style—all the fashionable young women are wearing them this way."

His Adam's apple rose and fell as he assessed the problem, the heat of his gaze on my skin making me feel flushed.

"It won't do for her to outshine the bride."

"Surely you do not mean that mademoiselle is more beautiful than your fiancee?" Madame feigned shock.

"No, of course not—"

"You do not wish your cousin to be a laughingstock, do you?"

"No, but . . ." His pupils dilated as he contemplated my neckline again. "Oh, very well. Have it boxed—but do select a suitable wrap for her to cover herself with during the ceremony."

Madame flashed a Mona Lisa smile. "*Oui*, monsieur. But of course. Shall I add a matching reticule?"

"Yes, of course."

"She'll need gloves, shoes, and an enameling set," she said, using the Edwardian term for a makeup kit. "I notice you drive a motorcar. A lady must have a broad-brimmed hat with a full veil in front to protect her delicate skin from the sun, not to mention goggles to shield her eyes."

"Yes, yes, I'll take it all." Nathaniel waved his hand dismissively. "Whatever she needs." Turning to me, he asked, "Is there anything else you would like?"

Levi's and a sweatshirt, I thought. Aloud, I

asked for the closest available substitute. "If it's not too much to ask, I'd really like a pair of those bloomers, with a shirtwaist and maybe some plain shoes."

"Bloomers!" Nathaniel stiffened.

I lowered my eyes. "I was thinking a bicycle ride might do Victoria some good, help her feel better. But if you disapprove . . ."

"Bicycling . . . Hmmm, Victoria would like that." A thoughtful expression came over him. "Yes, you would need some practical garments for that. Very well, you may have the bloomers."

"Thank you," I said, smiling. He wasn't really so unreasonable after all.

"While you ladies choose the accessories, I believe I'll go see if I can find a gift for Victoria, something to cheer her up," he said. "I'll be back in a short while."

After he left, Mme Riviere helped me select the accessories I'd need. She all but corralled me into selecting at least one set of earbobs, convincing me I'd disgrace the Stuart family name if I wore my pink plastic hoop earrings.

At the jewelry counter, a salesclerk was showing a piece of jewelry to a blond man wearing a fawn-colored suit with velvet lapels. "Here is the brooch you ordered to go with those earrings, Mr. Fenniwick," the clerk was saying.

Fenniwick! The man who would marry Prudence and bankrupt Westwind Shipping to pay his gambling debts, I thought, recalling Victoria's long list of Fenniwick's faults. The same man who would destroy Stuart House to line his own pockets. . . .

I edged closer, spying on him while pretending to look at earbobs. He had pretty-boy good looks, clean shaven and baby faced. He was a flamboyant dresser with an arrogant stance, cocky from the tips of his kid leather shoes to the top of his green felt bowler hat. If I didn't know better, I might have thought he'd just walked out of a gay bar in the Castro District.

"Exquisite." He turned the brooch over with gloved fingertips and held it up to the light. "The lady will adore it, I'm certain."

I gasped, then faked a cough to cover myself. The brooch, crowned by a pink pearl amid clusters of diamonds in an ornate gold setting, was identical to the earrings Prudence had been wearing earlier. Could it be coincidence? It was possible Fenniwick was buying the brooch for someone else. After all, I thought, a department store like this must sell dozens of sets like that one.

"You're making a wise purchase," the salesclerk was saying. "A flawless pearl that size and color is rare, and this setting is one of a kind."

I nudged Mme Riviere and asked under my breath, "That man, what can you tell me about him?"

She smiled knowingly. "Ah, quite the dandy, is he not? A real ladies' man. He is a manager at Pratwell Bank of Commerce."

What was Fenniwick doing buying such an expensive gift for a woman engaged to marry another man? Was he already her admirer, or something more? Maybe Prudence didn't love Nathaniel at all, but was only interested in his money. She seemed to have quite a high upkeep cost. Yet as a bank manager, Fenniwick was no pauper, and Prudence herself stood to inherit a mint from her father someday. If she had the hots for Fenniwick, why bother to marry Nathaniel? It didn't make any sense.

Fenniwick glanced up then; I looked away, but not before he glimpsed my face. Fortunately, he had no idea who I was. After paying for his purchase, he slipped the velvet box containing the brooch into the pocket of his brocade waistcoat and sauntered out the door.

My thoughts were interrupted by Nathaniel's arrival. He was carrying a large doll in a velvet dress with a red ribbon in her hair. Victoria would be thrilled. I was thrilled, too, just to see him, and surprised to realize I'd missed him even though we'd been apart only a short time.

"Great Scott, is this really my cousin?" he jested to Madame, a mischievous twinkle lighting his dark eyes. I was wearing my new bloomers, a white shirtwaist with leg-of-mutton sleeves, oxford shoes, and a hat the size of a small dog.

Apollo . . . had he managed to dig out from his pen yet? I wondered. I pushed aside visions of Nathaniel's carefully tended rose garden being uprooted in an exuberant orgy similar to the one the dog had displayed when trashing the bedroom earlier.

"Should I change?" I asked, thinking he disapproved of my bloomers.

He flashed a devilish grin. "No need. Your sporting attire should be most practical for what I have in mind."

"What's that?"

"A surprise."

As he settled the bill, I wondered just what sort of sport he had in mind.

"Where are you taking me?" I asked for the tenth time as the Silver Shadow sailed over the open road south of the city limits. Nervously I fiddled with my hat, tightening the veil tied under my chin to keep the whole thing from flying off in the breeze.

He shrugged. "Don't worry, it's a pleasant surprise. I guarantee it."

"Nathaniel . . ." I broached the subject that had been on my mind all afternoon. "What do you know about a man named Quentin Fenniwick?"

His mustache jerked. "That primping peacock! Thinks he's the Almighty's gift to women, though what any female would see in the odious fop is beyond me. Why do you ask?"

"Just wondering. I, um, saw him in the department store and the salesclerk told me he worked for Prudence's father." I considered telling him the details, but decided against it. Better to wait until I could confront him with proof of my suspicions. A witness—I needed a witness to Prudence's unfaithfulness, if in fact she was two-timing Nathaniel. On the other hand, if I accused her wrongly, how could I ever expect Nathaniel to believe the even more far-fetched stuff I had to tell him?

"Hmmm. Well, see that you keep your distance from that one," he cautioned. "Your reputation doesn't need any more tarnish."

Taking a deep breath, I turned toward him. "Nathaniel, about my reputation . . . there's something I haven't told you."

"Whatever your secrets, keep them. I've no wish to know."

"But—"

Before I could finish, he jolted off the road and onto a bumpy dirt lane leading up a grassy hill. I gripped the leather seats, wondering how anyone could drive such an expensive car over such a pothole-riddled trail. The lane was rough, making it impossible to carry on the serious conversation I'd intended. Nathaniel might be ready to show me his surprise, but my bombshell for him would just have to wait a little longer.

At the top of the hill he stopped in front of a large wooden building, a tall shed of some sort. Nathaniel killed the motor and came around to assist me down from the car. Seeing the impish grin spreading across his face, I had a sudden inkling of what must be inside.

Without a word he crooked his arm through my elbow and led me to the padlocked doors. He unlocked the lock and pulled open the doors, displaying his masterpiece inside.

"Your plane!" I stared openmouthed at the fragile-looking biplane crisscrossed by dozens of metal cables, the name *Victoria* emblazoned on its nose. "Nathaniel, it's spectacular!"

He smiled, clearly pleased by my enthusiasm. "I thought I'd try those changes you suggested. I still don't understand how you know so much about flying machines, but your ideas sounded sensible."

A strange tingling made me tremble from my toes to my ears. "Are you going to fly it today?"

He nodded. "I thought perhaps you'd like to watch. But if you'd rather not . . ."

"Watch? I want to come with you," I blurted out. I'd never actually flown with Alex, since his planes were owned by the studios. I'd pleaded with him to take me up, but he'd always refused. Still, I'd always longed to try it.

Nathaniel raised his eyebrows. "I admire your spirit, Miss James—"

"Taylor. I'm your cousin, remember?"

"You are not my cousin," he said brusquely, "as you well know. As for that particular idea of yours, it isn't safe."

"It's safe enough for you to try," I countered. "Surely you didn't build that thing as a two-seater for yourself?"

The muscles in his cheek grew taut. "I'd hoped that after I'd perfected the device, Prudence might be persuaded to accompany me. But . . ."

I nodded in understanding. Was Prudence right? Could he break his neck—and if so, didn't I have an obligation to stop him? "Nathaniel," I asked cautiously, "were you planning to make this flight today before you met me—or did my comments affect your plans?"

"I've been planning this for weeks, if you must know," he replied. "I've been studying wind velocities, weather patterns. . . ." He droned on as my mind eased. Nathaniel didn't vanish until the earthquake, which meant he must survive this first attempt at flight. But since I'd never read about his success in any history book, the effort must have been a failure.

"Would you mind tossing me the keys for that box in the backseat, please?" I asked him.

He gave me a quizzical look. "The tonneau? It's not locked. Get whatever you need while I inspect the aeroplane."

I opened the tonneau and rummaged through the clothing boxes until I found what I needed— a pair of leather goggles and a wool scarf. I put them on, then glanced up to make sure Nathaniel was preoccupied with his plane before I lifted the car's hood and removed a little something for insurance. I wasn't about to give Nathaniel the chance to speed off and leave me in the field after he heard what I had to say.

Closing the hood soundlessly, I stuffed the item in my pocket, then walked over to where Nathaniel was hitching the plane to the car's bumper. He raised his head from his toolbox and nearly bumped it on the propeller when he saw me.

"What the devil . . . surely you're not serious about flying?"

"I'm perfectly serious," I assured him. "You've obviously designed your flying machine to evenly distribute the weight of two people. I suspect the back won't hold the weight of a full-grown man, since you designed it with a woman in mind."

"True, but—"

"So if you fly solo, it's liable to be front-heavy."

"Possibly," he frowned. "So?"

"So if you crash and break your fool neck, you'll just prove Prudence right—though I'm sure she'd prefer you show up at your wedding in one piece," I concluded.

He frowned. "For a woman, you certainly know how to speak your mind. I believe you could out argue the devil."

"I'll take that as a compliment."

He seemed to debate my proposition mentally before speaking. "Are you certain you can control yourself up there—no whimpering or hysterical crying?" he asked. "As pilot, I cannot tolerate any distractions."

"I'm certain," I said, smiling victoriously as my heart took flight.

"In that case, Miss James," he said, bowing low and doffing his hat in a mock-formal gesture, "I'd be honored to have you as the first passenger aboard the *Victoria*."

Chapter Seven

After towing the plane to the center of the field, Nathaniel motioned me to join him. There was a long strip of bare ground where the grass had been cut, forming a makeshift runway. The wind had picked up speed, blowing briskly across the isolated field. I pulled the scarf tighter around my neck and, at Nathaniel's suggestion, tucked it into the top of my shirt so it wouldn't catch on anything and strangle me. Nathaniel donned a pair of goggles and adjusted his sleeves.

He lifted me around the waist and boosted me over the lower set of wings, the warmth of his hands lingering as he lowered me into my seat behind the pilot's chair. He climbed into his seat, moistened a finger, and raised it in the air to gauge the wind direction, then glanced at the red rag he'd tied on the elevator in front for confirmation. Finally he started the engine and leapt to the ground.

My heart soared as he moved to the huge propeller and spun it, using the full force of his upper body. I marveled at the solid mass of muscles rippling under his white shirt.

A more disturbing thought brought a lump to my throat. What if the plane took off before Nathaniel could jump back in? I couldn't fly a plane if my life depended on it . . . which of course it would.

With the propeller spinning at full force, Nathaniel ran alongside the plane and leapt up, grasping cables in his powerful grip as he pulled himself into his seat. I was surprised to note the bronzed color of his arms; he was obviously a man accustomed to hard work outdoors, whether aboard his ships or working on his flying machine.

We plowed forward over bumps and brambles, gathering momentum. Faster and faster; my hair swirled around me, half-obscuring my vision despite the goggles. My hands clenched the struts so hard that my knuckles turned white, finally, I felt the wheels lift free of the ground.

"We're airborne!" Nathaniel exclaimed as the earth receded beneath us. He glanced back at me; I flashed the *V* for victory sign, figuring he'd get my drift whether or not the symbol was in use yet.

The wind whistled in my ears, sending a chill straight through me. I felt exhilarated, as though every pore were wide open and absorbing the sensation of absolute freedom. I dared a glance down and saw the grass swaying beneath us in great golden waves. Above, the afternoon sun shone between tufts of clouds drifting on a sea of blue.

We climbed higher, the flying machine vibrating like reeds on an orchestra of wind instruments. We were surrounded by a chorus of rattles and clatters from the plane's skeletal wood frame, accompanied by the flapping sound of wind billowing beneath giant canvas wings. Nathaniel's enthusiasm was contagious; I wanted to shout and sing for joy. I felt like Icarus, the legendary Greek so obsessed with flight that he soared too close to the sun and melted his wax wings. . . .

Too close. I was getting much too close to Nathaniel. I'd be leaving in a few days, going back to my own time, yet I found myself more and more disturbed by the prospect. Was I, too, in danger of getting burned?

Nathaniel's booming voice rang out over the wind. "How are you holding up?"

"Fine," I shouted back. "Wonderful!"

He lowered the nose and we leveled off, soaring into the sun. I closed my eyes and imagined what it would be like to stay here forever, sailing like a bird without a care in the world.

"Hold on," Nathaniel's voice warned. The plane lurched, dipping sharply to one side. I opened my eyes, grabbing for a strut as I felt myself slide toward one wing. The plane had no seat belts; what if it flipped over? We're going to fall from the sky, I thought, panicking. I shouldn't have come along. . . . I shouldn't have interfered with history.

Nathaniel shifted his weight to one side, adjusting the ailerons on the wingtips. The plane jerked downward, lurching toward the opposite side. Fighting to regain control, Nathaniel shoved hard on the wheel in front of him to activate the rudder.

My pulse slowed to a gallop when Nathaniel finally righted the plane and guided us into a more gradual, if bumpy, descent. A few moments later, the wheels touched down on solid earth, jolting us forward until Nathaniel braked to a halt at the far end of the field.

He yanked out his pocket watch and read it, then leapt down. Ripping off his goggles, he waved the watch over his head. "Two minutes, fifty-seven seconds!"

"You did it!" I pulled off my goggles and shook my hair free, giddy with excitement. "You broke the Wright brothers' record!" And changed history—because of me, I realized with a jolt.

Nathaniel lifted me out by the waist and spun me around, then pulled me into his arms and hugged me with the exuberance of a conquering hero. My arms closed around his neck in return as I savored the intoxicating taste of victory and the protective feel of his embrace. I buried my head against his chest, unable to catch my breath.

He lifted my chin with his fingertip to meet his gaze. Suddenly there was no laughter, no celebration in his eyes, but only one unmistakable emotion—desire. "No," he corrected me, his voice husky. "We did it. I couldn't have done it without your help."

"I—it was nothing."

"You're wrong." He brushed a stray lock back from my cheek with his hand and leaned forward, his mouth hovering a hairbreadth above mine. "It was everything."

He kissed me then, and the dizzying feelings I'd felt when flying were nothing compared with the primitive emotion that tore through me when his lips met mine. His arms tightened around me as he drew me toward him, the full length of his body pressing hard against mine. I sifted my fingers through the thick tangle of hair at the back of his head, marveling at the surprising softness of his mustache and the rough texture of his unshaven chin that brushed my skin as his tongue parted my lips, exploring, discovering, conquering. I trembled like the slender wooden frame of Nathaniel's flying machine. I'd been kissed before, of course—but never like this, with such . . . ardor, to use an old-fashioned word. But then, Nathaniel was no modern-day man.

No modern-day man . . . I pulled free, my mind reeling. "No," I heard myself say. "This can't be happening. . . . I'll be gone in a few days; I'm not supposed to get involved with you."

Holding me at arm's length, he stared at me in wide-eyed astonishment. My heart fluttered like the canvas wings on his plane; I didn't trust myself to speak again.

"Taylor." His breath was ragged as he spoke my first name. "I don't know what—"

"I didn't—"

"We shouldn't have—"

"We did." My voice wobbled; I wanted to be kissed again.

Slowly he let go of me. We stood at arm's length, not touching, as I saw him struggle to control his emotions, which if they were at all like mine must have felt like a plane in a tailspin.

A shadow passed over his face. "I'm practically a married man," he said. "This shouldn't have happened."

"No," I said, wishing just the opposite even as I questioned my sanity. This was crazy—becoming emotionally involved with a man born nearly a century before me, a man I'd never see again after the next few days. Even if I could fix things so he wouldn't disappear during the earthquake, I still had to return to 1989. There were people depending on·me—my parents . . . Victoria. That is, assuming she was all right, and the earthquake hadn't flattened her run-down apartment, with her inside. I shivered at the thought.

Nathaniel paced restlessly. After a few moments he went to the car and opened the tonneau, taking out a wicker basket and a patchwork quilt. I swallowed hard, trembling. Had he decided to throw caution to the winds? Was he planning to make mad passionate love to me on that quilt, here in the field? The prospect made me feel hot all over.

Or did he intend to just satisfy his needs and be done with the problem, as if I were a common whore? Which, I reminded myself, was exactly what he thought I was. I tensed; no way was I about to sleep with a man who didn't love me, who only wanted sex. It was, after all, the reason I was still a virgin. Not that I hadn't wanted to, plenty of times. I'm not a freak. But none of the guys I went out with ever quite measured up. I'd dated my share of football jocks with no brains, computer hacks with no brawn, and history students who lived vicariously through their books. A couple of them even professed to love me, but I couldn't return their feelings. Not that I was frigid. The truth was simple: All my life, I'd been waiting for the right man to come along. He never had. . . .

Until now.

The realization shook me to the bone. I was falling for Nathaniel. Nathaniel! The one man I could never have. It had been one thing to flirt with him when I thought I was dreaming, or to want to stop him from marrying a woman who was obviously wrong for him. But to want him for myself? The idea was crazy. Insane. Wacko!

"Miss James?" Nathaniel's voice derailed my train of thought. He was, I noted, back to using my last name. Looking toward the sound of his voice, I saw that he'd spread the quilt under an oak tree at the edge of the field and was removing a block of cheese, a platter of smoked ham, and a loaf of sourdough bread from the wicker basket.

I walked toward him, wary of my own feelings as much as his intentions. "You brought lunch?"

He motioned me to sit. I did, on the edge of the quilt opposite him. "It will be nearly dinner-time by the time we return to the house; no point going hungry."

"No." I accepted a wedge of cheese and slice of ham he offered and tore a chunk of sourdough bread from the loaf.

Next he uncorked a bottle of red wine and poured a cup, offering it to me. "To celebrate," he said, then added hastily, "Our flight, that is."

"None for me, thanks," I said, my nervousness increasing. What was Nathaniel like when he started drinking? I thought of my father's drunken behavior and prayed Nathaniel handled his liquor better.

"Water then." He pulled out a jug and poured some for me. I accepted it, trying hard not to let my trembling hands spill any.

"Nathaniel—"

"Miss James—"

He set down his cup. "It seems I owe you an apology. I'd no right to take such liberties. You are an attractive young woman, Miss James."

"You don't have to apologize," I said, touched that he was concerned about my feelings.

"I confess to having certain . . . unchaste feelings toward you. I'm a man of the world—over the years I've enjoyed my share of women in your calling." He coughed, clearing his throat.

I felt a blush cover my cheeks as I imagined what he must be thinking . . . and feeling.

"I've been giving some thought to your future," he said.

"My future?" I swallowed hard. Things were certainly moving fast—and after just one kiss.

He looked at me as though reading my thoughts. "It will be an adjustment for you, naturally. In some ways, you may find your new life more . . . confining. I expect you've been used to speaking your mind a good deal more where you're from."

"That's true." I nodded, wondering where all this was headed.

He took a bite of crusty sourdough with a slice of ham on it, chewing with maddening slowness before finally swallowing. I forced myself to sample a bite of cheese, but my nerves were so taut I didn't taste a thing.

"I've been honest with you about my feelings," he said, unnerving me with his penetrating dark eyes. "Yet you've told me almost nothing about yourself. I can't help wonder what sort of family you were brought up in. You told me earlier that you know what it's like to lose someone you love. Are you an orphan, then?"

Uh-oh, I thought. Reality check. "No," I answered, dreading how he'd react when he heard about my family tree full of actors and actresses. "Look, the truth is, my dad's an alcoholic actor and my mom's an actress, when she can find work, that is. But they're both very much alive— at least, they were the last time I saw them," I amended, swallowing hard as I recalled the earthquake.

A vein in his temple throbbed. "A family of thespians . . . no wonder you wound up a fallen woman," he muttered, obviously thinking of Jessica. "Did they force you to sell yourself for money?"

"No, of course not!"

"Your brother, the aeronaut. Surely if he could indulge such an expensive pastime he ought to be able to care for his sister," he persisted.

I was silent a moment, reflecting on what might have been. "We were very close. He died last year."

His tone softened. "I'm sorry."

I'd tried not to think of Alex lately, as though blocking him from my memory could blot out the bad memories of how he died. I still found myself blinking back tears at the mere mention of him. If only I had Alex to talk to . . . He would have known what I should do. He'd always been the smart one, the one with all the answers, the one who could solve any problem—not at all like me.

Nathaniel leaned closer, his concern apparent as he drummed the quilt with his fingertips. "I want to do the right thing, Miss James. But my . . . attraction to you is getting in the way."

"Attraction?" I gulped. So this was it. Nathaniel was going to tell me he'd decided to dump Prudence for me. I felt an odd warmth spread through me and wondered what it would be like to lie in his arms and let him kiss me again, and again. . . .

He closed his hand over mine; my heart beat a

cha-cha rhythm as he continued. "You and I were caught up in the moment—the elation over a successful flight, nothing more."

I felt the bottom fall out of my stomach and glanced away to hide the hurt I was sure must show on my face. "Nothing?" I echoed. "What we shared meant nothing to you?"

"I don't fault you for what happened between us," he said, his voice ringing in my head. "If anyone's to blame, I'm the guilty party. You have a zest for life that I find refreshing; there's an aura of innocence about you that belies your jaded history—enough to make me momentarily forget your past. But I'm an engaged man, and we both know there can't possibly be any future for us. After what's transpired, I'm sure you'll agree that you cannot stay on any longer."

I choked on my water. Nathaniel reached forward and thumped me on the back. "Miss James, are you all right?"

"Y-yes. That is, no. I mean, I don't know," I stammered.

"It goes without saying that what happened between us here must not occur again," he informed me. "I simply cannot have you under my roof once Prudence and I are man and wife."

The wedding night . . . I saw then where his thoughts had turned, and felt my stomach tie itself into a knot. The thought of lying in his guest room knowing that he was making love to Prudence in the master bedroom down the hall didn't exactly appeal to me, either.

He bent forward, studying me. "You are still

intent on reforming your ways, are you not?
Surely you don't wish to go back to whoring?"

"No . . . That is—"

"Good, then I've a solution in mind. My uncle
Ephraim—that's my late father's brother—and
his wife, my aunt Faith, are arriving from Sausalito this evening for the wedding."

"Swell." I'd heard all about Uncle Ephraim and
Aunt Faith—the loving couple who took in Victoria after the earthquake, locked her in the
closet, and did who-knows-what-else to the poor
kid. Not exactly my nominees for parents of the
year.

"Aren't you going to finish your meal?" he
asked, looking at my nearly full plate. I shook my
head, my appetite gone.

"My uncle is a bit on the stern side, but Aunt
Faith is a good-hearted woman, and a remarkable seamstress," he said. "I plan to ask her to take
you under her wing. You could leave Saturday
after the wedding and stay with them in Sausalito while Aunt Faith teaches you to sew. In no
time you'd be ready to ply a new trade."

"No!" I exploded. If I let Nathaniel ship me off
to Sausalito, I'd never be able to save him—or
return to my own time.

He lowered his brows. "I don't understand.
Have you changed your mind? Do you wish to
return to your former life?"

"No, that's not it at all . . . I'm not what you
think I am. Nathaniel, I'm not a prostitute—I
never have been."

A frown creased his face. "You needn't deny it.

I'm not condemning you for your past."

"You don't understand—my past hasn't even happened yet! In fact, I won't even be born for another sixty years."

He lowered his cup, sloshing several drops of wine onto the grass beside the quilt. "What did you say?"

I steeled myself to go on. "I know it's hard to believe, but the truth is, I'm from the future. See, I was in the attic of your house in October, 1989—only it wasn't your house anymore, it was abandoned—when an earthquake hit. It must have disrupted the geomagnetic forces somehow; next thing I knew, you opened the door and I wound up in your bedroom in 1906."

Nathaniel knelt beside me, placing a palm on my forehead. "You've had too much sun—the altitude must have affected your mind."

"I'm not crazy!" I leapt to my feet, standing just inches from him. "You've got to listen to me. Think about it; it all makes sense. The unusual clothes I was wearing—the zipper." I felt myself redden at the memory.

"Obviously the apparel of a wanton woman," he said, his frown deepening.

"The medicine I gave Victoria," I rambled. "Apollo—my dog, a breed not introduced in this country until the 1970s or 1980s. All that stuff about the flying machine; don't you see? In my time airplanes are common—big ones that fly hundreds of people at a time all over the country. Why, we even have rockets that can fly people to the moon. . . ."

He shook his head and reached toward me as though intending to restrain me. "You need to see a doctor at once."

I ducked beneath his outstretched arm, reached into the pocket of my bloomers, and closed my fingers around the engine coil I'd removed from his car earlier, then turned to face him. "I'm not sick—and I'm not a nut case."

He eased toward me, his voice soothing even as the look in his eyes told me he thought I'd gone off the deep end. "Calm down. I'm not going to hurt you. But I do think a doctor ought to—"

"No doctors." I clutched the coil and held it over my head.

"What are you doing with that? The car won't start without it."

"I know."

"Now see here, Miss James. You're being most unreasonable—"

"No doctors." With my free hand, I unbuttoned the top two buttons on my blouse.

His eyes grew as round as the wheels on his Rolls Royce. "You wouldn't dare. . . ."

I met his stare with the sanest gaze I could muster. "You're going to hear me out, or you'll have to retrieve your coil yourself. Now"—I dropped the coil down my blouse until it settled safely—if uncomfortably—between my breasts, the one place I knew he wasn't about to venture—"are you ready to listen or not?"

Chapter Eight

He crossed his arms in front of him, looking like a cop preparing to grill a suspected criminal. "Very well," he grumbled. "I'm listening."

"I was born in 1966—"

"That's preposterous," he interrupted.

"I'm a student, a history major," I continued cautiously, keeping one hand on the button of my blouse. "That's how I know so much about your house. I met your sister, Victoria, when she was a frail old woman in her nineties—"

"You're mad!"

"I'm as sane as you are. Now, will you knock it off with the wisecracks and let me finish?" I drummed my fingertips lightly on the bulge in my blouse where the coil rested.

He swallowed his rage. "Go on."

"She asked me to take down her memoirs. She

told me everything about your family history, your house. Look, I won't go into all the details, but let's just sum it up by saying I know what's going to happen in the future. Your future."

"First a gypsy. Now a traveler in time?" His tone was mocking.

"Nathaniel," I continued, struggling to keep my voice steady, "the only reason I'm telling you all this now is to warn you."

"Warn me?"

"Yes. There's going to be an earthquake—a terrible one—next Wednesday. If you don't do something, you're going to disappear and your business is going to be destroyed."

His eyes narrowed. "Are you on Ruef's payroll? A spy for my enemy—working to discredit me, ruin my business? It seems implausible, but . . ."

"Wouldn't a spy come up with a more believable story than this?"

He looked doubtful. "Yes, I should think so. However—"

"I'm no spy. I'm just a perfectly normal woman who doesn't fit in here because I'm used to living in the 1980s!" My frustration got the better of me. "Prudence is going to remarry Fenniwick and they'll ruin everything. And if you won't believe me, help me change things, your sister will be burned in the earthquake. You've got to save her, and yourself," I shouted. "You have to—"

He jumped me then, knocking me to the ground before I knew what hit me. Pinning me down with one hand, he slipped his other down my blouse and closed his fingers around the coil, sending a hot flash across my chest as the back of his hand brushed the tops of my breasts. The full weight of his body collapsed on mine, squeezing the breath out of me. "You're h-hurting me. . . ." I gasped.

"Don't toy with me again," he warned, his face hovering just above mine. I could smell the scent of wine on his breath, rich, intoxicating. He shifted his weight and suddenly the sensation of having him lying on top of me didn't seem so bad. Maybe I *was* crazy, I thought, my senses inflamed.

He slipped the coil into his waistcoat pocket, keeping a firm grip on me. "It's for your own good," he informed me. "You're clearly suffering delusions. . . . I can hardly expect Aunt Faith to cope with your fits of raving—perhaps you do belong in a madhouse."

The look in his eyes sent a chill through me. He thought I was nuts. What if he had me committed? I recalled the horror stories I'd read about turn-of-the-century insane asylums, where patients were often kept chained, naked and drugged. . . . I might never get out—certainly not in time to save Nathaniel and Victoria, or get home when the earthquake hit on Wednesday.

"No! Not a madhouse—I'm not crazy," I said quickly, racking my brain for a way out.

"What possessed you to make up such an outrageous tale?" he asked. "Do you still believe I would send you back to the bordello you've run off from? I'm not such a monster, you know."

"I know," I said, intensely aware of every pore

in his far from monstrous body pressing down on me. "That's why you won't send me off to a madhouse—why, it would be an even worse place than a bordello," I improvised. "Besides, I'm not crazy."

"How can I be certain of that after your bizarre behavior?"

"I'll show you," I hedged, knowing I had to buy time somehow.

"Liar."

"I'm not a liar!"

"Prove it."

I took a deep breath. "Okay, I will. I'll make a deal with you."

He let out a hearty guffaw. "A deal? I'd say you're in no position to be bargaining just now." Heat rushed to my face as he tightened his grip on my wrists and his weight shifted, pressing the full length of him against my abdomen.

"Look, all I'm asking is that you don't ship me off to the loony bin just yet," I said rapidly. "Don't say anything to your aunt and uncle about my, uh, past until after the . . . wedding," I said, choking on the last word. "I'll be on my best behavior; I promise I won't embarrass you—"

"Why should I agree?" he asked. "Not that I'm saying I will, mind you."

"Give me two days to prove to you that I'm not crazy—that I can be trusted. If I succeed, you let me stay on until next Wednesday."

"And if you don't?"

"Then I'll go away after the wedding, just as you wish. With your aunt and uncle—or to the madhouse. Your choice."

I held my breath for what seemed forever. Finally, his eyes narrowed. "No more tricks?"

My heart jumped. "None. Honest—I promise."

He released his hold on me. "Very well, then. I'll give you one last chance, seeing as you seem to have come to your senses. Though I'm warning you—don't breathe a word of this rubbish about the future to my relations or I'll deliver you to the madhouse myself."

"I won't," I promised, wondering how on earth I was going to persuade him to trust me within 48 hours.

He offered me his hands and helped me up. His touch was an electric jolt, zapping me of reason.

"I still don't understand why you would spin such wild tales if you're not daft," he said, shaking his head as he packed away the picnic items. "You're quite an actress, I'll grant you that much. It must run in the family. For a moment, you almost sounded as though you believed that cock-and-bull tale."

"Sometimes truth can be pretty unbelievable," I said.

He gave me an odd stare as we walked together back to the Silver Shadow. "For now, it would be best to get you out of the sun. Make sure you put on that broad-brimmed hat with the veil for the return trip."

I nodded dumbly. I'd jumped out of the frying pan and into the fire, it seemed. Now Nathaniel was more convinced than ever that I was a fallen

woman—and maybe a deranged one, at that.
How on earth was I supposed to change history
when the hero of this story was so darned un-
cooperative?

The sun was low in the sky by the time we arrived back at Stuart House in the late afternoon,
after a long, tense ride. Nathaniel had answered
my questions about the visiting relatives and upcoming wedding in monosyllables. I managed to
learn that besides Victoria and Nathaniel's aunt
and uncle, no other Stuarts would be in atten-
dance, easing my concerns as to whether I'd be
able to pull off my "cousin" imposter act in front
of bona fide members of the family.

As Nathaniel pulled the Rolls into the driveway
and parked it inside the carriage house, I noticed
a black horse-drawn rig was stabled inside. "Ah,"
he noted as he helped me out. "It appears Uncle
Ephraim and Aunt Faith have arrived."

"Nathaniel," I began, recalling what Victoria
had told me about the uncle who'd mistreated
her in Sausalito after the earthquake, "if anything happened to you, Victoria'd wind up with
your aunt and uncle, right?"

"Of course. They're my closest living relatives.
Why do you ask?"

"I wouldn't trust them with her, especially your
uncle. The guy's no white knight."

"I'll not have you bad-mouthing my relations
in my own house," he warned, scowling. "My uncle can be dour at times, but he's not a bad sort.
You haven't even met the man and already you're

145

jumping to conclusions."

"But he—"

"Can I trust you to conduct yourself properly or not?" he demanded, freezing me with a look.

I bit back my words. "I'll be good," I promised.

"Now *that* would be a refreshing change."

We climbed the steps to the front porch and Mrs. O'Hara swung the door open wide. "There ye are—I heard ye drive up. We've got company, we have."

Behind her, Uncle Ephraim and Aunt Faith stepped forward to greet Nathaniel. Faith, dressed in a somber high-necked gown, gave Nathaniel a welcoming hug as her husband, a stern-faced man whose black suit reminded me of an undertaker's, slapped his nephew heartily on the back. "So, Nathaniel, some wench has got her hooks into you at last," he chuckled. Spotting me, he asked, "Is this the unlucky young la—"

His words caught in his throat as he stared at me, looking as though he'd just bitten into a jalapeno pepper. If I hadn't known better, I'd have sworn he knew me from someplace—and hated my guts. My discomfort grew as his gaze darted from the traces of engine oil stains on my blouse—souvenirs of the coil—to the similar stains on Nathaniel's hands, then back again.

Nathaniel came to my rescue. "This isn't Prudence, Uncle Ephraim. I'd like you to meet Miss Taylor James, a distant cousin."

"On your mother's side?" Faith inquired.

"Father's," Nathaniel repeated my lie.

The red color gradually faded from Ephraim's

146

age-spotted face, but his expression was far from satisfied. "That's odd," he said, leaning on an ivory-handled cane for support. "My father was an only child, and Josiah and I were his only children. How is it I never heard about any cousin?"

Nathaniel tugged at his collar, looking decidedly uncomfortable. "Your grandfather, my great-grandfather, had several sisters back in the old country, right?"

Ephraim grunted and nodded.

"Taylor is descended from one of them," he concluded.

"Which one—"

"Taylor, you must be exhausted," Nathaniel said, cutting short Ephraim's interrogation. To Aunt Faith, he explained, "My cousin had her clothes stolen in a train robbery. She's spent the afternoon shopping and now I'm sure she'd like some time to get changed before dinner."

"Poor dear." Faith clucked sympathetically. "Such an ordeal." Did she mean the shopping or the robbery, I wondered? She didn't seem the witch I'd envisioned; more like Edith Bunker. "Go on upstairs, Miss James," she urged. "I'm sure we shall have ample opportunity to get acquainted later, over dinner."

My stomach rumbled, but I ignored it. "Swell—I mean, that sounds fine." The idea of going away with these two gave me the creeps. I'd better find a way to make Nathaniel trust me, and fast.

Nathaniel ushered me through the foyer to the bottom of the stairs. "Wear something appropriate for dinner," he whispered. "And for God's sake, keep the conversation away from the family tree."

"Don't worry, I'll manage." As he started to turn, I caught his sleeve. "Nathaniel." I paused. "Thanks for not telling them about me. I noticed your uncle didn't exactly seem thrilled to meet me, as it was."

He brushed a stray curl away from my face. "Don't mind him. He means no harm."

"I suppose not. But remember—a deal's a deal. You won't rat me out, will you?"

"I'm a man of my word," he assured me. "I won't reveal your soiled dove identity to anyone before the wedding—even though you've told me nothing but lies and half-truths since I met you. But remember, show me good cause why I should trust you, or you'll leave me no choice but to send you packing before I bring my bride home on Saturday."

Two days from now. How could I make Nathaniel trust me in so little time? He'd refused to listen to the truth, nor would he pay attention to even the slightest criticism of Prudence. Still, he left me little choice but to agree to his terms.

"I understand," I said, though I felt as if I were walking blindfolded through a minefield. Things were ready to explode, I sensed. But who would be the first casualty?

Nathaniel was holding a black box under his arm when I came downstairs later. "Come on outside, into the evening light," he was saying to Aunt Grace and Ephraim.

"What's that?" I asked, pointing to the box as I followed the three of them out onto the front porch.

He stared at me curiously. "Haven't you ever seen a camera before?" he asked, motioning for Aunt Grace and Uncle Ephraim to have a seat on the porch swing.

I blinked in surprise. "Not like that one," I said, looking closer at the black box he held. I knew cameras had been invented, of course, but I'd envisioned one of those clunky things with bellows and a hood, the kind that required a tripod and exposures of several minutes.

"It's a Kodak box camera, invented by a fellow named George Eastman," Nathaniel explained as he squinted through the viewfinder.

"How does it work?" I asked, fascinated.

"Simple." He shrugged. "Here, you try it."

He handed me the camera, which was much heavier than the kind I was used to. I peered through it and saw Uncle Ephraim sitting stone-faced beside Aunt Faith, who was puckering up her face from the setting sun that was no doubt in her eyes.

"First you pull this cord on the top of the camera," he instructed. "Then you turn that key next to it. Good. Now all you have to do is hold it steady while you press the button—no, not on the top. Here, on the side."

The inside of his forearm brushed tantalizingly against mine as I pushed the button and heard the shutter release. "That's all there is to it," he said, grinning. "Revolutionary, isn't it?"

"Amazing," I agreed, wishing I had a Polaroid to show him. "Do you do your own developing too?"

"Not with this camera. It has one hundred frames on a roll. Once that's finished, I simply mail the whole thing back to Mr. Eastman. He then returns the prints, along with the camera, loaded and ready with a new roll."

"Unreal," I acknowledged. So much for being invited into Nathaniel's darkroom. Flushing at the memory of our kiss, I found myself feeling curiously disappointed at being deprived the chance to be alone with him in the dark.

To cover my unease, I backed up to the street and took some shots of Stuart House, until Mrs. O'Hara informed us that dinner was ready.

Decked out in the blue tea gown with the scooped neckline, I sat at the dining room table between Nathaniel and Victoria, who had made a remarkable recovery.

Across from me, Aunt Faith prattled on endlessly about the wedding, salting her conversation here and there with choice tidbits about Nathaniel's childhood.

"Do you know, when he was three years old he tried to jump off the roof with a sheet draped across his shoulders, like wings? Said he thought he could fly." Aunt Faith chuckled, her eyes crinkling at the memory.

"No kidding," I said, exchanging a knowing smile with Nathaniel, who looked handsomer than ever in the dark suit, starched white shirt, and black cravat he wore. My gaze wandered to his lips as he savored an oyster and I found myself recalling the warm pressure of those lips on mine. Quickly I glanced down at my plate to hide the pink color I was sure my face must be turning.

Throughout the meal, Nathaniel endured his aunt's embarrassing disclosures and deflected the conversation away from probes into my background with the skill of a master fencer. Uncle Ephraim occupied the far end of the polished mahogany dining room table, sneaking glances at my cleavage whenever Nathaniel wasn't watching. Aunt Faith caught him in the act at least once and gave him a knock-it-off-or-you're-dead-meat stare. I wanted to run upstairs and escape the whole ordeal, but one thing stopped me: I was starving, since I'd hardly eaten a bite of my picnic lunch.

Fortunately, there was no shortage of food. First came an assortment of appetizers I couldn't pronounce but which tasted wonderful. Next came cioppino, a San Francisco specialty. The piping hot tomato-based stew laden with whole clams, mussels, and chunks of fish was served up in hollowed-out individual loaves of sourdough bread. The main course, a crown roast of pork garnished with a flaming orange-brandy glaze, made my mouth water just looking at it, not to mention the new potatoes, scallions, and succulent hearts of artichoke. But the grand finale was dessert, an elegant fruit torte served with enough whipped cream to top a small mountain. I slipped a portion of mine into a napkin to smuggle to Apollo later in lieu of our daily doughnuts. After all, dessert was his favorite.

After dinner, I excused myself from polite conversation, pleading exhaustion. As I walked past Uncle Ephraim, he leaned toward me and hissed, "You don't fool me for a moment."

"Excuse me?" I whispered, unnerved. Had Nathaniel told him of my supposed profession?

"I know what you are, and if my nephew had any sense, he would too," he said, leering at me with yellowed teeth.

"I don't know what you're talking about," I said, brushing quickly past him. Something about him gave me the willies, even then.

Upstairs, I noticed that someone had replaced the quilt Apollo had shredded with a rose-colored comforter. Turning down the covers, I saw fresh linens—crisp, cool, and inviting. I yawned, stretching my aching limbs.

I stripped off my clothes, except for a thin cotton chemise, and flopped down on the bed. I'd just rest for a few minutes before washing up and getting into my night things. The room was warm, so I didn't bother to pull the covers over me, luxuriating instead in the freedom from all those hot, heavy clothes.

I must have been more tired than I thought. It seemed like no time before I was deep into a disturbing dream, waltzing across the ballroom in Nathaniel's arms. The chandelier above cast a glittering reflection on us, illuminating the depths of his hauntingly dark eyes as he dipped me backward and crushed his lips against mine.

"I want you, Taylor," his rich voice whispered as he caressed my face. His lips traveled downward, etching a white-hot trail from my neck to the tender skin just above the low-cut gown I wore.

"Touch me. . . . Kiss me again," I moaned, arching backward, aflame from his hot breath on my bare skin.

The pain awoke me—a sharp pinching sensation in both nipples. My eyes popped open and I found myself staring at the leer on Uncle Ephraim's face.

"Enjoying it, aren't you?" An ugly laugh escaped his broad lips. "I might have known. You're just like Jessica—the likeness is unmistakable."

"Get out of my room!" I sat up and grabbed at the sheet, but he yanked it away.

"You don't fool me," he snarled, rubbing his bulbous fingers across my cheek. I edged backward until my spine banged against the bedpost. "You're no Stuart. You're kin to Jessica. . . . She's too young to have a daughter your age, so you must be her sister—trying to get your hooks into my nephew just the way Jessica did with my brother, Josiah. I'm here to see that you don't." He leaned over me, moving his cracked lips toward my face.

"No!" I slammed the heel of my palm up under his nose, grateful for that self-defense class I took on campus last semester.

He groaned in pain. "Bitch . . ." He slapped me hard across the face. I screamed. He shoved a

153

beefy forearm down on my mouth, muzzling me. Fear welled in my throat as he pinned my wrists behind me and I saw him unbuttoning his trousers. God, no—not him. . . .

"We'll just see if your favors are as satisfying as your whoring sister's." He pawed at the front of my chemise, momentarily freeing my mouth. "Help!" I yelled. "No—you're wrong. . . . Get away fr—" He stuffed a handkerchief in my mouth and climbed on top of me.

The door slammed open. I heard the threatening growl an instant before I saw Apollo barreling toward my attacker, Victoria two steps behind him, with Nathaniel a close third. Apollo launched himself at Uncle Ephraim, sinking his teeth into the seat of the old lecher's pants.

"He's hurting her, he's hurting her!" Victoria bobbed up and down, pointing at her greatuncle. "I heard her screaming 'no' and telling him to leave, but . . ."

Nathaniel lurched forward and pulled Apollo loose, along with a sizable chunk of Uncle Ephraim's trousers. Then he pulled back his fist and swung hard, smacking a hard right hook on Uncle Ephraim's jaw that smashed the old pervert against the wall.

"Get out." Nathaniel's voice was low and menacing, like a snake's rattle.

Uncle Ephraim staggered to his knees. "Now see here, Nathaniel, this was just a little misunderstanding. . . ."

"I said get out!" Nathaniel grabbed his uncle by the collar and hauled him to his feet. "If you so much as lay a hand on her again, I'll fix it so you won't be capable of molesting a woman again."

"I won't. You have my word," Uncle Ephraim wheedled. "You wouldn't—that is, Faith has her heart set on staying for the wedding. . . ."

Nathaniel released him with a thud. "I wouldn't shame Aunt Faith by telling her what I've just seen. You'll stay for the wedding and you will conduct yourself like a gentleman, or I'll throw you aboard one of my ships and have you keelhauled."

Ephraim backed toward the door, clutching his sore backside. "I'm still your uncle, so I'll give you a piece of advice," he muttered, throwing me a threatening stare just before stumbling into the hall. "You're making a mistake, Nathaniel, trusting the likes of her."

Victoria shut the door the instant he was gone.

"Taylor, are you all right?" She rushed to my side.

Nathaniel was already there, gently removing the gag from my mouth. I clutched at my chemise, burying my face in my hands. Seeing my distress, Nathaniel pulled the sheet up to cover me. I was shaking uncontrollably.

"There, it's all right." Nathaniel pulled me against him, comforting me by his mere presence. I felt safe in his arms, knowing nothing bad could happen to me as long as he kept holding me. Insanely, I wished he'd never let me go.

"My uncle, he didn't—?"

"No. I wasn't . . ." I glanced at Victoria and the

word *rape* froze on my tongue. "He didn't . . . violate me."

He exhaled a relieved sigh, his fingers instinctively combing my matted hair as he murmured some soothing words. Apparently realizing the impropriety of his actions, he dropped his hands to his sides.

Victoria looked from me to Nathaniel and back again, an inquisitive look on her face. Something about her disturbed me; at times she seemed altogether too worldly for a 12-year-old child.

Apollo hopped onto a trunk at the foot of the bed and scrambled up onto the covers. A moment later he was climbing over Nathaniel's arms, licking my face.

"Whoa—easy, boy." I laughed. "How'd you get in here, anyway?" I asked, recalling suddenly that Apollo had been banished to the pen out back earlier.

Victoria grinned sheepishly. "He kept howling all day long. I felt sorry for the poor thing, so I sneaked him inside to my room. We were sleeping together when we heard you cry out."

Nathaniel scowled and looked as though he were about to scold the girl, but stopped himself. Apollo was now a household hero and, apparently, above criticism for the moment.

"Can I keep him, Nathaniel? Can I?" Victoria begged, throwing her arms around Apollo, who had wormed his way out of my face and onto her lap.

"He isn't yours to keep, Victoria," Nathaniel reminded her.

She pursed her lips. "True. But I thought perhaps he could stay upstairs tonight, if it's all right with Taylor. I promise I'll help keep an eye on him, and he can protect her again if—"

"All right, I surrender." Nathaniel emitted a low chuckle. "It seems I'm outnumbered by the females in this house. Just see to it the young rapscallion isn't left untended. And for heaven's sake, don't let him anywhere near Prudence."

Apollo snorted loudly. Being caged in a goose pen was now beneath the dignity of a hero, it seemed.

"I'm glad to see you're feeling better," I said, noting the spots of color on Victoria's face.

She beamed. "Those pills you gave me worked like magic." Turning to the dog, she instructed, "Come, Apollo, I'll tuck you back in." Obediently, he trotted out the door behind her.

Perhaps he was trainable after all, I thought, shaking my head in disbelief.

Nathaniel laid me down gently and tucked the sheet up under my chin, then sat beside me. "I'm so sorry—I've no idea what got into my uncle to make him behave so reprehensibly." A frown creased his face. "You didn't let slip about your occupation, did you?"

"The subject never came up."

He nodded. "Best it doesn't, after what happened tonight." After a pause, he added, "You were right about my uncle. I should have trusted your intuition."

"Than you admit you can trust me?" I pounced on the opportunity.

He shifted awkwardly. "Enough to know you're not crazy, at least," he conceded.

It was enough for now, I decided as I looked into his eyes and saw the depth of his concern. "Thank you," I said, my voice shaky as the full impact of what nearly happened sank in. "I never expected to see you come charging in to defend my virtue."

We shared a smile over the irony. "Lord knows you're beautiful enough to drive any man wild. Still, if I didn't know better," he said, giving me a stare so intense that it made me shiver, "I'd almost believe you were never a harlot at all, that it was just another of your wild tales."

"You said something earlier about my intuition," I said carefully. "Maybe it's time you start to trust your own instincts."

"Perhaps," he said. "But at least this proves one thing. I know now beyond a shadow of a doubt that your intent to reform is genuine. If it wasn't, you'd have soaked old Uncle Ephraim for everything in his wallet in exchange for a lively romp between the sheets."

I shuddered. "He was so awful. . . ." Snatches of the nightmare floated in my mind. "He kept comparing me to Jessica, for some reason."

"Jessica? Odd. He scarcely knew my stepmother. She ran off when Victoria was an infant, as you know. As far as I recall, Uncle Ephraim only met her once or twice."

I frowned. "It didn't sound that way to me."

Nathaniel released my hand. "Well, it doesn't matter anymore," he said, rising. "After all, that's all in the past. Right?"

Chapter Nine

As soon as Nathaniel left, I dug out the night-gown Mme Riviere had selected for me, trudged off to the bathroom, and filled the tub with steaming hot water, eager to scrub off the imagined filth that clung to me wherever Uncle Ephraim had touched.

This time I borrowed Apollo and posted him just inside the bathroom door to keep out intruders. Not that he'd deter Nathaniel—but somehow I doubted if Uncle Ephraim would risk crossing the dog's path after his earlier close encounter.

I closed my eyes, my thoughts a muddy jumble. Thank God for Nathaniel. If he hadn't come in when he did . . . He must have *some* feelings for me, the way he'd decked his own uncle. He'd protected me, stuck up for me the way nobody ever had, except maybe Alex. He was even starting to doubt his own conclusion that I was a not-so-happy hooker. Flashes of my earlier dream came to mind, of Nathaniel's lips closing over mine as he waltzed me across the ballroom. . . .

What was I doing, allowing myself to become hung up on Nathaniel, dreaming of intimate moments with a man I couldn't possibly have a future with? It was nuts. I had to quit fantasizing about a relationship going nowhere. He was bound and determined to marry Prudence on Saturday—and even if he weren't, he would never allow himself to act on his "unchaste feelings" toward me. I was damaged goods in his eyes. A scarlet woman, an improper influence on his impressionable younger sister.

Forget about him, I told myself. Just concentrate on making Prudence show her true colors before the wedding, so Nathaniel will call it off. That would take care of saving his house and fortune; then all I'd have to do would be to convince him to let me stay on here until Wednesday—and somehow keep him out of the attic and Victoria away from her candles.

Fat chance. I sighed, overwhelmed by the steep road ahead.

A banging sound from next door caught my attention. Just as long as it wasn't Uncle Ephraim again . . . Suddenly I was grateful for Apollo's presence, even if he was scattering crumbs and frosting all over the bathroom floor from the leftovers I'd smuggled upstairs.

I finished bathing, shampooed my hair, and climbed out of the tub—careful not to slip this time. I missed my blow-dryer and hot rollers, settling instead for a towel wrapped turban-style around my head. After toweling dry the rest of me, I cleaned up the mess Apollo had made, changed into my new white nightgown and robe, and walked back to my room with the dog.

Victoria was waiting for us in my room, perched on the edge of my bed. "How are you?" she asked, swinging her heels back and forth. Apollo waddled to her side and nuzzled her ankles; she stroked his chin indulgently and slipped him a bit of roast pork that I'd seen her remove from her dinner plate before.

"I'm all right. Really."

She tilted her head to one side. "Nathaniel seemed quite worried about you. He's grown to care for you a good deal, you know."

I rested my hands on the back of the vanity chair for support. "Well, that's to be expected. I'm his cousin."

Victoria looked skeptical. "That isn't how things ought to be, not at all."

Before I could comment on her strange remark, she reached into the folds of her skirt and pulled out a worn leather volume. "I brought you a book. I hope you'll enjoy it; it's from Nathaniel's library. He told me you have a gift for storytelling, so I assume you enjoy reading. I do too—I adore Gothic novels, though this book on the ancients is a favorite of mine."

I accepted her offering, turning it over in my hand. It was a book on mythology, depicting legends of the Greek and Roman gods. "Thank you,"

I said. "But should you be taking books from your brother's library without asking him first?"

She evaded my questioning stare. "There's no harm done," she said. She hopped up and skipped to the door, Apollo close behind her. "By the way, Nathaniel installed a lock on your door while you were bathing. It should keep you safe . . . just in case."

So that's what the banging sound was. I glanced at the gleaming brass lock and nodded. "Good."

An impish twinkle gleamed in the girl's eyes. "Sweet dreams, Cousin Taylor. I hope they all come true."

"Same to you."

Grinning like a Cheshire cat, she vanished into the hall and pulled the door closed behind her.

I combed my hair out, then sat reading the book for an hour or so until my hair was dry. Visions of Nathaniel filled my mind despite my best efforts to concentrate on the urgent problems to be solved. Finally, I turned down the covers, ready to hit the sack.

A flutter of white pinned to my pillow caught my eye. It was a folded piece of paper with my name on it. I removed the pin and unfolded the paper. It was penned in ornate lettering on Nathaniel's monogrammed stationery:

My dearest Taylor.
I must see you alone. Meet me in the gazebo
in the dark before the dawn. I shall count the

hours until we meet.

—Nathaniel

My heart stopped, then started with a jolt. He wanted to see me, alone, at a time when the rest of the household was sleeping. He called me *dearest*—said he was counting the hours until he'd see me again. . . .

If he meant to send me away, he'd never phrase a summons that way. I clutched his letter to my chest, scarcely able to breathe. From the tone of it, he sounded as though he meant to tell me how he felt about me. My run-in with his uncle must have made him realize that he could trust me after all. . . . Did that mean he was ready to dump Prudence? I sat down on the bed, trembling. Could this be the way to save Nathaniel—by making him fall in love with me? Love. Was that what I felt for Nathaniel? It couldn't be. I'd just met him; it couldn't be love. Lust, perhaps. Lust? Yes, that was it, I thought, letting my mind roam into forbidden regions.

I laid my head on the cool linen pillowcase, imagining the feel of Nathaniel's broad, hairy chest against my cheek. It could never happen, of course. Nathaniel would never give up Prudence for me. He might have his doubts about me, but he'd still been too bullheaded to really believe me when I told him I wasn't a prostitute. Small wonder, after all the other far-fetched stories I'd told him.

Too bullheaded to believe . . . A dangerous idea snaked its way into my head. Desperate situations called for desperate measures, I rationalized as I sat up in bed, my emotions springing cartwheels. Nathaniel cared about me; he might even love me. But he would never dare admit it.

Not as long as he thought I was a prostitute, at least. I could think of only one way to prove him wrong.

I hardly slept a wink and woke up a full hour before 5:00, clicking off the timer on my watch before it had a chance to buzz. I brushed my hair a couple of hundred more strokes and carefully applied a light touch of color to my cheeks and lips from the enameling kit Mme Riviere had thankfully provided for me. I wondered if I should get dressed, but decided against it. If anyone should see me wandering the halls before dawn, it would be awkward to explain why I wasn't still in nightclothes.

If anyone should see me . . . Uncle Ephraim. What if Nathaniel's uncle was up early and found me alone? Just in case, I decided to bring Apollo along. I doubted if Uncle Ephraim would risk another meeting between his backside and Apollo's teeth. I slipped into the hall, wondering how I might rouse Apollo from Victoria's room without waking her. To my surprise, I found him poised just outside her door, ears cocked, as though he'd been waiting for me.

My pulse felt as if it were running a relay race as we crept down the stairs, freezing when my step creaked a floorboard. Apollo whined; I put my hand over his mouth to muffle the sound.

When no one emerged, we continued our descent. On the second-story landing, I saw a faint light flickering from beneath the door to Nathaniel's private study and heard a rustle of movement inside, but resisted the urge to surprise him there. Better to let this act play out according to his script.

With Apollo at my heels, I slipped out the kitchen door and made my way through the garden, breathing deeply as I inhaled the potent aromas of roses and honeysuckle. Moonlight cast a silver halo of light, adding a surreal effect to the night's already dreamlike happenings.

Finally I reached the gazebo. To my surprise, Nathaniel was already there, pacing, arms crossed. Waiting. So it wasn't him in his study . . . he must have left the lamp on. The noise I'd heard had to be a mouse or something. Who cared? Nathaniel was here, waiting for me, wanting me.

I took the steps swiftly as my white robe billowed out behind me on the faint breeze. Belatedly I realized that in the moonlight, my figure must be silhouetted through the filmy fabric. I resisted the impulse to cover myself, knowing I'd need all the ammunition I could get in order to seduce Nathaniel. Instead, I untied the sash of my robe, letting it fall open.

"I'm here," I said breathlessly, halting two feet in front of him. Apollo lay down on the step behind me, a monument to discretion.

Nathaniel lowered his arms to his sides, his gaze sweeping downward, then up to meet my

165

eyes. "So I see," he whispered. The intensity of his stare made me shiver in anticipation. "Taylor, this isn't proper. I shouldn't be here with you, but there's a matter we must sort out."

"Sort away," I said, stepping closer.

A low groan escaped his lips. "Lord, you're beautiful," he said softly. He lifted his hand, sweeping away the long strands of hair that the breeze had blown in my face.

My heart hammered in my chest as I stood on tiptoes and touched the coarse stubble on his chin. "What is it that you want?" I asked, tracing his smooth-as-velvet lips with my fingertips.

"You know damned well what I want," he said, his breath ragged. "I'm finding it damned near impossible to resist your temptations. Ever since we flew together, since I tasted your charms, you've haunted my thoughts and tormented my dreams."

"I have?" I whispered, dizzy. Without waiting for his reply I wrapped my arms around his neck and pressed my lips against his. I felt him stiffen in response as a low groan escaped him. Deftly I slid my tongue between his lips.

He pulled me into his arms, crushing me against his rock-hard chest. My cheek brushed against the satin lapel of his smoking jacket, the rich scents of smoke and brandy engulfing me. This was crazy—insane . . . yet I didn't dare stop. I'm not sure I could have even if I'd wanted to. I hardly knew Nathaniel Stuart, yet I felt as though I'd known him all my life.

Without warning, he tore himself free and set

me at arm's length. "Your madness has be-witched me," he said, his voice husky with emotion. "But I can't allow things to go further; I won't. That's what I came to tell you, face-to-face, until you made me lose my wits again. It's the only reason I went along with your headstrong game—"

"Game?" I asked, my mind spinning out of control.

"The note you sent me. Asking me to meet you here."

"*I* sent *you*? I never sent you any note. It was you who sent one to me. . . ." Realization flooded into my brain; I felt my face turn scarlet. "Oh, God. You thought—"

I reached into the pocket of my robe and pulled out the note I'd received, handing it to him. As I did so, I detected a flicker of movement behind a curtain in the second-story turret window. Victoria's window.

Nathaniel scanned my note, his eyes taking in the direction of my gaze. "It seems," he said, stuffing my note in his pocket, "that we've both been had."

"And I've got a pretty good idea who's responsible," I added, silently resolving to have a long, hard talk with Victoria later.

He cleared his throat. "It appears I owe you an apology."

"No—I'm the one who should be sorry. I never would have acted like this if I'd realized . . . I should have known—"

"Don't." He cut me off. "Stop blaming yourself

for my sister's pranks. The child is willful, always has been. But this time she's gone too far. I'll see that she's disciplined appropriately for her mischief."

"Don't be too hard on her," I pleaded as we stepped down together from the gazebo. "I'm sure she only had your best interests at heart."

He frowned. "That, as I see it, is precisely the problem."

The sound of footsteps from the vicinity of Victoria's playhouse diverted my attention. I glanced toward the sound in time to see a shadow pass behind the trees, moving rapidly away. Apollo stood up, the hairs on his spine rigid.

"What was that?" I asked, halting in midstep.

"What was what?"

"Over there. By the playhouse. I could swear someone was there."

Motioning me to stay put, he went inside the playhouse and checked things out, then forged into the trees behind the structure. A low growl curled from the dog's throat; I held on tightly to his collar, not about to be left alone in case Uncle Ephraim was prowling around nearby.

Nathaniel emerged several minutes later. "Nothing. Must have been your imagination. I'd say we both need to go back to bed—to clear our heads."

I nodded, my senses numbed.

As we reached the kitchen door he motioned for me to go inside. "I'll wait here until you're safely upstairs. And Taylor"—he met my gaze, his dark eyes warning me of something—"make sure and keep your door locked."

I agreed, thinking of Uncle Ephraim. But who, I wondered as I made my way shakily upstairs, was Nathaniel really trying to protect me from? Or, for that matter, was it himself?

Equally troubling was the prospect that someone other than Victoria had witnessed tonight's little tete-a-tete. Who was out there in the playhouse? I couldn't see any reason why someone should spy on Nathaniel and me. Recalling the noise I'd heard coming from the study earlier, I wondered if the same person was responsible for both occurrences. But if so, who was it? And more important, what were they doing skulking around here in the middle of the night?

Somehow I managed to drift off to sleep after lying awake until past sunrise. Sheer exhaustion, I suppose. I awoke midmorning feeling tired, frustrated, and totally humiliated. I'd all but thrown myself at Nathaniel, all because of Victoria's dumb note. Not that he'd exactly run from my advances . . .

My thoughts lingered on the delicious taste of him, the warm feeling that suffused my limbs when he'd held me in his arms. I found my mind wandering into areas better left alone, imagining what it would be like if Nathaniel weren't quite so honorable—if he had let things go further.

All of a sudden, returning to the future didn't sound so great. In fact, to my amazement I realized I wasn't looking forward to the prospect one bit. I'd never been very close to anybody in my own time, other than Alex, and he was gone. My parents cared about me, of course, but it was a sort of benign neglect that in my confusion I'd mistaken for love. The truth was, I'd never really been loved before—or felt the way about a man that I was feeling toward Nathaniel. Was it love? I was afraid to hazard a guess. Even though I knew he'd never be free to love me, the thought of leaving him made something shrivel inside me.

Cool it, Taylor, I told myself. You've got to forget about him. A disturbing thought took root in my mind. Was I allowing my own feelings for Nathaniel to color my thinking about Prudence? After all, I had no proof that my suspicions about her were true. It wasn't her fault that Nathaniel vanished during the earthquake; her only real crime was in marrying the wrong second husband. But maybe if Nathaniel never disappeared, he and Prudence would simply live on, happily ever after together.

I had to find out about Prudence. If my suspicions were justified, I could show Nathaniel proof and he'd call off the wedding. But if I was wrong, I owed it to Nathaniel to step back and let him marry Prudence. I could find some other way to prevent him from entering the attic next Wednesday, then get out of his life and leave him—and Prudence—alone. Go back to my own time and forget I ever met him.

Yet even as my thoughts formed the words, I knew that I would never forget Nathaniel Stuart.

Chapter Ten

"Miss Pratwell stopped by earlier, while ye were sleepin'," Mrs. O'Hara informed me as she placed a plateful of hot buttered waffles and a glass of orange juice in front of me. Quite a change from my usual instant breakfast drink. "Left her calling card. Said she hopes ye'll accept her invitation t' tea this afternoon."

"Oh?" I drizzled syrup over my late-morning breakfast, pondering Prudence's motives. Was she suspicious of me? She had a right to be jealous, I supposed. Maybe she'd picked up on my feelings for Nathaniel even before I was aware of them myself. Or maybe she was just trying to be polite. After all, I was her fiance's cousin. In theory.

"Send word to Miss Pratwell that I'd be delighted to accept," I said. At any rate, it would give me a chance to get to know Prudence better and find out if my suspicions were justified.

What would Nathaniel say about me having a private chat with his fiancee? I wondered. Somehow I doubted he'd approve. "Where is my cousin?" I asked.

"Gone t' take care of some business matters. He said he'd be back this evening."

"Oh." I couldn't help feeling disappointed at the prospect of not seeing him all day, even though he'd made it clear he had no intention of spending time alone with me. But at least his absence left the coast clear for me to check out Prudence.

Aunt Faith entered the dining room and settled into the chair opposite me, instructing Mrs. O'Hara to bring her a plateful of buttered scones with marmalade, whipped cream, eggs Benedict, and two sausages, browned crisp. Pure cholesterol—the woman was a heart attack waiting to happen.

"My, you must have been tired too, sleeping so late," she said to me as a servant poured her a cup of coffee. She raised her eyebrows and peered at me over her spectacles. "Long night?"

The waffles felt dense in my mouth. "Why do you ask?"

"No reason." She plopped three lumps of sugar into her china cup, then added a spoonful of real cream. I could practically hear her arteries harden. "It's just that I saw your light on late."

"I was reading."

Had Aunt Faith been the mysterious predawn

visitor spying on Nathaniel and me? It seemed unlikely, but then again, she had noticed that her hubby couldn't keep his eyes (not to mention hands) off my anatomy. If she heard me come out of my room, she might have thought I was going to meet him, and followed me.

Uncle Ephraim hobbled stiffly into the room—still sore, no doubt, from his run-in with Apollo's teeth. "Ah, there you are, Faith. So—" Seeing me, he tightened his grip on his cane.

"Yes, dear?" Aunt Faith gave him a puzzled look.

Had Uncle Ephraim been the nocturnal spy? Perhaps he saw me wander into the garden and decided to finish what he'd started before. The thought sent a shudder through me.

I stood up, not about to make small talk with a would-be rapist. "Aunt Faith, it's been lovely talking with you but if you'll excuse me, I've got to go find Victoria."

She took a long, slow sip of her coffee. "If I were you, I'd try the playhouse," she advised, leaving me to wonder just when was the last time she'd visited there.

I found Victoria curled up in the loft of her playhouse, chin drawn up to her knees, Apollo guarding the base of the ladder below. "Did Nathaniel send you here to scold me?" she asked when I climbed up.

"No. I came on my own."

She peered at me around her knees, clutching a porcelain doll. "Are you angry with me too?"

173

I waded through the layers of carefully arranged dolls and toys and knelt beside her. "I'm not angry. Disappointed, perhaps, but not angry. Victoria, you shouldn't have written that note. You'd no right to interfere in your brother's personal life." Or mine, I added silently.

Her lower lip jutted out. "I was only trying to help him."

"Help?"

She nodded petulantly. "And it was working too! He was kissing you—at least, until you two spotted me at my window."

"Victoria—" I felt my face redden. "You musn't say anything about that to anyone, especially Prudence. It shouldn't have happened—"

"Why not?"

"Because I'm going away soon, and Nathaniel is going to marry Prudence."

"But I don't like her."

I sighed, crossing to the window. "Sometimes we have to adjust to things we don't like."

"You like Nathaniel, don't you?" She followed me to the window.

I turned to face her. "Of course I do, but—"

"And I know he likes you. He told me so. So why is it so wrong to want the two of you together?"

"Victoria." I knelt in front of her, taking her hands in mine. "There's nothing wrong in wanting. It's acting on what we want that's wrong, when it can hurt someone else. Like Prudence."

She wrinkled her nose. "I don't want to talk about her."

A sudden thought struck me. "Victoria, were you in Nathaniel's study last night—borrowing some more books, perhaps?"

"No, of course not." Her eyes narrowed. "All the best books are in the library. Besides, you know perfectly well where I was last night. So why do you ask?"

"No reason. I heard something, probably a mouse, that's all." I scanned the loft. "You've got quite a doll collection up here. How many do you have?"

"Seventy-three. It should be seventy-four, but I lost one when I was a little girl. My favorite—a colonial doll with a red calico dress and a Martha Washington cap."

I felt sorry for her, alone with no one but her dolls for company. She needed other children to play with, to make her feel more like a child instead of a miniature adult. "Victoria, would you like to go bicycle riding?" I asked impulsively.

She lowered her head. "I can't. Nathaniel told me I can't go anyplace until after the wedding . . . as punishment."

"Grounded, eh? What a bummer."

"Bummer?"

"The pits. Crummy. No good."

Victoria cracked a grin. "Bummer." She tried out the phrase, elongating the first syllable. "I like that."

I stayed with her a while longer, until she got hungry and decided to go back to the main house for a snack. As I descended the ladder, my foot stepped backward off the bottom rung onto the playhouse floor and I felt something crunch under my shoe.

I picked it up and turned it over in my hand. "A button," I said, holding the ornate gold object up to the light. "Victoria, did this come off one of your dolls?"

She looked at it closely. "No, I'm certain it didn't. Nathaniel never buys me dolls with button eyes, and this is too big to have come off any of my dolls' clothes. It looks like a button off a man's jacket, or perhaps a lady's coat."

If the button didn't come from Victoria's dolls, it must have come from somewhere else. Someone else. Whoever was watching from the playhouse last night, perhaps?

I tousled Victoria's hair as we stepped outside. "Good work, Sherlock."

She grinned. "Elementary, my dear Watson."

A cool blast of air hit my face as I stepped outside, haunted by the uncanny sensation that I'd just stepped into one of Victoria's Gothic novels.

"Miss James, I'm so glad you agreed to come today," Prudence greeted me cordially after a servant ushered me into her parlor.

"Thanks for inviting me."

We sat on matching cherrywood Chippendale chairs with embroidered cushions, a half-moon–shaped French provincial table between us. Prudence dismissed the servant and poured tea from a sterling silver pot.

"I owe you an apology, actually," she said, offering me a cup. "I'm afraid I behaved rather dreadfully yesterday morning."

This was a surprise. "You had a right to be upset," I said. "My dog wasn't exactly on his best behavior, either."

She smiled, holding up a small silver pitcher. "True. Cream?"

"No thanks."

"Sugar?"

I started to ask for Sweet'n Low, but caught myself in time. "Sugar sounds fine."

She passed the bowl. I used a pair of silver tongs to lift two lumps of sugar, dissolving them in my tea with a sterling silver spoon.

"As I was saying," Prudence began, stirring her tea, "I didn't mean to be rude to you. It's just that I'm frightened of dogs, and I took out my vexation on you. I'm sorry, and I'd like us to start with a clean slate."

"Sure," I said, wondering if her sincerity was just an act. "Why not?"

A relieved smile tilted the corners of her delicate little mouth upward. She really was gorgeous—a regular drop-dead beauty. I tugged at the whalebone collar constricting my air; it felt as though I'd stuck my neck in a noose.

"I see you've been shopping," she noted. "That's a lovely dress—the color suits you."

"Thanks. Yours is nice too," I said, feeling dowdy compared to her. "You know, those were really pretty earrings you had on yesterday. The pearl ones. Do you mind if I ask where you got them?"

She touched a strand of pearls at her throat.

"Why, thank you. They were a gift from someone dear to me. Pearls are my favorites. They're so lustrous—like miniature crystal balls."

I had a pretty good idea who the "someone dear" was who'd given her those earrings, but her mention of crystal balls reminded me of something else. "Prudence believes in spirits," Nathaniel had told me when he found me in the attic.

I'd tried everything I could think of to stop him from marrying her—telling the truth hadn't worked; neither had lying, and I'd failed miserably at seduction. What the heck. If Nathaniel wouldn't buy my psychic act, why not give it a shot with Prudence?

"May I see your hand?" I asked, forcing a polite smile. "I read palms, you see. Mom says I should have been born a gypsy—so many of my predictions have come true."

"A palmist!" Prudence tittered with excitement. "How divine. I simply adore having my fortune told." She laid her hand on the table, palm up, and I took it in mine.

"I see a long lifeline," I began.

"Oh—that's good," Prudence fanned herself with her free hand. "What else do you see?"

I bent forward, squinting as I pretended to study her cold, manicured hand. "That's odd," I said. "Your love line is split. Can you beat that?"

Her face turned chalk white. "Well, obviously that part must be wrong. I'm being married on Saturday."

I shrugged. "I don't interpret this stuff; I just

178

read 'em. Hmmmm." I traced a line in her hand and wrinkled my nose. "See this? It means a troubled marriage."

"What?"

"I'm sorry to break the news, but I see great sadness in store for you."

"Sadness?" Her hand trembled. "Won't my new husband treat me well?"

I nodded. "At first."

"And then?"

"In time, he will tire of the parties and dancing you love." I scrunched my eyes, peering closer. "I see you confined to your room, forbidden to go out. . . ."

"Nathaniel would never do that!" Her hand flew to her throat.

"No more beautiful gowns—or jewelry. I see your husband putting you on a budget. A stringent one . . ."

Behind me, I heard the sound of a man's voice. "Rubbish! My dear, whatever are you doing paying good money for such drivel from a con artist?"

Turning around, I saw Quentin Fenniwick standing behind me. The color drained from his face as he recognized me from the store.

"Mr. Fenniwick!" Prudence's face flushed. "My guest is not a con artist. Why, she's practically a relative."

"Pardon me," Fenniwick said, nodding to me. "I was merely looking after Ms. Pratwell's interests—for her father, you understand. Speaking of which"—he turned toward Prudence—"I, ah, had a message from your father. Perhaps I'd best come back later—after your guest leaves," he added pointedly.

"Nonsense." Prudence stood, gesturing toward a love seat. "Won't you join us for tea, Mr. Fenniwick? I was just having a fascinating conversation with Miss James. She's Nathaniel's cousin."

Fenniwick's Adam's apple bobbed up and down. "His cousin?"

"Why yes." Prudence smoothed down her dress. "I'm sure she has lots of fascinating stories to tell me about Nathaniel's childhood. Tell me, Miss James, was Nathaniel a naughty boy?"

I groaned inwardly. "Ask Aunt Faith. Nathaniel and I didn't meet until we were adults."

"Oh." She pursed her lips. "Well, I shall look forward to meeting Natty's aunt, then."

Fenniwick took off his hat and sat down. "It's a pleasure to meet you, Miss James. And you, Miss Pratwell, are looking lovely as a spring morning."

Prudence's cheeks flushed; she was practically glowing. "Why, thank you, Mr. Fenniwick."

I took a sip of my tea. It had a pleasant taste, minty yet not too sweet, with a hint of chamomile. "This is good tea," I said.

"It's a special blend. I'll send a packet home with you, if you'd like," she said, glancing away as if to avoid meeting Fenniwick's gaze. It was obvious the two of them couldn't wait to get me out of the room so they could be alone together.

"Thank you. That would be nice. I really should hit the road now, though—to give you plenty of time to get ready for the big party tonight," I said.

Prudence smiled gratefully. "Of course. But do wait a moment, while I fetch you a packet of tea to take home." Home. I felt an ache at the word. Would I ever see it again?

She swished out of the parlor, leaving me alone with the man responsible for Nathaniel's demise.

I smiled innocently. "You look familiar to me, somehow. I know—the department store yesterday. You were buying jewelry for a lady friend, weren't you?" I raised my eyebrows, questioning.

"You oughtn't to pry into a gentleman's personal affairs, Miss James," he said, flashing a disarming smile. Giving me a wink, he added, "But if you must know, I was buying a gift for my mother."

Right . . . and pigs could fly. "She's a very lucky lady," I replied.

"That she is." He stood up, evading my gaze. "I can't imagine what's taking Miss Pratwell so long with that tea. I believe I'll go check and see if everything's all right."

Nothing was all right, I thought as he left the room. Prudence behaved like a lovesick puppy around the smooth-talking Fenniwick, and I didn't for a minute buy his story about that brooch being for his mother.

My fortune-telling hadn't worked. But I'd gotten what I came for, it seemed. Now all I had to do was convince Nathaniel that his fiancee was in love with another man.

I'd sooner talk Apollo into eating ox bones.

* * *

Descending the stairs later dressed in the blue satin evening gown selected by Mme Riviere, I drew in my breath at the sight of Nathaniel.

He stood at the base of the stairs, looking more handsome than any mortal should in his tails and silk top hat. I felt my pulse beat faster as I slowly moved toward him.

His eyebrows lifted in approval. Silently he held out a gloved hand to take mine. His touch sent a warm ripple through me as he tucked my arm beneath his and escorted me onto the porch and down the pathway to the waiting Rolls.

A liveried servant held open the front passenger door open for me and I stepped inside while Nathaniel ushered Aunt Faith into the seat behind me and positioned Uncle Ephraim behind the driver's seat—as far away from me as possible, I noticed gratefully. Then Nathaniel slid behind the wheel, with Victoria between us.

"So," Nathaniel broke the ice, nodding toward Victoria and me, "how did you ladies occupy yourselves all day?"

I stared ahead through the dash, not sure this was the best moment to fill him in. I'd rushed home and dressed a full hour early, hoping to get a few minutes alone with Nathaniel to tell him what I'd learned. But he arrived home late and screwed up my plan.

"I didn't do anything, since you said I had to stay home," Victoria complained. "It was frightfully boring. Taylor wouldn't even let me go with her to Prudence's house—"

"Where?" Nathaniel leaned forward, gripping the wheel.

"Prudence invited me to tea," I explained. "I saw no harm—"

"Saw no harm? No harm! What if she'd asked you about—"

He stopped, as though suddenly remembering the presence of the others in the car.

"About what?" Victoria asked, peering at me intently.

"Gracious, child, hasn't anyone taught you that children are to be seen but not heard?" Aunt Faith scolded.

"The child has a point." Uncle Ephraim's stale breath scalded the back of my neck. "Tell us, Nathaniel, what does Taylor have to explain?"

"Nothing. Never mind." Nathaniel sat back, his spine rigid. "So, how was this . . . tea party?"

"Everything went fine." I rushed to put his mind at ease. "We had a lovely talk—and I certainly got to know Prudence a lot better." The sordid details about her infatuation with Fenniwick would have to wait, at least until Victoria and the dynamic duo in the backseat were out of earshot. Maybe I'd even have the chance to round up some more ammunition during the party. If Fenniwick showed up, I'd have to keep a close eye on him.

Nathaniel's frown softened. "Good. Then you can see now what a lovely person she is."

"She's a real beauty, all right," I observed. "So how was your day?"

His jaw tensed. "There was a fire at one of my warehouses."

"A fire?" Uncle Ephraim leaned forward, sputtering. "Did it do much damage? How did it start?"

"Burned several crates of imported goods, but fortunately it was contained before it could do any real damage. The fire marshal believes it was arson."

"Arson!" I burst out. "But why would anybody want to burn down one of your buildings?"

"I believe it was a warning," he said darkly. "From an enemy who isn't accustomed to losing."

Ruef, I thought, recalling the threats Nathaniel had mentioned receiving over his mysterious dealings with Mr. Spreckels. Before I could learn more, we pulled into the circular drive in front of the Pratwell mansion.

"I thought this was supposed to be a small dinner party—you know, for friends and family," I whispered to Nathaniel as we passed through the marble foyer big enough to house my family's entire apartment and were ushered into a ballroom crowded with a hundred or more elegantly dressed guests. The ballroom was opulent to the point of ostentatiousness, with gilt ceilings, marble pillars adorned with carved grapevines, and a sunken champagne fountain in the center of the room crowned by a white pedestal supporting statues of three Grecian cherubs, naked except for a long strip of strategically placed alabaster drape.

"The Pratwells have a lot of both," he replied.

"Look." Victoria stifled a giggle with her gloved hand as she pointed at two young women decked out in gowns far too frilly for their severe features. "There are Prudence's sisters. Don't they remind you of the stepsisters in *Cinderella*?"

"Victoria, that's a cruel thing to say," Nathaniel chastised her.

"What are their names?" I asked.

"Prunella and Priscilla," he replied.

Victoria winked at me and held her nose. I bit my lip to keep from smiling.

Prudence swished toward us, her face lighting up as she set her sights on Nathaniel. I couldn't believe my eyes.

She was wearing the brooch. So much for Fenniwick's phony story about giving it to his mother. How tacky could you get, wearing jewelry that was a gift from another man to your own prewedding party? I couldn't wait to get Nathaniel alone and tell him about Prudence's imprudence.

"There you are, darling," she cooed, linking arms with him as she drew him away from me. "I thought you'd never get here. You simply must come with me and meet everyone. My out-of-town relatives are dying to meet you." Glancing at me and the rest of Nathaniel's entourage, she added, "And your family, of course."

I felt a sharp stab of jealousy. Stop it, I told myself. You've got to keep a cool head tonight.

Uncle Ephraim cackled a dirty-old-man laugh. "That's a mighty fine filly that young stallion of ours has corralled, wouldn't you say, Faith?"

"I'd say you're too old to be chasing after young fillies," Aunt Faith said, tightening her hold on his elbow.

I clenched my hands at my sides, digging my nails into my palms. If only I could get Nathaniel aside for a few minutes to tell him of my suspicions. Would he believe me? I wanted to believe so, though looking at him now, with Prudence, I had to admit he might not.

A stir rippled through the crowd at the arrival of the next guest. "Who's that?" I asked Victoria, staring at the slightly built man with dark hair and a bushy mustache.

"Boss Ruef," Victoria said. "Nathaniel despises him. Says he'd like to be the one to tie a knot in that snake's tail."

He might be a snake, but like any politician, Ruef certainly knew how to work a crowd. He slithered his way through the room, exuding charm with the ladies and political muscle with the men. I was introduced formally to the rest of Prudence's relatives and then to Boss Ruef; even his lips felt slimy when he kissed the back of my hand. The man reeked of power but it was a tainted scent, like that of a freshly dug onion with dirt clinging to its roots.

Victoria struck up a conversation with some preteen cousins of Prudence. Soon the group of young people headed for a buffet table spread with trays of appetizers and a silver punch bowl.

The orchestra struck up a waltz. Aunt Faith dragged Uncle Ephraim onto the dance floor, but his gaze wandered to several young women nearby, lingering on the exposed cleavage waltzing past.

Nathaniel asked Prudence to dance, leaving me standing alone. The green-eyed monster inside me breathed fire at the sight of his hands on her slender waist and bare shoulders as he swept her across the ballroom. How many times had I stared at that old photo of him and dreamed of waltzing across the Stuart House ballroom with him, to have him staring into my eyes the way he was now staring into hers, with loving adoration?

I turned away, unable to watch. A haze of tobacco smoke drifted across the room; where was a nonsmoking section when you needed one? Air. I needed some fresh air. I drifted toward a set of French doors at the back of the ballroom that led out to a terraced veranda. Walking down to the lower level, I found a quiet corner behind a marble colonnade and sat down on a wrought-iron bench. Leaning forward, I rested my forehead in my hands.

Get a hold of yourself, Taylor, I told myself. You're losing your grip . . . you can't have Nathaniel Stuart, even if Prudence loses him. You've got to accept that.

The sound of hushed voices from the level above caught my attention. ". . . still don't like it. Spreckels and Stuart together spell trouble," said the first voice, which I recognized from earlier as

Boss Ruef. Why was Ruef concerned about Nathaniel's business?

"Don't worry. I'll take care of it," the second voice assured. I froze in shocked recognition. What was Mortimer Pratwell, Prudence's father, doing in league with Ruef? I lowered myself to the ground and crept closer as the two men walked several paces away.

"The way you 'took care' of those papers?" Ruef's voice needled.

"We'll find them—"

"See that you do," Ruef snapped, adding in a threatening tone, "Stuart must be stopped at all costs."

Was Ruef the enemy Nathaniel suspected was behind the fire earlier? Not to mention the ship that was sabotaged. I held my breath as Boss Ruef went inside, followed by Mortimer Pratwell. So Ruef was after some papers Nathaniel had, and Prudence's father was in on it, too. The papers Nathaniel had dropped at Mr. Spreckels's house? I recalled the noises I'd heard in Nathaniel's study the night before. Not a mouse, but an intruder searching for those papers, perhaps?

I slipped inside. Nathaniel was waltzing with one of Prudence's ugly sisters and seemed oblivious to my presence. But Fenniwick, who was dancing with Prudence, did a double take when I walked in. He whispered something to Prudence and left her standing on the dance floor as he strode over to her father and spoke rapidly. Mortimer Pratwell glanced at me and turned the color of the white marble pillar behind him.

Swell, I thought. Busted. Well fine, but they couldn't stop me from telling Nathaniel what I'd overheard.

"Oh, there you are, Taylor," Victoria said, intercepting me. "I've been looking for you everywhere. Do you know I heard—"

"Victoria, please. Not now. I've got to talk with your brother—"

"But Taylor, it's something scandalous about Prudence."

My ears pricked up. "Oh?"

She leaned toward me, her pupils dancing. "I was in the library, checking out the Pratwells' book collection, when—"

"Victoria! It's not polite to wander through other people's homes."

She shrugged. "I guess not. Sorry. Anyhow, I heard someone coming and didn't want to get caught, so I crawled under the desk. Guess who it was?"

"Prudence?"

She nodded. "And that handsome fellow who works for her father."

"Quentin Fenniwick?" This had potential. I only hoped Victoria hadn't overheard anything too adult between the two. "So what happened?"

"He was angry with her. Said he'd told her not to wear that brooch tonight and she said she couldn't see the harm in it. Can you imagine, Prudence accepting jewelry from another man when she's engaged to marry my brother?"

"Was there anything else?"

"Prudence sounded perturbed. She said Mr.

Fenniwick was being unreasonable."

"Hmmm." That didn't make sense, but Prudence wasn't exactly noted for being prudent. "Anything else?"

"Not really. Prudence marched out in a huff. Of course, she was already peeved because my brother told her they'd have to delay their wedding trip because of some business problem." An impish twinkle gleamed in her eye. "Do you suppose we ought to tell Nathaniel?"

Before I could answer, I felt someone tap my shoulder. I turned to see Nathaniel bowing formally. How much of the conversation had he overheard, I wondered?

His resonant voice sent a ripple of pleasure through me. "Cousin Taylor, may I have the pleasure of this dance?"

Chapter Eleven

A warm sensation shot through me, only to fizzle out as reality sank in. Embarrassed, I admitted in a whisper, "I've never actually learned how to waltz."

He looked at me with compassion. "You needn't worry," he said, taking my hands tenderly. "Just follow my lead."

He led me onto the dance floor, resting one hand on my waist and entwining the fingers of his other hand in mine. I lifted a gloved hand and placed it on his muscular shoulder, tingling at his touch as he pulled me closer. God, but he was handsome—his white starched collar sharply contrasted with his bronzed face, black coat, tails, and cummerbund.

With a firm hand, he guided me through the steps, leaning forward to whisper in my ear. "Back-two-three, side-two-three . . . that's it, turn—relax. Don't try to lead—for once, follow my directives," he instructed with a twinkle in his eyes.

I did. It was remarkably easy, like floating on a cloud, I thought as we swirled together across the dance floor. I'd never felt this way before— not even when we were flying. Nathaniel was a superior dancer; he made me feel beautiful and graceful, like some enchanted fairy-tale princess. Only this Cinderella couldn't live happily ever after with her prince. Not when I had to return to my own time in just a few short days. . . .

"Tell me," he said, "are you enjoying the evening?"

"It's been quite an eye-opener," I said, discovering how very much I enjoyed being in his arms again. It was as though I'd had a magic spell cast over me, one that made me feel warm and safe and . . . desirous. Closing my eyes for one indulgent moment, I recalled the magic of our kiss earlier, wishing the moment never had to end.

Nathaniel's voice, deep yet soft, lingered in my ear. "So," he whispered, "what was it that my sister thinks I ought to be told?"

I opened my eyes, the spell broken. "It's about Prudence," I said hesitantly.

"What about her?"

"I—there isn't any easy way to say this. Nathaniel, I think there's something going on between Prudence and Quentin Fenniwick. Even Victoria senses it."

"Fenniwick?" His palm pressed harder against

my back. "That's absurd. I thought you and Prudence were getting on better—at least, she had only glowing things to say about you. How can you see fit to malign her character this way?"

"I'm not maligning anyone. Look at them together." I nodded my head toward where Fenniwick was twirling Prudence around the dance floor. "She's staring into his eyes like a starstruck schoolgirl."

He saw it too; I could tell by the frown lines around the corners of his mouth. But he wasn't ready to admit it, even to himself. "She's just being polite—Prudence has a way of making everyone feel special; it's one of her many gifts."

"Speaking of gifts, that brooch Prudence has on was a gift from Fenniwick."

Gold flecks shone in his dark eyes. "Prudence would never accept a gift from another man."

It was growing warm; the music throbbed in my head as Nathaniel swept me around the room. "If you don't believe me, ask Victoria. She overheard them talking about it."

His frown lines deepened, then relaxed. "My sister shouldn't be eavesdropping. Besides, Fenniwick is employed by Prudence's father, after all. Mortimer must have asked Fenniwick to purchase the trinket on his behalf. Yes, that must be it."

"But—"

"No buts." His voice was firm. "You've got to quit deluding yourself, Taylor. Prudence is a lady. She would never compromise herself by so much as the appearance of impropriety."

Holy cow, what would it take to get through to him—videotapes of Prudence and her boyfriend in the sack together? With great effort I held my tongue, realizing that any further criticism of Prudence would fall on deaf ears.

"Whatever you say." I dismissed the subject, for the moment. "But I do have some news that should interest you. A little while ago I heard your future father-in-law talking with Boss Ruef out on the veranda. Ruef seemed awfully eager to get his hands on some papers of yours. Something to do with that business deal you're involved in with Mr. Spreckels."

"What? Are you sure?" His voice had an urgency I hadn't heard before.

"I'm certain. Nathaniel, I didn't want to say anything before, but last night I thought I heard someone in your office. At the time I thought it was you, or maybe Victoria hunting for a book. But now I think someone else was in there, going through your things."

"Ruef and I have never seen eye to eye, but I'd no idea Mortimer was involved with that scoundrel. I wouldn't put breaking and entering past Ruef for a moment, if it served his purposes." A look of concern flashed across his face. "Taylor, do they know you overheard them?"

"I'm not sure. When I came in the room Fenni—"

Just then, Fenniwick tapped Nathaniel on the shoulder. "May I cut in?" he asked, smiling suavely.

Nathaniel warned me off with a stare, but I

nodded. If I could coax or con Prudence's beau
into giving me some more information, it would
be worth enduring a dance with the slimeball.
Seeing my approval, Nathaniel grudgingly relin-
quished me to Fenniwick. Belatedly I realized I
hadn't had the chance to warn him about Ruef's
threat to stop Nathaniel at any cost. That much
would have to wait until later.

"You seemed to be having quite an intense conversation with your cousin," Fenniwick said as
he steered me away from Nathaniel. "What were
you discussing?"

"Oh, this and that." I smiled sweetly. "You
know."

"No." His mouth formed a hard line. "I don't."

Suddenly my foot stepped back onto nothing;
I stumbled backward, landing smack on my
backside in the middle of the Pratwells' tacky
fountain. My face burned as the whole roomful
of people stared at me, their hushed snickers echoing in my ears as I dragged myself to my feet.
Champagne gushed down the back of my dress
and streamed down my legs; I smelled like a wino
and my gown was soaked from the waist down,
clear through to my drawers.

"How terribly clumsy of me," Fenniwick said,
one corner of his mouth turning upward with a
hint of mockery. "I daresay the gown will be ruined unless you rush back to your cousin's house
at once. Pity you'll miss the rest of the party.
Shall I escort you?"

"No thanks," I said quickly. "I'll manage."

Aunt Faith bustled over, fretting over me as a

servant blotted at my clothes with a towel. An instant later I was surrounded by a cluster of servants and guests.

"Taylor—what on earth happened?" Nathaniel knelt beside me and brushed my soggy skirt with his hand. It squished beneath his touch, sending a stream of pale gold liquid onto the polished wood floor.

"I, um, fell."

"Not again!"

"Look, if it's all the same to you, I think I'll just go back to your house."

"I'll escort you. Prudence will understand."

I shook my head. "Don't bother. Stay and enjoy your . . . wedding party." I nearly choked on the words.

"You could change clothes and return."

"To tell you the truth, I've had enough partying for one night. I think I'll just go back to your place and crash out."

Prudence, of all people, came to my rescue—sort of. "Oh, my poor dear, you'll catch your death of cold. Nathaniel, you simply must see your cousin home at once. Besides"—a seductive look sparked in her eyes as she exchanged a smile with her fiance— "it's important that you get a good night's sleep—so you'll have plenty of vigor come tomorrow."

Victoria chimed in, "Guess that means the party's over, right?"

Nathaniel guided his little sister firmly toward the door. "For us, yes, I suppose it is."

Victoria flashed me a thumbs-up sign behind her back and sighed loudly. "Bummer."

Prudence's words grated on my nerves as Nathaniel escorted me up the walkway to Stuart House, his aunt, uncle, and sister behind us. The image of Nathaniel making love to his bride on their wedding night made my stomach feel queasy. I reminded myself for the thousandth time that I had no claim on him—I was from another time, and with any luck I'd be going back soon.

But that didn't change the fact that Nathaniel didn't love Prudence, and worse than that, she didn't love him. She couldn't, not the way she was leading Fenniwick along, accepting his gifts of jewelry—and God knows what else. I'd tried to give her the benefit of the doubt, but she was worse than the airhead I'd originally imagined her to be. Unless there was some weird explanation I hadn't thought of, Prudence was being unfaithful to Nathaniel before she'd even said "I do."

"You're shaking," Nathaniel said, his concern evident as he wrapped his coat around me.

"Th-thanks," I said through chattering teeth.

Mrs. O'Hara opened the front door, Muffin peering out from behind her apron. "My, sure and I hadn't expected ye back so early. How was the par—" Seeing me, she stepped forward and rushed me inside. "My stars! Miss James, ye look as though ye've been swimmin' in the bay, ye do."

"More like a little too much champagne," I

said, still irritated with myself for not seeing Fenniwick's plan to dunk me until it was too late.

"Quentin Fenniwick pushed her into the fountain," Victoria said indignantly.

"Victoria!" Mrs. O'Hara exclaimed. "Surely it must have been an accident."

"The man has the grace of a buffalo," Nathaniel groused. "Show Miss James upstairs and see that she gets into some warm clothes and a dry wrapper."

"Right away, sir." The housekeeper nodded. Turning to another servant, she instructed, "Stoke a fire in the parlor. Miss James'll want to be warmin' herself after she's changed. Sure and a spot o' tea will take the nip out o' her bones as well."

"I'll instruct the kitchen help to brew some," Aunt Faith offered.

"Where's Apollo?" Victoria asked.

As if on cue, the dog padded out from the kitchen. Mrs. O'Hara blushed. "The little mite's been keepin' me company in the kitchen—samplin' everything, he does. Sure an' he's even learnin' to get on with Muffin, here, may the devil strike me if that isn't God's own truth." She stroked the cat at her feet.

Now I'd seen everything. Apollo was certainly learning to fit in here. He seemed to have a real knack for getting people to care about him.

Sadly, I found myself reduced to envying my dog.

* * *

The fire warmed the soles of my feet through the borrowed slippers I wore as I clutched the teacup, letting its warmth permeate into my palms.

"Thanks," I said to Mrs. O'Hara as she filled a china saucer for Apollo and set it down on the hearth beside me.

She seemed flustered at being caught catering to a dog. "He's not such a bad little mite, after all," she said. "Will there be anything else for ye, Miss James?"

I shook my head. "No, I'll be fine."

"Very well. Ring if you think of something you need."

I lifted my teacup, recognizing the fragrant aroma of the chamomile blend Prudence had given me. I wasn't too keen on accepting a token gift from the woman who was about to marry Nathaniel, but the thought of the warm liquid soothing my churning insides had an irresistible appeal.

Apollo sniffed at his bowl and emitted a low growl.

"What's wrong?" I asked. "Bored with chamomile? Sure, I know. Consider the source. But what the heck, I'm half frozen and it's warm. Cheers." I raised my cup in a mock toast and touched it to my lips.

Apollo vaulted into my lap and sent my teacup clattering to the floor. I jumped up, blotting up the puddle of tea on the parlor floor with my napkin as Muffin, the cat, lapped at the spilled liquid. Had Victoria spoiled the cat on tea as well?

"Apollo!" I scolded. "What's wrong with you? If you're trying to get yourself banished to the backyard again, you're on the right track."

I pulled the bellpull and summoned Mrs. O'Hara. The cat, meanwhile, lapped up more of the puddle, shook its head, and let out a loud meow.

Mrs. O'Hara appeared a moment later. "What can I get for—oh, my!" She exclaimed, rushing forward.

I turned around. Muffin was staggering as if drunk; the cat's eyes were glazed.

"What's happened to my cat?" The housekeeper's voice trembled as she knelt down, stroking the animal's white fur stained pale green in patches from the tea.

"I don't know. He was fine a minute ago. . . ."

Muffin's ears twitched; he made a strangled sound and lay down. His paws jerked and a trickle of green tea drizzled from the corner of his mouth.

"Saints preserve him. . . ." Mrs. O'Hara crossed herself, tears forming in her eyes as she scooped the cat into her arms. "What happened? Muffin, wake up. Can you hear me, love?"

Muffin's furry body convulsed, then stiffened. I bent over the cat and pressed my ear to his chest, listening for a heartbeat. There was none.

"No, not my little Muffin." The housekeeper blinked through a haze of tears, a dazed look on her face as she cradled the dead cat tightly against her chest. "How could the little mite up'n' take sick so quickly? It isn't natural, I'm tellin' you. . . ."

The tea. I stared at the spilled liquid, dumbstruck.

"Mrs. O'Hara, I'm very sorry about your cat. It drank some of the tea that was meant for me."

Her eyes widened. "Are ye sayin'—"

I nodded. "Apollo tried to warn me. He growled and knocked the teacup out of my hands. Dogs have a keen sense of smell—I think he knew someone had . . . tampered with it."

"But that's madness. Why would anyone want t' harm ye?"

"I'm not sure. Tell me, who had access to that tea?"

"Well"—she scrunched up her forehead, wiping her eyes with a hanky as she thought—" 'twas the master's aunt who ordered a kitchen maid to make it. Though I'm sure she wouldn't—"

"Who else?"

She frowned. "The teapot was simmerin' on the stove a bit with no one tendin' it. Come to think of it, that bag o' tea was sittin' out on the sideboard all afternoon. Most anyone could have gotten to it, I suppose. . . ."

Anyone, including Prudence. She was the one who gave me the tea. Not to mention Nathaniel's lecherous uncle and his wife, who'd both been downstairs when I was up changing for the party earlier. Fenniwick might have hired someone to do me in, after what I'd learned about him and Prudence. For that matter, Boss Ruef and Mortimer Pratwell also had ample motive to want me out of the way after what I'd overheard earlier. Any one of them, or someone else entirely, could have bribed a servant to slip something into my tea.

A horrible thought struck me. Could Nathaniel be so anxious to have me out of his house before his wedding that he tried to poison me? I rejected the thought as quickly as it had come. Whatever his faults, I knew in my heart that Nathaniel was no murderer.

"But where would 'most anyone' obtain poison?" I asked, hoping for a reassuring answer.

"Arsenic." Mrs. O'Hara pursed her lips. "I keep some in the pantry, for the rats, don't ye know." Wiping away a tear trickling down her cheek, she turned and disappeared into the kitchen.

She emerged several minutes later, her face pale. "I sifted through what was left of the tea in the bag Miss Pratwell gave ye. I found traces o' rat poison in it, all right. Enough t' set you in your grave, if you'd drunk the whole cup."

My hands trembled as the full realization of what had nearly happened hit me. Someone had tried to kill me. The question was who? And would they try again before I could find out?

"Poisoned! Are you sure?" Nathaniel's voice boomed as he bolted to his feet, his broad form silhouetted by the misty morning light filtering through the window behind him in his study.

"Positive," I confirmed. "If it hadn't been for Apollo, I'd be pushing up daisies along with Mrs. O'Hara's cat."

"It's true, sir, I'm sorry to say." Mrs. O'Hara set her jaw squarely. "After what happened to poor Muffin, I examined the tea left in the bag. I found traces of arsenic, sure as I'm standin' here before ye."

"Good lord." He moved around the desk and knelt beside the chair I was sitting in, taking my hands in his, turning them over as though to check my circulation. "Are you all right? You're certain you didn't drink any of that foul brew? If you feel any ill effects we must summon a physician at once."

The warmth of his hands radiated up my arm, sending soothing heat straight into my heart. He believed me—for once, Nathaniel wasn't accusing me of being crazy or imagining things or suffering from heatstroke. He believed me. A stirring of joy fluttered deep inside me, like a butterfly emerging from its cocoon.

"Mrs. O'Hara." He stood up and turned to address the housekeeper. "From now on you're to personally handle anything my cousin is given to eat or drink. See to it that no one else touches her food. Question the servants about anyone who might have been handling the tea, and instruct the rest of the staff that no strangers are to be permitted in this house for any reason." His voice softened as he added, "I'm sorry about Muffin. If it will help ease your loss, I'll buy you a new cat. Your choice—pick of a litter."

The housekeeper blinked back a fresh round of tears. " 'Tis kind of ye, Sir."

"You may go now."

"Yes sir." She bobbed her head. "Right away, sir."

The instant Mrs. O'Hara left the room, Nathaniel's eyes were upon me, searching for answers I wish I could give him. "Taylor, what reason would anyone have to want you dead—did you make some enemies in your past? Is that why you were running away?"

I shook my head, touched by his concern. So he *did* care about me, after all. "One thing I'm sure of is that nobody who knew me before I came here has any idea where I am right now."

He stroked his chin, a troubled look in his eyes. "Ruef knows you overheard his conversation last night."

"Probably," I admitted. "Fenniwick saw me come in off the veranda right after Ruef and Prudence's father, and rushed right over to talk with them. Ruef looked ready to choke. But I told you everything I know about their conversation already—" I stopped short. "Except one thing. Ruef said he wanted you stopped at all costs, and Mortimer Pratwell agreed."

Anger flashed in his eyes. "You've confirmed my suspicions that Ruef was behind the fire yesterday. No doubt he sees you as a threat; maybe he thinks you overheard more than you did. Something that links him to the fire."

I considered the comment. "That's possible, I suppose. They were talking on the far end of the veranda before they walked over to where I could hear them. But why—"

"Ruef is a ruthless scoundrel with a small fortune at stake." Nathaniel scowled. "If he's behind this, you won't be safe in this town until he's behind bars."

I recalled my history textbooks. "He will be, in just a few—"

"I won't risk your neck on suppositions. There's only one sane course of action to take. You must leave town—today."

"What! But the wedding . . . It's only a couple of hours from now. I can't—"

"You will." He put his hands on my shoulders and locked his gaze on mine; I could see the turbulence churning in the depths of his midnight-black eyes. "Taylor, you know I've grown fond of you these past few days. More than fond. The truth is,"—he paused, looking at me with a lingering tenderness that sent a ripple down my spine—"I can't bear the thought of anything happening to you."

"It won't. I'll be careful. I'll—"

"No." He pressed a finger to my lips to silence me. "I can't let you take that chance. This charade has gone on long enough. Victoria and I aren't your real family; I won't allow you to put your safety in jeopardy for the sake of appearances. Before the wedding starts, I'll tell Victoria you've taken ill and had to go home. By the time the ceremony is over, you'll be gone."

The walls seemed to be closing in on me. "Don't you understand? I can't go home! I c-can't. . . ."

"There now, don't worry." I felt his mustache brush my cheek as he bent forward, his arms closing around me to draw me against the comforting warmth of his chest. "I promised you I'd never send you back where you came from, and I meant it. But I will help you to build a new life for yourself. I'll buy you a train ticket and give you a tidy sum of money, enough to start over— any place in the country you want to go, or overseas, if you prefer. I'll gladly grant you passage on any ship in my fleet, just as long as I know you're safe."

I felt the floor crumbling under my feet, worse than in the earthquake. If I slipped through the crack Nathaniel was opening up, I'd never find my way back. "Don't you see?" I whispered hoarsely, staring up at him.

"See what?" He ran his hand gently through my hair, his fingers lingering at the base of my neck. My eyes burned from the effort to keep tears from dimming my vision.

"See that I don't want to leave you," I said, my lower lip trembling like a violinist's vibrato.

His lips brushed my forehead; then he stepped back, holding me at arm's length. "Ah , Taylor— can't you see that's part of the problem? We're growing to care for each other far too much. It's best this way, best for you to go away and forget you ever met me."

"I can't just put you out of my mind the way I'd pack away a pair of old sweatsocks!"

"Stockings," he corrected me, the corners of his mouth turning upward wryly. "You're a lady now, remember? And you will forget me, in time."

"The way you'll forget about me?"

He swallowed hard, releasing me. "I won't forget you. But in a couple of hours, I'll be a married man. I've a duty to remain true to Prudence, and keep the sacred vows I intend to take. And frankly"—he looked at me one last time with agonizing deliberation—"I'm not sure I could do that with you living under the same roof."

I looked at the floor to hide the tremor I felt. I was losing him—in more ways than he knew.

"Tell me where you wish to go," he said. "Chicago? Denver? New York? Or somewhere more exotic—Hawaii, perhaps, or Singapore?"

"Any of them . . . none of them. It doesn't matter," I said dully. There had to be another answer, another way to save him. I looked up suddenly. "What if I won't go?"

"Taylor." His voice was low, insistent. "I'm not asking you to leave. I'm telling you. You've no choice in the matter. I'll have the servants dig out some baggage for you from the attic. You're to have your bags packed by the time the rest of us leave for the wedding. I'll send my business manager to pick you up at two o'clock and take you to the port or train station, whichever you choose. By this evening, when I bring home my bride, I expect you to be gone."

"Then it's over," I murmured, dazed. Was I destined to be trapped here in the past—away from Nathaniel and his family? This couldn't be the way things were meant to happen . . . assuming there was a method to this madness, which I was beginning to doubt.

He bent low and kissed my hand, his lips smooth as velvet against my skin in one final act of chivalry. "Alas, my lady, it is."

Then he turned and walked out, pulling the door shut behind him. Numb, I slumped forward in the chair, fighting to regain control of thoughts spinning dizzily toward a crash.

Chapter Twelve

Perched on the guest room bed, I rested my head on my arms and peered longingly out the window. Even from three stories up, Nathaniel looked more handsome than the groom on the top of a wedding cake in his morning coat and tails. In less than an hour he'd be married to another woman; I had to get him out of my mind, yet I couldn't help peeking out the window for one last look at him before he and the rest of his family drove away in his Silver Shadow—off to the church, and out of my life.

Saying good-bye to Victoria had been almost as hard, though at least I hadn't had to fake an illness. Hearing my sniffles and seeing my red-rimmed eyes, she accepted Nathaniel's explanation that I was in need of prompt medical attention. But she pleaded with me to come visit her again soon, then cried, pouted, and turned away when I couldn't promise what she wanted.

Before she left with the others, I did my best to warn her about the earthquake. Not with the whole truth, of course. She'd never have believed that. Instead, I told her that a fortune-teller had foretold that the earth would tremble early Wednesday morning, with dire consequences. I made her promise not to burn any candles for a week, but from the stubborn way she stuck her lower lip out I was afraid she was only humoring me.

The minute the car pulled away from the curb, I exhaled the breath I'd been holding. No way was I going to let Nathaniel ship me off while he destroyed his life.

He'd left me a packet of money and instructions to be ready when his business partner arrived at 2:00, but that still gave me plenty of time to figure out a way to jam the attic door. With luck, Nathaniel would be so caught up in his newlywed activities that he wouldn't get around to trying the attic door for a few days.

That was step one of my plan. Step two called for me to hop off at the first train station out of town and catch the next train back to San Francisco. I'd hide out someplace until Tuesday night, when I'd come back here. With luck, by then I'd have figured out a better way to save Nathaniel and Victoria. I'd keep him out of the attic somehow, even it meant reasoning with Prudence. Nathaniel once mentioned that she believed in spirits; maybe I could play on her superstitions to convince her of what the future would hold.

But for now, I had to come up with a stopgap measure. I took Apollo downstairs and asked Mrs. O'Hara to keep an eye on him, explaining that I didn't want to be disturbed while I was packing. As soon as I was back upstairs I raced into Nathaniel's bedroom, clutching the reticule—the Edwardian term for a purse too small to hold much—into which I'd dumped the contents of my fanny pack. Maybe my chewing gum or hairpins would come in handy on the lock.

I started by digging around on the shelves. If I could find the key to the attic, I could lock up the attic and steal the key. If not, I'd have to figure out some way to jam it from the inside—a tough trick, since I'd have to make my exit through the roof door and down three stories to the ground.

No luck. I pulled open the armoire and yanked out its drawers, rifing through its contents. No key. Carefully putting the drawers back in place, I reached my hand underneath the down-filled mattress. Still no key.

My breath came in shallow, rapid motions. It had to be here somewhere. My gaze fell upon Nathaniel's spyglass, propped up in a corner next to the armoire. I picked it up; sure enough, in a leather-bound box underneath sat a ring of keys.

I grabbed the heavy keys and ran to the attic door, trying them one by one. Time telescoped in on itself, and I was running out of it. Already it must be after 12:15; the wedding would start at 1:00, and by 2:00 Nathaniel's business manager would come to take me away.

The first seven keys didn't fit. But the eighth slid in like a charm; I heard the lockworks clicking as I turned the key. I pushed on the door; it opened. Thank God I'd found the key in time. . . . Now maybe I could check out the attic and try to figure out exactly where I'd been standing when I got transported back in time—and where, presumably, I'd have to be again next Wednesday morning if I wanted to go back to the future.

"There's got to be a way back," I mumbled aloud, stepping inside.

"For you, Miss James, I'm afraid there's no way out," a familiar voice behind me said.

I jerked my head around. "Fenniwick!"

He closed the gap between us in two paces. "My, you don't look at all ill. Pity, it would make things easier for you."

"How did you get in here?" I asked, feeling the blood rush to my head. He stepped toward me; I stepped backward, away from him—and further into the attic.

"A simple matter, really. I climbed the tree outside the window of the room you've been staying in. When you weren't in your chamber I heard sounds coming from your cousin's room, and decided to investigate."

"What do you want?" I asked, edging away from him.

He yanked the door shut behind him and pulled out a knife. I screamed. He lunged toward me in the darkness; I shoved something into his path and ran toward the roof door, my heart racing. I flung it open and ran onto the roof.

He grabbed my wrist and twisted it. "There's no one to hear you. The servants are all on the first floor, making ready for the newlyweds. I checked. All the same, if you scream again I'll have to end this the messy way."

It was then that the glint of metal on his overcoat caught my eye. "You're the one," I said, fear flooding through me as I recognized his buttons. "You're the one who was in Victoria's dollhouse the other night, spying on Nathaniel and me."

"Spying is such a derogatory word." He dug his nails into my wrist and nudged me up a step with his blade. "I prefer to think of it as keeping an eye on my investments."

"Your investments?" Keep him talking, I thought. If I could get him to confess to whatever he'd been up to, I could go to Nathaniel and he'd have to listen to me. Assuming I could get out of here in one piece. "The trolley company," I guessed aloud, "That's it, isn't it? You're on Ruef's payroll. You're the one who was searching Nathaniel's office, looking for those papers." Whatever they were. "I'll bet you even started the fire in Nathaniel's warehouse."

"Very good, Miss James." A dark light glinted in his eyes. "You'd make a first-rate detective— which is why I can't afford to let you go around spreading such tales."

If I could convince him I'd already spilled the beans, maybe he'd cut his losses and let me go. "I've already told Nathaniel everything," I lied boldly, feeling my face grow hot. "By now he's

213

notified the cops. Any minute now, they'll be coming to haul you off to jail."

He shook his head. "Pity you're such a poor liar, Miss James. If it weren't for the way your face reddens when you stretch the truth, I might have been tempted to believe you."

Fear knotted in my chest. "I might be willing to keep my mouth shut—for a price," I said, knowing he wouldn't believe I'd keep quiet for nothing. It was time to play by his rules. "I could be a mole—you know, spy on Nathaniel for you and find out where he's hidden these papers you say you need."

His laugh had a sinister undertone that made my skin shrivel. "Nice try."

"The poison. You're the one who put arsenic in my tea, aren't you? I'll bet you stole some rat poison from the Pratwells' kitchen and slipped it into the bag of tea before I even left their home."

"I'll confess I was startled this morning to hear you were abed ill." His voice grated on my jangled nerves. "Obviously you didn't drink the full cup. Such a pity—it would have been much easier for you if you had."

"You bastard!"

"Enough small talk." He nudged me in the ribs, jerking my arm up behind me until the pain was almost more than I could stand. "Now, you're going to take a little walk—up there, to the widow's walk."

His knife blade felt ice cold as he nudged the small of my back. "You're going to throw me off the roof," I said, full realization hitting me with

214

the force of a 9.0 quake. I took a stab in the dark. "The same way you're planning to kill Nathaniel next Wednesday morning—before he and Prudence leave on their wedding trip." I nearly choked on the thought.

"A for effort, Madame Sleuth," he said in a startled tone, forcing me up the steps. "Though I can't fancy how you found out. I hadn't confided my plan to a living soul. It's so simple, really— all I have to do is hide in the attic while he and his bride are asleep, then finish him off when he's distracted by his astronomy pursuit at five A.M."

So Nathaniel didn't disappear during the earthquake, as Victoria had believed. He'd been murdered—it was only a stroke of fortune for Fenniwick that the earthquake had occurred and covered up his crime, burying Nathaniel's body beneath the rubble. A surge of anger jolted through me. I had to stop him; I had to save Nathaniel.

"Keep going," Fenniwick's voice needled behind me. "Class is over. Now it's time to teach you a lesson."

I swung my reticule, smacking him in the head. He knocked it out of my hands and slashed my arm; I felt a warm ooze of blood as he jerked my hair, dragging me forcefully over to the railing. I forced my thoughts away from the three-story drop below me and made myself keep talking.

"If you're going to kill me, you may as well tell me the truth," I gasped. "You want to have it all, don't you? Your pay from Ruef, Pratwell's daughter, and Nathaniel's money."

"And why not? I've earned it," he said, pressing the knife blade under my chin.

"You're in this with Prudence, aren't you? The two of you want to kill off Nathaniel so that you can be married and keep all his money."

"Prudence is a naive little twit." He twisted my hair to lean me backward over the railing, his blade cold against my throat. "It was easy to make her fall in love with me. Once I'd won her heart, I played the cad and told her I'd never marry her, which is why she accepted your cousin's proposal."

"Then you seduced her?" I guessed.

"It was child's play," he gloated. "After your cousin is dead I've no doubt she'll fall into my arms and let me comfort the grieving widow. Marriage is only a matter of time."

"So when did you talk her into killing him?" Blood rushed to my brain as he leaned me farther back over the rail; I fought the dizziness imposed by my precarious position.

He snorted derisively. "Prudence wouldn't kill a flea. The murder was entirely my idea. That's why I was monitoring your cousin's movements—to determine the safest time to finish him off. Fortunately, his habit of stargazing before the rest of the household arises each morning will make my task simple."

"You'll never get away with it," I said, frantically clutching the railing behind me.

He cocked an eyebrow. "No? Nathaniel's poor half-crazy cousin, distraught over the man she loves marrying another woman, leaps to her death. Don't protest—your feelings for the man were obvious to more than me. Even Prudence noticed."

I was too scared to blush. Then I caught a flicker of movement out of the corner of my eye and saw Victoria peering up over the top of the stairs. My fear shifted from my safety to hers— if Fenniwick spotted her, he'd kill her.

"What about Nathaniel?" I said, distracting him. "Do you really expect people to believe he killed himself after you push him off the roof too?" The can of Mace, I remembered suddenly. If I could reach my reticule, maybe I'd have a fighting chance. With the toe of my shoe I tried to hook the handle of the reticule to drag it to-ward me, praying Fenniwick wouldn't detect the movement. But the purse lay hopeless inches out of reach.

"A tragic accident. That's how it was planned, though now after your suicide I suppose I'll have to come up with some other means of doing in your cousin. Two falls from the same roof might seem a bit coincidental."

He grabbed my shoulders and shoved me over the side. I felt my grip on the rail loosen; another second and I'd be history—for good. Forcefully I kicked Fenniwick in the shin and twisted away from him and onto solid footing, feeling something tear in my ankle.

"Interfering bitch!" He backhanded me across my jaw and knocked me down—smack onto my purse. Reaching a hand beneath my dress, I unclasped it and wrapped my fingers around the Mace can just as Fenniwick lunged at me. I dodged the blow, deflecting his knife with my elbow. He swore and grabbed my hair, forcing me back over the rail, the knife blade at my throat. Clutching the rail with one hand, I raised the can of Mace and fired.

Fenniwick gasped and stumbled backward as the cloud of gas enveloped him. Coughing, I closed my eyes, tears burning them.

A loud thunk made me open my eyes just in time to see Fenniwick drop to the floor in a heap. Behind him, Victoria stood holding Nathaniel's telescope, a triumphant grin on her face.

"He looked positively panic-stricken when Aunt Faith told him you were ill," she explained. "Especially when she said she expected you'd recover. I realized maybe he was the one who poisoned you, since you knew about him and Prudence—"

"How did you know I was poisoned?"

She blushed. "I listened in when you were talking to Nathaniel about it. So when I saw Mr. Fenniwick slip out of the church just before the ceremony, I told Aunt Faith I had the curse and absolutely had to go to the powder room. Then I sneaked out and followed him."

"Good thing you did," I said, knowing how a prisoner spared from death row must feel. I took a step forward and a bolt of pain shot up my leg. Ignoring it, I bent over Fenniwick, checking to make sure he was really unconscious. "He's out cold," I said. "Victoria, is there some rope around here somewhere?"

Catching my drift, she nodded. "There's an old jumping rope of mine in the attic. I'll go fetch it."

Five minutes later, we had Fenniwick securely tied up, gagged, and tethered to the railing.

"We'll lock him up here for now and have the servants summon the police," I said.

"Yes, of course. But we've got to reach Nathaniel," Victoria urged. "He'll never marry Prudence now, not after we tell him about—" A depressed look fell over her face. "But the car's not here."

"I hate to say it," I said, gritting my teeth to block out the pain, "but I think I sprained my ankle."

"So we can't walk, either." Victoria groaned. "It's too far, anyhow. How will we get there in time to stop the wedding?"

I looked at her, an outlandish idea forming in my brain.

"Victoria," I asked, forming a smile. "Are you feeling up to a bicycle ride?"

Chapter Thirteen

My ankle throbbed as Victoria and I pedaled pell-mell uphill and downhill toward the church. At least the bikes weren't the type with one big front wheel like you see in museums, but they were surprisingly heavy and awkward to maneuver. I found myself reaching for a gearshift that wasn't there. "Why the heck couldn't your brother have invented a ten-speed?" I muttered to Victoria as we pulled up in front of the church at last.

We parked our bikes on the church steps. My traveling dress was spattered with stains, I noticed as I climbed off the bike, despite the fact that I'd hitched it up well above the ankle-level considered decent. Too bad there hadn't been time to change into my bloomers.

Victoria ran up the steps and bolted through the massive oak doors. White-hot pain seared my ankle as I hobbled after her, my heart thumping in my chest. What if we were too late? What if Nathaniel and Prudence were already married?

The church was packed; there must have been at least 300 people there. As Victoria and I burst in, several dozen heads turned toward us, gawking in disapproval. Not caring about the commotion we were causing, I half-limped, half-stumbled down the aisle after Victoria, bracing myself against the edges of the pews to keep from falling.

"Do you, Prudence Elizabeth Pratwell, take this man to be your lawfully wedded husband—to love and to honor, to have and to hold, in sickness and in health, for better or for worse. . . ." The minister's voice droned on.

Victoria reached the altar first. Prudence gave a shocked gasp as she caught sight of Nathaniel's sister from beneath her elaborate white lace veil.

"I do," she said quickly.

The minister glared at me as I lurched forward but repeated his question to the groom, who had not yet noticed our intrusion.

Nathaniel nodded slowly. "I d—"

"You *can't*," Victoria shouted, hurling herself at her brother. He spun around and dropped his jaw.

"Victoria! Taylor? What the devil has gotten into—"

"I can explain," I said. "Fenniwick—"

"Tried to murder Taylor by pushing her off the roof," Victoria interrupted, placing herself between the bride and groom. "I saw him—he said

Prudence is in love with him and that he's going to marry her, after he kills you too!"

"It's true," I confirmed. "Fenniwick was on Ruef's payroll. He's the one who poisoned my tea and set fire to your warehouse. He admitted it to me just before he tried to push me off the widow's walk."

Nathaniel's face drained of color. He turned toward his almost-bride and lifted her veil. "Prudence, what do you know of all this?"

Prudence flushed the color of a ripe strawberry. "I didn't know anything about a murder—Quentin never told me a thing about that!"

"Quentin, is it?" A grim look settled on Nathaniel's face. "Then you admit you've been . . . seeing him?"

She covered her mouth with her hand. "Oh, Natty, I never intended to hurt you," she said softly. "You've got to believe that. I couldn't help loving him—I never could. But Papa never approved; he said Quentin was beneath me."

"And I was right." Mortimer Pratwell scowled at his daughter from the front pew. "The man was a reprobate and a gambler—though he seemed a dependable enough employee. Apparently I've sorely misjudged the man."

"It didn't sound that way when you told Ruef you'd have my cousin taken care of," I said, confronting him as I ignored Prudence's squelched sobs. "Then you hired Fenniwick to torch Nathaniel's warehouse."

"That was Ruef's idea! I'd no idea he or Fenniwick intended bodily harm. I still don't comprehend what drove the man to such avarice. He was paid well enough for his services to me."

Nathaniel's mouth was a hard line. "I suspect if you examine your books you'll find your trusted employee has been embezzling funds to cover his gambling debts. Word is that the wretch is indebted up to his miserable neck."

Prudence wadded her handkerchief into a dripping ball. "Oh, Natty—you've always been so good to me, a proper gentleman; I d-don't deserve you. . . ." In a burst of sobs, she scooped up her lace train and ran out of the church. Grace Pratwell shot up and rumbled out after her daughter with Prudence's father close at her heels.

Nathaniel never gave any of them a second glance, instead closing the gap between the two of us in a single stride. He took my hands in his as the churchful of spectators stared in stunned silence.

"Taylor, I've been a fool. I never should have left you alone," he said in a low voice only I could hear. "You tried to warn me—I should have listened. To think I almost lost you. . . ."

I looked up at him and saw my own crazy feelings mirrored in his eyes. A strange warmth flooded me from head to toe and then it hit me—I was in love with Nathaniel.

"It's okay," I whispered, dazed.

I started to step forward into his arms, when my ankle gave out and I stumbled.

"You're hurt," he observed, steadying me as the

223

Miriam Raftery

lines around his eyes deepened in concern before hardening to anger.

"It's just a sprain," I said, embarrassed.

"Where is that scoundrel, Fenniwick? I'll thrash the miserable life out of him."

"Victoria and I tied him up and gagged him, then locked him in the attic. By now the police should have hauled him off to jail."

His eyebrows shot up. "You and my little sister did what? Two females—alone?"

I felt the corner of my mouth lift in a told-you-so grin. "Like I said, women can do anything men can do."

"Yes," he said, staring at me with a respectful glint in those dark eyes of his. "So you did at that. Though I'll wager some things are best done together."

Someone in the church cleared his throat. Nathaniel turned to face the onlookers. "What are all of you gawking at?"

An astonished murmur swept through the crowd. Raising his voice to be heard over the commotion, he roared, "What are you waiting for? Go on home—all of you. The wedding is off!"

A shock wave ran through me as the full meaning hit with the force of a tsunami. Nathaniel had called off his wedding, so Prudence couldn't hurt him anymore and Fenniwick was no longer a threat, which meant Stuart House could be saved—

And I had changed history.

* * *

224

"You don't have to do that—actually, it's feeling much better," I said on Tuesday afternoon as Nathaniel propped another pillow up under my slightly swollen ankle.

During the three days since the wedding, he'd hovered over me, refusing to leave my side except to sleep. We'd talked for hours, sharing our thoughts and feelings on many things—though not, of course, on everything. I'd even talked him into letting me borrow his camera to shoot some photos of the neighborhood, or at least as much of it as I could photograph from his porch and rooftop, since my ankle was too swollen to hobble more than a few yards. We'd grown quite close and I found myself dreading the prospect of stepping into that attic the next morning before dawn and leaving him—assuming my theory about returning to my own time during the earthquake would work, which I nearly hoped it wouldn't.

Since the wedding, he hadn't spoken another word about me leaving and I, in turn, had quit trying to convince him the world was coming to an end. After all, I'd succeeded in altering his fate. Sometime tonight I'd have to do something about Victoria's.

He set down a bed tray on my lap. On it was a bowl of steaming chicken soup, a sourdough roll, and a doughnut. "Eat this—it should help you regain your strength." He picked up the doughnut. "This is for Apollo."

The dog accepted the offering from Nathaniel's hand and wolfed down the doughnut ungraciously. "You're welcome," Nathaniel mocked, pulling a chair closer to my bed to sit down.

"Thanks," I said for both of us, savoring the aroma of chicken broth. I motioned to the newspaper tucked under his arm. "So what's new in the world?"

"Let's see," he began. "Roosevelt's raising hell with the muckrakers, Caruso opens tonight at the Grand Opera House, and in Italy—"

"Mount Vesuvius has erupted, killing hundreds."

His brow lifted. "How the devil did you know about that? The news has only just reached the West Coast."

"I have my ways," I said in a mysterious tone, preferring not to press the point just yet.

"Can you imagine an entire city wiped out by a natural disaster like that?" He shook his head. "The concept boggles the mind."

"It certainly does," I said edgily, knowing I'd have to tell him about the earthquake soon. "Speaking of disasters—"

"One more item you might be interested in," he interrupted. "Fenniwick's trial starts next week."

If the courthouse doesn't burn down first, I thought. Aloud, I asked, "What do you suppose will happen to him?"

"He'll spend the rest of his days in prison—that is if he doesn't hang."

I nodded. "Couldn't happen to a nicer guy."

He reached forward and stroked my cheek with the back of his hand, wrapping a curl of my hair around his fingers. "You use the most curious turns of phrase. At first I found it odd, but I confess I now find the habit most endearing. In fact, I find nearly everything about you to be captivating beyond words."

His words and touch lit a flame inside me. "You do?" I whispered.

"I do," he replied, gazing steadily into my eyes. I remembered the last time he'd spoken those words—or nearly, and felt myself tremble at the implications. "Taylor," he continued, taking my palms in his broad hands, the rough texture of them coarse yet stimulating against my skin. "I've been wondering if you feel up to a night out yet."

"A night out . . . with you?"

"Who else?" A smile tugged at his lips, making the corners of his mustache tilt upward. "*Carmen* opens tonight. I'm hoping you'll do me the honor of allowing me to escort you."

"You're asking me for a date?"

He squeezed my hands, his thumb rubbing lazy circles in my palm that set my pores on fire. "That's one way of putting it."

I felt joyous and bittersweet at the same time; I'd dreamed of just such a moment—the idea of a night on the town with the most handsome man I'd ever known was like something out of a fairy tale. Yet now that I was on the brink of leaving him for good—at least, assuming it was possible to go forward in time during the earthquake—the smart thing to do would be not to get involved any deeper with Nathaniel than I already was.

"Yes," I heard myself say. "I'd love to hear the opera with you." In truth, I realized, I'd have gone with Nathaniel Stuart to a hog-calling contest if he'd asked. Luckily for me, his taste ran more toward cultural affairs than swine.

A frown crossed his face as he glanced out the window at the gathering clouds. "I only hope it doesn't rain."

"It won't. The weather will be clear and crisp, a perfect spring evening," I said, recalling the descriptions I'd read of the night before the quake.

"Let us hope so. Until tonight, then." He lifted my hand and pressed his lips to my palm, sending a red-hot current up my arm.

"Until tonight," I replied, seeing stars long before the darkness fell.

As I was dressing for the opera, Victoria knocked on my door. "Taylor, can I come in?"

"Sure," I said, opening the door. At the sound of Victoria's voice, Apollo perked up his ears and trotted to the door to greet her.

Victoria's eyes widened at the sight of me in the peach-colored dress Nathaniel had purchased for the wedding, but which I'd never had the chance to wear. "Gracious—Taylor, you're beautiful!" she exclaimed.

"Do you think this dress is all right?" I asked, self-consciously fiddling with the lace at the low-cut neckline. "I'm afraid it's too light and frilly for evening wear, but I don't have anything more appropriate."

"It's perfect," Victoria declared with a decisive nod. "All those old biddies in their dark gowns will be green with envy, mark my words." She held out a hand and opened it, displaying some leftover ibuprofen pills. "I won't be needing these anymore, for now. It worked like a charm—thank you for lending them to me."

"Sure, anytime," I said, plunking the pills down on my nightstand as Victoria rubbed Apollo's ears, eliciting a satisfied grunt.

"Well," she said with a knowing twinkle in her eye, "I'd better let you finish getting ready. You know my brother doesn't like to be kept waiting."

"I'll keep that in mind," I said as she skipped out into the hall with Apollo at her heels.

After she left, I dropped the pills in the ibuprofen bottle and started to put it back in my fanny pack, when my eye fell on the expiration date: July 31, 1990. Here was the proof I'd been looking for—I could go to Nathaniel and convince him now that I really was from the future.

So why didn't I feel overjoyed? I should feel elated—excited, thrilled, at the very least relieved. But if anything I felt let down.

It was, I realized to my amazement, because suddenly I didn't want to tell Nathaniel where I was from—or that I'd soon be leaving.

I wasn't ready to break the spell between us. I couldn't; not yet. The earthquake wouldn't hit until 5:13 tomorrow morning. There was plenty of time yet to hide Victoria's candles and keep her safe. But first I wanted one night of magic together with Nathaniel. Tonight.

Just one night, I thought, before Cinderella goes back to her rags—or in my case, spandex. But sometime before sunrise, I'd have to tell my newfound prince the truth about where I'd really come from.

The opera house was packed as the stage lights dimmed. Beside me in the darkness, Nathaniel reached for my hand and took it in his own, radiating warmth through me. "They say Caruso has the voice of an angel," he said under his breath.

"An angel who won't be back," I said idly, recalling the stories I'd read of how Caruso, terrified after the quake, ran to the window of his hotel room and sang at the top of his lungs to make sure his voice hadn't been scared out of him.

Nathaniel scoffed. "Why, it would take an act of God to keep a man of Caruso's stature—not to mention conceit—away from this town."

"You've got that right," I said, suddenly edgy. This didn't seem the right time to mention that the opera house, along with every other theater in San Francisco, would soon be burned to rubble.

Caruso's interpretation of Don Jose was inspired. I found myself caught up by the story of the prostitute, Carmen, recognizing the ironic similarities between Bizet's heroine and myself. At one point, I was so moved by Carmen's plight and Caruso's soul-stirring interpretation that I found myself blinking back tears.

"Don't," Nathaniel whispered, brushing my tears away with his fingertips. "I don't ever want to see you unhappy again."

His words warmed me even as a tremor ran through me at the thought of leaving him at dawn. What would he say, I wondered, when I told him the truth—would he believe me this time?

More important, I thought as the curtain fell, would he want me to go—or stay?

Chapter Fourteen

The house was dark when we returned after the opera. It was late—past eleven, I judged. Nathaniel, handsome as any fairy-tale prince in the waistcoat and tails that seemed to accentuate every muscle in his lean, hard torso, escorted me through the foyer. He flung open the doors to the grand ballroom, motioning me to follow, and revealed a blaze of light from the glittering chandelier.

The one that would shatter at dawn.

I watched, fascinated, as Nathaniel moved to a small table and lifted the arm on a phonograph that looked like one straight out of an old RCA ad, minus the dog. He placed the needle on a record and a moment later the melodic strains of Strauss's *Blue Danube* waltz filled the ballroom.

"Taylor." His voice was husky, welcoming me

as I stepped into the circle of his arms. He pulled me close against him, his masculine scent distorting my reasoning as we glided across the dance floor, just as we had in my dreams. I ignored the soreness in my ankle, reality intruding on my fantasy. I knew I had to speak up, and soon. . . . But not yet, I thought, unwilling to end the giddy sensation of waltzing in his arms. I closed my eyes, allowing my imagination to picture what my life could be like if I stayed here—if I didn't go back.

Didn't go back? How could I even think such a thing—Mom and Dad must be frantic worrying about me after the earthquake, I reminded myself. And there was my degree to think about, and Victoria.

"The opera was stirring, but all I've been able to concentrate on all evening is you." Nathaniel's breath was warm in my ear, derailing my common sense. It was crazy to think of staying here, and yet . . .

He twirled me about with a flourish as the music stopped and we came to a halt, standing just inches apart in the middle of the ballroom floor as the lights from the chandelier cast a thousand shadows that made his expression unreadable.

"Nathaniel—"

"Taylor—"

He took my hands in his, looking at me with an intensity that made me quiver. "In the short time since you've come into my life, you've made me realize how much I've been missing."

"I feel the same way," I whispered.

"After Fenniwick tried to push you off the roof, when I almost lost you, it made me realize just what you've come to mean to me—and to Victoria. Taylor, there's something I must tell you."

"That makes two of us," I said, feeling a rush of guilt at the mention of Victoria's name. "I've got to fill you in on a few things, too." What right did I have to lead Nathaniel on when come tomorrow I'd be gone? At least I thought I would, assuming my theory about traveling forward in time would work. I had to tell him about the earthquake now. Even though I'd managed to stop Nathaniel's wedding and save his house from Fenniwick, Victoria was still in danger. Unless we stopped her, she'd be burned when the earthquake struck at dawn. Taking away her candles was far from foolproof. I couldn't remember the exact extent of damage to the house. What if a ceiling collapsed, or she was cut by flying glass?

"Taylor—"

The doorbell sounded, halting Nathaniel's speech. He lowered his brows in annoyance as he strode to the ballroom doors, muttering under his breath, "Of all the ill-timed intrusions . . ."

A sleepy-eyed Mrs. O'Hara straggled down the stairs, tugging at the tie on her robe. "Now who on earth d'ye suppose would come callin' at this hour?"

A distant memory popped into my head. Victoria had told me something once about a late-night visitor the night before the earthquake. What was it she said? "A strapping young man, handsome as a bull . . ."

"Antonio," I announced.

"What?"

"Your business partner. He's here with news of an important business transaction you've been expecting." I hazarded a guess and jumped in with both feet. "It has to do with those papers about the trolley, the ones you've been working on with Mr. Spreckels."

He stared at me. "By God, I hope you're right."

Mrs. O'Hara opened the door to admit a towering broad-framed Italian who matched Victoria's description perfectly. "Well, Mr. Giuseppe do come in. The master's waitin'."

Antonio removed his hat and stepped inside Nathaniel met him in the foyer and ushered him into the parlor while Mrs. O'Hara bustled off t get some tea. Glancing at me, Antonio shifted from one foot to the other. "I have news—*mag nifico*," he began. "But now perhaps is not the time. . . ."

"You may speak freely in front of Miss James," Nathaniel assured him. "What is this news?"

Relaxing, Antonio unrolled a sheaf of papers in his hand and thrust it into Nathaniel's hands. "The letters of incorporation for your new trolley company—they've been signed!"

"New trolley company?" I looked at Nathaniel, startled to discover just what the mysterious trolley papers were all about.

A satisfied grin spread over his face. "Well and good. Ruef and his cohorts were set on making a tidy fortune running trolleys on overhead wires, you see. They spread rumors and planted bogus newspaper stories indicating that it would be impossibly expensive, even dangerous to run a network of trolleys on underground lines. So Spreckels and I called his bluff by forming our own company to accomplish the impossible."

"And that's why Ruef torched your warehouse and tried to have you killed?"

"Pushing me off the roof was Fenniwick's idea. Apparently the scoundrel intended to double-cross Ruef and Prudence's father, after pocketing their money, of course. He bled dry the bulk of Pratwell's fortune through his embezzling; then after he'd gambled that money away he decided he'd woo Prudence to get to my money. Fortunately"—he squeezed my hand—"you put a halt to his madness."

From the corner of my eye, I spotted Victoria kneeling on the third-story landing, spying on us. Antonio saw the affectionate look that passed from his employer to me and cleared his throat. "I should go now. I apologize if I've intruded at a bad time. *Arrivaderci.*"

"No, don't go." Grabbing Nathaniel by the arm, I whispered in his ear, "I've got to talk with you— now."

Giving me a puzzled glance, he turned to Antonio. "Kindly excuse us a moment."

We stepped into the ballroom and he closed the door. "Nathaniel," I began breathlessly, "there isn't time to explain, but you've got to send Victoria away with Antonio."

"What? Send her away!"

"Look." I took a deep breath. "You didn't believe me before, when I tried to warn you about Prudence. But I know what's going to happen in the future—I'm serious. Tomorrow morning at 5:13 there's going to be an earthquake, and Victoria will be burned terribly. You've got to believe me."

He started to protest, but stopped. "You knew Antonio was at the door with those papers," he said, stroking his chin thoughtfully. "Just as you knew about Prudence and Fenniwick, and that he meant to kill me."

"That's right," I said, my voice rising along with my impatience. "Don't forget the airplane— how do you suppose I knew how to make it fly? Or how to cure Victoria's cramps, or what the weather would be like this evening?"

"An uncanny series of coincidences . . ."

"How do you explain the fact that I knew Mount Vesuvius had erupted before I'd read the newspaper?"

After an awkward pause, he said, "I'll admit I can't fathom the explanation, though of course there must be one."

"There is. I'm telling you, I've seen the future— and there's going to be an earthquake worse than any this city has ever seen."

A troubled expression lit his eyes. "Perhaps you are indeed gifted with second sight. I'll concede it's possible. . . ."

I could see faith battling common sense in his eyes. He needed proof. I considered the bottle of ibuprofen but decided not to confuse the issue by bringing up the fact that I was from the future just yet. "Her room," I said decisively, praying Victoria would forgive me for betraying her confidence. "Victoria is reading a racy novel she thinks you won't approve of. That's why she'll be up at dawn, reading by candlelight when the earthquake strikes."

"And the candle—"

"Will set her hair on fire. Her face will be scarred for life."

A look of horror came over him. Barging past me, he ran out of the ballroom and up the stairs, passing a startled Victoria on the landing. I ran after him, nearly colliding with him as he came out of Victoria's room a moment later carrying the evidence in his hand.

"Victoria, haven't I told you not to waste your mind reading this rubbish?" He waved the romance novel in front of her.

She looked at me as if I were Benedict Arnold. "Taylor, I thought you were my friend."

"I am," I protested. "I'm doing this for your own good. You'll understand in the morning."

Nathaniel turned the book over in his hand as if it were bewitched. "How do I know you didn't plant this in Victoria's room yourself?" he asked me.

"You don't. But are you really willing to bet your sister's safety on the chance that I'm lying?"

Silence.

"What do you have to lose?" I challenged, sensing victory. "If I'm right, and you send her away, you'll save her from . . ." Glancing at Victoria, I softened my words. "You'll keep her out of

238

harm's way when the earthquake hits. But if I'm wrong, Victoria will have lost nothing but a couple of days away from school on a short vacation."

"Earthquake! What is she talking about?" Victoria tugged at Nathaniel's sleeve.

He turned to me, a deceptive calm in his voice. "It seems I can't afford not to believe you. But if there is to be an earthquake, as you suggest, how can you be certain Victoria will be safe if I send her away?"

I racked my brain, trying to remember what areas were undamaged by the quake. Then inspiration struck. Ships outside the harbor rode out the quake safely, I recalled. "Have Antonio take her out to sea aboard one of your ships."

"Antonio?" Victoria's eyes brightened. "You want me to go on a trip with Mr. Giuseppe?"

"Make him promise to keep her away for at least three days," I went on. Until the fires that will destroy the city have burned themselves out, I added silently. "If you're worried about what people will say, send Mrs. O'Hara along as a chaperon."

Nathaniel was silent, emotion battling reason on his face. Finally he nodded. "I could never forgive myself if anything happened to my sister. I'll speak with Antonio now and give him his instructions."

I exhaled the breath I hadn't realized I was holding. "You won't be sorry. Trust me."

He met my gaze steadily. "I do, Taylor. Lord knows why, but I do."

239

* * *

"The servants have been awakened and are busy packing," Nathaniel informed me 20 minutes later. "Though none of them understand why they've been sent off to stay with relatives at this late hour."

"It's for their own good," I assured him. "All those buildings out back are going to get wiped out when the quake hits, including the servants' quarters."

"Even my workshop?" His voice was strained.

"It's true," I said softly. "I wish it wasn't, but it is."

He wrapped an arm around me and pulled me against his comforting warmth. "We'll find out soon enough, won't we?"

Victoria's hastily packed bags were loaded into Antonio's carriage, along with a baffled Mrs. O'Hara. "Will you still be here when I get back?" Victoria asked me as we stood on the front porch a few minutes later. She was, I noticed, dressed up and had pulled her hair up into a bun, which made her look surprisingly grown-up.

"No," I answered, feeling more than a twinge of regret. "I won't."

Her eyes widened and she threw her arms around me, dampening my skirts with moisture from her tears. "I'm going to miss you, Taylor. Why do you have to go?"

I felt my own eyes start to water at the thought. "It's time, Victoria. I don't belong here—this isn't my home."

She looked up at me and blinked through

misty eyes, once more childlike. "It could be, if you wanted it to be."

Her statement shook me to the roots. Was she right? I felt a warm glow inside at the memory of Nathaniel's words earlier, when he'd told me all he could think about was me. . . . Still, even if he did have feelings for me, I could hardly chuck it all to stay in an era when women's thoughts were considered less important than the feathers in their hats. Could I?

Before I could reply, Nathaniel walked toward us. "Are you ready, Victoria?" he asked.

She nodded. Accepting his arm, she walked steadily toward the carriage door that Antonio helped open for her.

Apollo whimpered at my side, looking from me to Victoria and back again. "I know," I said, rubbing his ears. "I'll miss her too."

Suddenly my dog broke free and ran to Victoria, who turned and scooped him up into her arms. Could he sense, somehow, that this young girl would one day grow up to be the old woman who had raised him and given him to me in what seemed another lifetime? I bit my lip, surprised to find how much it hurt to see him go. Apollo cocked his head to give me one last lopsided grin out the carriage window before it clattered down the drive and off into the night.

And they say cats are fickle.

Nathaniel joined me on the porch and we stood together, watching in silence until the last echo of carriage wheels died on the night wind.

"You did the right thing," I assured him.

He wrapped an arm around my shoulder and pulled me close, infusing me with warmth. "I pray you're right."

"Your house will survive," I said as he held the door open for me to step inside.

"My father built this house," he said, a look of pride in his eyes. "Victoria was born here. I've a duty to save it, God willing. So I had the servants fill all the basins and tubs with water before they left, along with every pot and pan in the house, and soak several dozen sheets."

"Good thinking," I said, impressed. "I talked Mrs. O'Hara into letting me cut some spare sheets into long strips, for bandages, while she was packing. A lot of people are going to be hurt before this is all over. I've laid out all the antiseptics I could find and borrowed some brandy from your study, in case it's needed as a pain-killer."

He frowned. "I don't know whether to wish you're sane or mad. Antonio thinks I've gone around the bend, but he promised to send a shipment of wine casks from the warehouse anyhow."

"Smart move." I nodded approvingly. "Some of the Italian neighborhoods were saved from burning by residents who soaked their homes in wine. Now then," I said, starting down the walkway, "we've got to warn the others."

"Others?" He protested, overtaking me as I reached the end of the walkway, "No one will believe such a cock-and-bull story."

"It's not a story. It's history," I insisted,

crossing the street as Nathaniel tugged at my elbow. "If we warn your neighbors, maybe they can save their homes. With your car, we could ride through the city and sound an alarm—sort of like Paul Revere. . . ."

"Now you really do sound crazy. But if you're bound and determined to rouse the neighborhood, I'd best come along to make sure no one throws you into a madhouse."

I grinned. "That's the spirit."

We marched up to a modest Victorian home across the street. "Let me do the talking," he said under his breath, then rang the bell. No answer. He rang again. After a moment, an old man in a nightcap poked his head out an upstairs window. "Nathaniel Stuart? D'you have any idea what time it is?"

Nathaniel took a step back and craned his neck, looking up at the grumpy-looking old man. "Sorry to wake you, Dr. Greely," he said, hesitating. "I don't have time to explain, but an experiment I've conducted indicates that an earthquake is going to strike early in the morning."

Wow, I thought, startled anew by his inventive mind. Way to go, Nathaniel.

"Shortly after five o'clock," he was saying. "I'd advise you to—"

"An earthquake? That's rich," the old man said, yawning. "You wake me up from a sound sleep to tell me another of your wild-eyed theories?"

"A highly probable theory. I know it sounds far-fetched, but the evidence indicates—"

"Be off before I summon the police." He slammed the window shut to punctuate his point.

"Wait—" I started to shout, until Nathaniel clamped a hand over my mouth.

"He's set in his ways; no amount of arguing will change a closed mind. Getting us hauled off to jail won't help anyone."

I had to admit he had a point. "I'll try the next house," I volunteered. It was a three-story brick home trimmed with white shutters and an immaculate flower garden in the front yard. I rang the bell and, when no one answered, pounded on the door. Finally, it opened a crack and two plump old ladies peered out at me. "Is something wrong?" the shorter one asked, recognizing Nathaniel beside me.

"Yes," I began. "I'm Nathaniel's cousin. I'm sorry to wake you, but there's going to be a terrible earthquake. I had a vision—"

"Vision my eye," the taller woman snapped. "I told you we shouldn't have answered the door, Mabel."

"You were right, as usual, Millicent," Mabel said, looking down.

"I'm telling you, it's true!" I argued. "But if you'll fill your bathtubs and start soaking some blankets—"

"It sounds as if you're the one besotted." Millicent looked down her hawklike nose at me, then turned to Nathaniel. "I'd heard some wild rumors after your wedding to that lovely Miss Pratwell was called off, young man, but I never! This young woman you've taken up with is clearly deranged."

That did it. "I am not—"

"My cousin is used to speaking her own mind"—Nathaniel interrupted, firing me a warning glance—"sometimes more than is welcome. But I've good reason to believe what she claims is true." His voice took on an almost seductive tone as he added, "That rose color becomes you, Millicent. It brings out the color in your face."

Millicent turned pink as the geraniums in her flowerpots. "Flattery will get you nowhere, young man." To her sister, she added in a whisper, "It's that young woman he's taken up with—she's affected his judgment. I heard she was an odd one; now I know it's true."

"I'm not a kook!" I argued. "I—"

Nathaniel dug his fingers into my elbow and dragged me off the porch, apologizing to the two old women for interrupting their beauty sleep.

"Where are you taking me?" I protested as we reached the sidewalk. "We haven't gotten anyone to listen. . . ."

"Give it up, Taylor," he said gently. "Their minds are closed. No one wants to believe it's possible to predict the future. Would you, if someone else tried to tell you your whole life was about to turn upside down?"

I bit my tongue. "No," I admitted. "I guess not."

He draped his arm around me to shield me from the chill night air. "Come on," he said. "Let's get you tucked into bed." A ripple ran through me as he shepherded me across the street and up the walkway. The prospect of sleeping alone in the guest room waiting for an earthquake to strike suddenly sounded far from appealing.

"Nathaniel," I said as we stepped over the threshold. "I—"

He raised a finger to my lips, brushing them to silence me. Slowly, his gaze probing mine, he lowered his head until his firm, warm lips covered my mouth in a kiss full of promise. "Enough talk. If it's true that an earthquake will strike at dawn, I don't want to waste another precious moment of our time together."

Closing the door behind us, he pulled me into his arms. "I need you, Taylor."

"You what?" I asked, stunned.

"I need you. I have from the first moment I laid eyes on you." He bent his head forward and pressed his lips to mine.

"But you don't know me. . . ."

There was, I realized as I tightened my arms around his neck, only one place in the house that I knew for sure was safe during the earthquake. Nathaniel's bedroom, where Prudence had been sleeping when the quake hit—at least, before I changed history.

"I know all that I need to know," he murmured between kisses. "Your past is just that—history." Before I could protest he kissed me again, separating my lips with his tongue, searing and probing as his hand pressed against the small of my back, pulling me hard against him. I felt the pounding of his heart that matched the rhythm of my own and knew that he wanted me as much as I wanted him. As my breathing came harder and harder one thing became crystal clear—more than anything, I wanted to make love to Nathaniel Stuart.

A man who thought I was a prostitute.

"I'm not what you think I am," I protested, tilting my head back.

"And what, pray tell, are you?" he asked, cocking an eyebrow as he raked me with his eyes, turning my knees to jelly. The idea that he still thought I was a hooker tore at me inside . . . then suddenly I realized that it didn't matter what he thought. In the morning I'd be gone, with nothing left of Nathaniel but a memory. So for tonight, I wanted to create a memory that would last for all time—a memory that would sear my heart with the permanence of a branding iron.

"You're right," I said softly, slipping my arms around his neck as my lips brushed his. "My past doesn't matter. Not now."

"This earthquake," he said, a flicker of concern darkening his eyes as his gaze paused on the chandelier. "You've said the chandelier will fall, though the house itself will remain standing. Is there an area within the house that you know to be safe?"

"Your bedroom will protect us from the quake," I whispered, tracing the rugged contours of his face with my fingertips. "Though I'm not sure safe is the word I'd choose to describe it."

Smiling broadly, he swept me into his arms and carried me up the stairs.

* * *

Miriam Raftery

I trembled with excitement and more than a touch of nervousness as Nathaniel untied my traveling cloak and laid it on the chair, then proceeded to unfasten the countless tiny buttons on the back of my gown. A warm ripple ran through me as he slid the dress down and caressed my bare shoulders, then slipped it off over my ankles and tossed it aside.

I watched, mesmerized, as he began to unbutton his shirt. Unable to stop myself, I slid my hands inside the front of his shirt and sifted my fingers through the thick tangle of dark hair on his chest. His hard, corded muscles tensed beneath my palms and a low groan escaped him as he ripped off his last remaining button and dropped his shirt to the floor. I drew in my breath sharply at the sight of him, bare to the waist.

He crushed his lips against mine with bruising force, sending a heat wave through me. Enveloping me in his arms, he dipped me backward until my back sank into the comforting softness of his feather bed. Impatiently he unlaced my shoes and removed them, then peeled away the seemingly endless layers of undergarments, down to my corset, drawers, and stockings.

"You're beautiful," he whispered, as he unlaced my corset ties, freeing my breasts from the uncomfortable confinement while I tingled in anticipation.

"Me? Beautiful?" I mumbled through a velvet haze. Even his words made me feel flushed; I'd never thought of myself as pretty. Presentable, yes, maybe even attractive, if I used enough stage makeup and hot rollers. But beautiful? Not in my wildest dreams.

"So beautiful," he murmured as he knelt and kissed first one breast, then the other, sending a white-hot flame through me wherever his lips and tongue touched—teasing, tantalizing, arousing. Okay, I thought, my mind growing fuzzy. Maybe in my wildest dream . . . which surely this had to be.

"This time must be different than all the others," he said, encircling me in his strong arms as I learned what heaven felt like. Deftly he slipped off my drawers, then unrolled my silk stockings and removed them, one by one. "I want to satisfy you as no man has satisfied you before," he whispered in my ear, then proceeded to caress me with fingers and lips and tongue until I thought I'd die from pleasure yet begged him not to stop—just like the wanton woman he thought I was.

When I was sure I couldn't stand another moment he did stop, then slowly took off his remaining clothes until, finally, he stood naked before me.

I drew in my breath at the sight of him, illuminated by the flickering gaslight from the wall sconce. He was magnificent—solid bands of muscle and sinew made his chest and shoulders gleam like a bronzed statue in a museum, tinged by dusky hairs that rippled when he breathed, tapering to a narrow triangle on his firm, flat abdomen, and below. . . .

Seeing the path of my gaze, he quirked an eyebrow playfully. "Is something wrong?"

I felt myself redden. "Wrong? No way. I was just, um, admiring your birthday suit."

The corners of his mouth tilted upward in a smile. "It isn't my birthday. But if you're willing, we can celebrate anyhow."

"I'm willing." He moved toward me as if stepping into my dream and pulled me into his arms, smothering me in red-hot kisses. The warmth of his bare flesh against my own made my pores steam as we sank together into the feathery depths of his bed.

"I want you, Taylor," he whispered, his hot breath ragged in my ear. I snuggled against his chest, tingling all over as he dipped his head and blazed a molten trail down my cheeks, neck, and shoulders. "More than I've ever wanted any woman before."

"I want you too," I murmured as I ran my fingers through the hair on his chest, then explored the muscled contours of his back, savoring the expedition. His face moved lower as his lips and tongue worked their magic on my breasts, then down the center cleft between my ribs. Covering my hand with his, he guided my palm lower, around the angular curve of his hip. Without warning his weight shifted and a burst of adrenaline shot through me as I sensed the swollen evidence of his desire. Nathaniel groaned, burrowing against me as his own hand trailed lower until he found the moist core of me and dipped inside. I writhed at his touch, driven wild with a passion I hadn't known was part of me, until I was sure I couldn't stand a moment more of such exquisite torture.

When he lowered himself onto me and entered me at last a lightning bolt ripped through me, filling me with heat and pain. Deep inside, a dry chafing ache made me feel as if I'd split in two. I bit the edges of my tongue, determined not to let him see my discomfort.

He paused, looking at me as though he were seeing me for the first time. He knows, I thought, dazed. Somehow Nathaniel knows that this is my first time. . . .

"I don't know where you've come from, but it sure as hell wasn't any brothel," he whispered, his voice husky, "How could I not have known?"

I trembled as he bent forward until his lips claimed mine, tenderly at first, then hungrily as his tongue slipped between my parted lips, stirring the embers of a fire smoldering deep within me.

A white-hot explosion erupted inside me as I wrapped my arms around him tighter and felt him start to move inside me, slowly at first, then faster. Instinctively I followed his lead, moving with him in a primitive rhythm until the pain receded and there was only pleasure—waves of it, cresting and falling, one after another, drowning me in a thunderous tide. I felt free, as if I were waltzing on a cloud, or flying above the clouds. . . . Though not even the joy I'd felt when rising into the sky with Nathaniel in his flying machine could match the dizzying sensation I felt as we soared together toward the sunrise. For the two of us, then, there was no past and no future—no yesterday or tomorrow, but only our incredibly glorious present together. A present I wished would never end even as his final, shuddering release lifted me closer toward heaven than I'd have believed possible.

Then something coiled deep within me, breaking free with a force more powerful than any earthquake. If only the night didn't have to end. . . . Sensing my need, Nathaniel answered my unspoken plea and began anew the timeless cycle of love between man and woman, the one thing that hasn't changed in a thousand lifetimes, nor will change in a thousand more. . . .

And the rest, as they say, is history.

Chapter Fifteen

"You've changed." Nathaniel, propped on one elbow in his bed, rubbed sleep from his eyes. A slow grin spread across his face as he raked his gaze over the curves in the leotard and hot pink spandex tights that I'd put on while he dozed. "Come to think of it, I believe I could use another lesson on how this 'zipper' works."

Reluctantly, I shook my head. "I've got to go now."

"Go?" Confusion, then anger, flashed on his face. "You can't mean to leave now—not after what we've shared. You've told me there's to be an earthquake"—he paused, glancing at his stopwatch—"in less than a half of an hour. Where the devil were you planning on going?"

I clutched the fanny pack strapped at my waist. "Back to where I came from."

He sat up straight and looked me in the eyes. "I think,"—he said, patting the covers beside him—"that it's high time you tell me where that is, don't you?"

Nodding, I approached the bed and sat down, heat staining my cheeks as I remembered the passion we'd shared there only a few hours earlier and envisioned him naked beneath the covers. With difficulty I resisted the almost irresistible impulse to climb under the covers beside him. "I tried to tell you once before," I said, "but you didn't believe me."

His eyebrows dipped, forming a vee. "That nonsense you babbled about being a gypsy fortune-teller—"

"I made that up because I didn't think you'd believe the truth."

"Why didn't you tell me before that you were a virgin?" he asked, his tone gentle as his thumb traced a circular pattern on my palm that burned like a brand. "What could be so terrible that you'd prefer to let me go on believing you were a woman of ill repute?"

"I tried to tell you, but you didn't want to hear."

"When I saw you in those clothes, I assumed . . ." He sighed. "All right, so I plead guilty as charged. Just what was this truth I was too bullheaded to let you tell me?"

I took a deep breath, dreading his reaction. "The truth is that I'm from the future."

A stunned look froze on his face. "All those absurd stories you told me about airplanes, and rockets to the moon . . ."

"They're all true. I swear it." Unzipping my fanny pack, I pulled out the bottle of ibuprofen and placed it in his hands. "Maybe this will help convince you."

He turned it over, disbelief obvious in his eyes. "What is this made of? I've never seen a material like it."

"It's plastic," I explained. "A man-made synthetic. Lots of things are made from it in my day—milk bottles, toys, even furniture. And medicine bottles, like this one."

"A pillbox?" He looked at me suspiciously. I felt my heart sink; he didn't believe me. He fingered the lid between his thumb and forefinger, a frown forming on his lips. "How does it open?"

"You line up the arrows, like this." I demonstrated. "It's called a childproof cap, so kids can't get into it."

"A worthy concept." He tested the opening device and popped off the lid, looked inside at the pills, then twirled the container in his hand. "Your potion cured Victoria, all right, though—" He stopped in midsentence as his eyes fell on the expiration date.

"1990?" He rubbed his fingers across the date, glancing from it to me. He laid down the bottle and stared at me as if I'd just sprouted angel wings and flown across the room.

He exhaled a long, slow breath, steadying himself. "You couldn't have tampered with this; it's a printed label. So that's how you knew about Mount Vesuvius, and the rest—"

"In my own time, I was a historian," I clarified.

"I was doing research for my master's thesis on restoring old houses from your time period. That's how I met Victoria."

"Incredible," he said, shaking his head. "If I hadn't witnessed your uncanny ability to predict future events, I'd never have thought such a thing possible. But . . ." He locked his eyes on mine.

"I know it sounds crazy," I said. "It's—"

"A miracle," he finished in an awed tone.

"Maybe," I admitted. "I don't pretend to understand it. I've read a little about plate tectonics, and—"

"Plate what?"

"Tectonics. It's a scientific theory about what causes earthquakes. Big plates crashing against each other until pressure makes the earth shift."

He nodded, a spark of scientific excitement lighting his eyes. "It makes sense. That would of course release a tremendous amount of energy. . . ."

"Enough energy to cause shifts in time as well," I said. "I was in the attic of this house when an earthquake hit in 1989. So the way I figure it, if I hang out in your attic when this morning's quake is due . . ."

"It will send you back to your own time," he finished, comprehension dawning on his face. "I'm beginning to understand that anything is possible. Yes, it's conceivable. There could be a place below the earth here where time has gotten out of alignment; the concept would explain why compasses have never worked right in this house."

"Geomagnetic forces out of whack—"

"Powerful forces," he agreed, pulling me against him.

"Very powerful," I whispered just before his lips descended upon mine again, capturing me in a lingering kiss that kindled embers still smoldering from the night before, as if he never intended to let me go. Feeling his arms around me again made me ache to lie back on his bed and have him make love to me now, and forever. I didn't want to go back to my own time—my parents could get by without me somehow, and Victoria . . . well, her life was nearly over, after all. The young Victoria needed me even more.

I held my breath as Nathaniel broke the kiss. "This future of yours—what is it like?" he asked.

I hesitated. "Well, there are good and bad points, I guess. Traffic and crime aren't so hot. But on the plus side, we have new technologies— cellular phones, laser surgery, microwave ovens—that make life more comfortable in many ways."

"Cellular phones? Lasers? Microwaves?"

"Portable telephones without wires—you can talk anywhere on one, even in your car. Lasers are concentrated beams of light. Surgeons use them instead of knives."

"Astounding," he said in an awestruck tone. "And microwaves?"

"Ovens that use radiation. I'm no Julia Child— she's a gourmet chef—but I can still cook a whole meal in a matter of minutes."

He was silent, absorbing my words. "It's clear

you miss all those innovations," he said at last.

"I'm getting used to doing things the old-fashioned way," I lied.

"And your family," he continued as if I hadn't said a word. "They must be half-mad worrying over you."

"Mom used to worry I'd been mugged if I was a half hour late getting home from school," I admitted.

Anxiously I waited to hear the words that would make me stay. All he had to do was tell me that he loved me, that he still wanted me now that he knew the truth about me.

I held my breath, watching his emotions battle visibly for a long moment before a look of resignation settled on his face. "I'll never forget you," he said, stroking my hair gently. "But it's clear you belong in your own time."

He might as well have taken a knife and stuck it in my heart. I buried my face against his shoulder, determined not to let him see how much I was hurting. My lip trembled; I fought down the urge to burst into tears.

Gently he released me and reached for his smoking jacket. He pulled it on, then took my arm and led me to the attic door.

He snapped open his pocket watch, studying it longer than was necessary. "It's nearly time." He held open my hand, laid the pocket watch in my palm, and closed my fingers around it. "To remember me by," he said, his voice pulsing with an emotion I hadn't heard before.

"Thank you," I said in a voice so hoarse I hardly

recognized it. I unclipped the odometer with a built-in compass from my fanny pack and handed it to him. "The compass won't do you much good in th-this crazy house of yours," I said, fighting to keep my voice steady even as my heart was breaking. "But the odometer might come in handy when you're flying. It t-tells you how many miles you've c-come—"

Unable to finish for fear I'd humiliate myself by bursting into tears, I clamped my mouth shut. Nathaniel looked equally uncomfortable. Finally he broke the awkward silence.

"Then there's nothing left to say."

I nodded. "Right. I guess this is it, huh?" I waited, praying he'd beg me not to go.

"Yes," he said, his eyes tugging at me like magnets. "Godspeed, my love."

I gripped the door handle and pulled it open. "Nathaniel," I half-whispered, turning to face him.

"Yes?"

I love you, my brain screamed. But I couldn't voice the words. I'd slept with him, fallen in love with him, but he didn't love me enough to ask me to stay. Or maybe he doesn't believe I could fit into his way of life, I realized, my mind spinning as I wondered if he was right, after all. He knows I don't belong here, and I never will. . . .

I stood on tiptoes and brushed my lips on his, then spun around and staggered into the attic, willing myself to push the stunned look I'd seen on his face out of my mind. I sensed rather than saw his gaze boring into me from behind, burning me with the intensity of a laser.

Blinking back tears, I forced myself to walk away from him and retrace my steps from the night of the last earthquake. Was it really just a week ago? I found a crate with a splintered board—the one I'd tripped over in the darkness, perhaps. Somewhere a horse whinnied; I heard the distant sound of dogs barking. The animals know, I thought. Somehow, their instincts are telling them that an earthquake is about to hit.

All of a sudden I found myself missing Apollo. At least before I hadn't had to make this trip alone. "This was all y-your fault," I rambled aloud to the missing dog. "If you hadn't gotten loose and run up those stairs—"

The floor rumbled. Visions of my old life flashed in my mind—a life without Nathaniel, the man I loved—a man who'd made it clear he wanted me to leave him, I reminded myself, digging my nails into my palms, willing the pain to bring me to my senses. Without him, I had nothing . . . yet I wouldn't turn back. I couldn't.

The sound became a roar; the floor beneath me lurched and I bolted forward over the crate. Panic hit me. What if my theory was wrong? What if I wound up in some other time, past or future? Or worse, returned to my own time, only to find out there was nothing left to come back to after the earthquake.

Behind me, a deafening crash followed by Nathaniel's startled cry of pain penetrated the foggy edges of my consciousness. I whirled around, struggling to keep my balance. Through the open attic doorway, I saw Nathaniel sprawled face-down on the bedroom floor. A wooden shelf had crashed down off the wall and now lay awkwardly across the back of his head, a heavy marble bookend next to it. A thin trickle of blood oozed onto the wooden floor. Fear washed over me. He was so still—unnaturally still.

I hadn't saved him at all—if anything, I'd *caused* this to happen to him. God only knew how badly he was hurt. Yet if I helped him, I'd lose my only chance to return to my own time. . . .

A wave of dizziness hit me and I felt weightless, as if I were being sucked into a giant vacuum with everything moving in slow motion. Terror flashed in my brain as the world spun around me, but one thought came through loud and clear—Nathaniel needed me.

Chapter Sixteen

I flung myself at the door frame, terrified by the realization that it might already be too late to turn back. Clawing for a handhold, I felt as if I were being ripped in half by some unseen force. The earth shook violently, pitching me forward onto my knees. "Nathaniel," I gasped, crawling to his side. As I brushed his temple with my fingertips, he groaned and shoved the bookshelf off his head, struggling to one knee.

"You're still here," he said hoarsely, staring at me as if I were a hallucination.

"You're not dead." Relief flooded through me as I stared at his blood on my fingertips.

He pulled a handkerchief out of the pocket of his smoking jacket and pressed it to his temple. "Just grazed. But you—" He raised his voice to be heard over the roar of the quake. "You didn't go back."

"I may still have time. . . ." Torn, I stood frozen like a rabbit about to be squashed by oncoming headlights while the earth shuddered and my heart broke. I had to go. Turning away, I took a determined step toward the attic.

Nathaniel lunged forward and tackled me, knocking me down and covering me with his body as a heavy oak beam over the attic door crashed down and a section of ceiling collapsed with it, burying the entrance—and my ticket to the future—beneath a heap of rubble. I stared at it, tears streaming down my cheeks as I realized it would be impossible to dig through it in time. Still, I couldn't help grasping a handful of fallen plaster, frantically digging deeper until Nathaniel's voice brought me back to earth.

"It's too late," he said, then lifted me onto the four-poster bed, his body forming a protective shield above me. I trembled in his arms as the bed shook and plaster rained down from the walls and ceilings. Reality hit me like a slab of falling concrete. I was stuck here, without my family. Forever.

Three stories beneath us, the ground still roared like a living thing, echoing my tumultuous emotions. In the distance I heard the ominous crash of a building crumbling to earth. The window shattered, spewing shards of glass across the room as a gust of cold air whistled in my ears.

Then just as suddenly as the earthquake had

started, it stopped. Nathaniel and I lay clasped together on the bed, staring at each other in disbelief as silence thundered in our ears.

"It happened just as you said." He shook his head, marveling at the seeming miracle of it.

"Heckuva morning after, isn't it?" I pulled the covers tight around me.

"Thank God it's over."

"It isn't," I said, remembering what Victoria had told me. "There'll be a second quake, even worse. That's why Victoria got burned—she came out of her room, carrying the candle, after the first quake hit, and then . . ."

The jolt banged us both against the headboard.

"Come on." Nathaniel grabbed my hand and pulled me out of bed and across the undulating floor, then shoved me under the sturdy door frame separating the bedroom from the hallway.

I buried my head against his chest and felt his arms close around me, protecting and comforting, blocking out the thunderous noise of earth splitting somewhere close by. Then the sound of shattering glass, louder than before, filled my ears. "The chandelier," I gasped, glancing up to see millions of glass shards scatter across the landing and the ballroom below. Far away a woman's cry pierced the night; the distant sound of a firebell clanged.

"It doesn't matter," Nathaniel said, shielding me with his arms as the earthquake shuddered to a stop at last. "The only thing that's important now is your safety."

Chivalrous of him, I thought. If only he cared

about more than just my safety. "I'm okay," I said, wishing it were true. "But I'm not so sure about the others out there."

"Come." Taking my hand, Nathaniel led me back into the bedroom, where we picked our way over fallen debris to the broken window and looked out onto a panorama of destruction.

"Merciful God." He drew in his breath, staring at the ghastly scene below. "Dante could have dreamed up nothing worse."

I could only nod, speechless. Even after all the photos I'd looked at, nothing could prepare me for the reality of the devastation I saw now.

A fissure split Van Ness Avenue, tilting cement squares of pavement up at alarming angles. A hiss of steam seeped out of the rift; a broken gas line jutted up and the sour odor of gas permeated the air. Across the street, the house owned by the crotchety Dr. Greely who we'd tried to warn the night before had collapsed. Mabel stood, dazed, in her front yard wearing only a flannel nightgown. One wall of her home was sheared off and lay in ruins, and the carefully tended flower garden lay buried beneath a pile of rubble marking what used to be a chimney.

In the gray predawn light we could see damage blocks away. All across town, homes and businesses lay in ruins. Dogs barked. Sirens wailed. In the distance, the downtown district looked like a scene after a Beirut bombing, with toppled high rises and skeletal remains of buildings sheared open, their insides exposed. Stunned residents wandered the streets; others knelt in piles of rubble. From everywhere the eerie wail of survivors mourning their losses drifted on the chill April wind.

Nathaniel squeezed my hands, warming them in the cold. "Thank heavens you talked me into sending Victoria to sea."

"It's the safest place." His touch was torture, a tantalizing reminder of a love I wondered if I could ever have.

"I'd better check out the damage downstairs," he said.

"I'm coming with you."

He tried to light a wall sconce, but the gas wasn't working. Groping in the darkness, he found some candles and lit them, then hastily pulled on trousers, shirt, and work boots.

"You'd best get dressed too," he said. "Wear something practical."

"Mrs. O'Hara washed my shirtwaist and bloomers yesterday and they're still damp. I'm not about to put on one of those long skirts and break my neck stumbling around in the dark over all this stuff." I motioned to a pile of rubble. "No way."

"You can hardly parade around like that outside," he said impatiently, gesturing toward my leotard and tights. "It's indecent." He grabbed my arm as I reached into his armoire and rummaged through his clothes. "What do you think you're doing?"

I pushed his hands away, scalded by the memory of those same hands holding me last night, stroking, caressing, enticing. . . . I pushed the images to the back of my brain and slammed the armoire drawer shut.

"Borrowing some of your stuff." I couldn't keep the sharp edge off my voice. "If you're ashamed to be seen with me in men's clothing, just pass me off as one of your deckhands."

He stared at me frostily as I pulled out a sturdy workshirt and pair of pants. "I was merely concerned for your reputation, not mine. At any rate, I've more important things to see to just now than arguing with you."

I buttoned up the shirt, which fell below my knees, and rolled up the sleeves to my elbows. Next I pulled on the trousers, which hung baggier than clown pants on me. I rolled up the cuffs and wrapped a belt around the waist, cinching up the excess fabric. Not sexy, but serviceable, I thought, which was probably just as well. I thought of borrowing a pair of boots, but decided my Nikes would be easier to walk in. Hastily I knotted my hair on top of my head and fastened it with bobby pins from my fanny pack, then grabbed Nathaniel's beret off a wall peg and pulled it on. It was too big, the brim slipping low to shade my face, but at least it would help keep dust and soot out of my eyes.

"No one will ever mistake you for a man, even in that getup," Nathaniel said, raising his eyebrows as he surveyed my outfit. He took my hand, sending a tingle through me that I tried to ignore as he led me downstairs, carrying a lighted candle in his other hand.

Damage inside the house was relatively minor.

Outside of some shattered glass and fallen plaster, the only real destruction was smashed crockery and a couple of hairline cracks that snaked their way up the kitchen wall.

As daylight began seeping through the broken windows, Nathaniel blew out the candle and we stepped outside into the garden. Or rather, what once was the garden.

A gigantic crevasse had formed 20 feet or so behind the house, just below where the rose garden used to be. On the opposite side of the crevasse, the earth had slid downward and now rested several feet below the near bank, burying the structures underneath. The smell of newly turned earth assaulted us as we stared at the playhouse where Victoria had played with her dolls, the servant's quarters, gazebo, and Nathaniel's workshop—all collapsed in crumbled ruins. Only the carriage house was still standing.

"My flying machine—it couldn't have withstood a quake of this magnitude. But the model, my plans . . ." Nathaniel rushed forward to the heap of debris that was once his workshop and began hurling aside splintered boards.

I laid a hand on his shoulder. "You won't find them in there."

"There must be something left," he insisted, stubbornly shaking me off to sift through more rubble.

I scrambled in front of him. "You won't find them because I took them out last night while you were helping Victoria pack. They're in your study."

He halted, lowering the board he held in his hands. My throat caught at the sight. His shirt and face were brushed with dirt; his hair was tousled and he looked sexier than ever. "You've thought of everything, haven't you?"

"I hope so," I said, glancing nervously at the horizon, where a thin plume of smoke drifted into the sky streaked with the first rays of daylight.

Nathaniel traced the path of my gaze. "Fire." He drew in his breath in a sharp whistle. "Will it do much damage?"

I braced myself to break more bad news. "That one must be the ham and eggs fire—so called because it supposedly started by someone cooking when the quake hit. There'll be others—dozens of them."

"The fire department will have their hands full."

"Worse. The earthquake broke the city water mains."

"Good God! Then that means—"

"The whole city will burn." Seeing the stricken look in his eyes, I stepped forward, resisting the impulse to stroke his unshaven jawline with my fingertips. "The downtown district, Chinatown, Nob Hill, virtually all that's left from the gold rush, and most of the waterfront," I rambled on. "But it will rebuild. You'll see—in a few years it'll be bigger than ever."

He shook his head. "It will never be the same."

"No," I conceded. "It won't. But sometimes change can be for the better." Not for me, I thought, digging my nails into my palms. My whole world had changed into a nightmare from which there was no escape.

"Yes." He flashed an expression I couldn't decipher. "I've noticed." A moment later he wiped his brow. "Are you sure this house will be safe? Even from the fires, and the gas leaking?"

"Positive. According to the history I learned, Prudence—she was your wife"—I almost choked on the words—"stayed in the house until the fires were put out, and she was fine."

The sound of a woman screaming riveted our attention. Nathaniel grabbed my hand as we turned and ran across the street, dodging the steaming fissure in the middle.

"It's Millicent," Mabel sobbed, throwing herself at Nathaniel. "She's under th-there, but I can't r-reach her!" She pointed toward a heap of unstable-looking rubble with a narrow tunnel underneath.

Nathaniel dropped to his knees and squeezed through the entrance. My heart thudded at the thought of the whole pile collapsing onto him, but after a moment he emerged, grimfaced.

"I can see her, but I can't reach her," he announced. "We'll have to dig down from the top. I'll round up some men."

I cleared my throat. "Let me try."

"That's no job for a woman! It's far too dangerous."

"I'm smaller than you are. I think I can fit through." Before he could stop me I squirmed into the tunnel and wriggled my way underneath a fallen timber that had apparently blocked Nathaniel's way. Above me, creaks and groans from tons of rubble made the hairs on my neck stand on end. Millicent whimpered and I inched forward. Just a little farther . . .

At last I reached her. Her arm was bent at an unnatural angle and she was crying incoherently.

"Calm down," I said. "We'll get you out of here."

A look of shock came over her as she glanced from my masculine clothing to my face, but at least she stopped crying. I tried to move the bricks that trapped her, closing my eyes and bracing for the worst at the sound of rubble shifting overhead.

"Taylor? Are you all right?" Nathaniel's voice carried from outside.

"For the moment. Millicent's okay too." Gritting my teeth, I pushed and pulled and somehow managed to unwedge her from the pretzel-like position she was in until she lay on her stomach, facing out. When I touched her right arm, she groaned. Supporting the arm as best I could, I guided her through the tunnel, one inch at a time. My mouth went dry as the earth rumbled and a shower of dust rained down on us. An aftershock! With my luck I'd be buried alive. . . .

Nothing ever smelled as sweet as the damp morning air when I emerged outside, even if it was tinged with the sharp odor of smoke. Nathaniel pulled me against him, his heart pounding in my ears like a hammer on an anvil. "Thank the Lord you're safe," he said, his voice choked.

"Don't ever try a crazy stunt like that again."

"I don't take orders—from you or anyone else," I answered on autopilot before his concern for me registered in my dazed brain.

Mabel fussed over Millicent, then noticed Dr. Greely limping over from next door in his nightshirt, his face the color of ashes.

"Millicent's arm's hurt," she moaned. "You've got to do something for her, Doctor."

"My home, my life's work—" the doctor moaned, staring back at the crumbled remains next door.

"There isn't time to feel sorry for yourself," Nathaniel said in a brisk tone. "You've a patient to tend to, and I'll wager you'll have plenty more before long."

The glazed look in Doc's eyes cleared. "Yes, yes, of course," he mumbled, stepping forward to examine Millicent. "Arm's broken," he announced. "Needs to be set. But my medical bag, my supplies . . ."

"We have a stockpile of bandages and some makeshift medical supplies at my house, thanks to Taylor," Nathaniel said. "You're welcome to them."

"This young man?" Doc Greely squinted, looking closer. "That was an admirable rescue, crawling in under all that rubble, lad. Took a heap of courage, if you ask me."

"This is Mr. Stuart's cousin," Millicent said, sniffing in disapproval. "A *female* cousin."

Apparently having her life saved hadn't improved her disposition any, I decided as Dr.

Greely did a double take and frowned, recognizing me from the night before.

"You—you knew this was going to happen," Mabel stammered, looking at me as if she suspected I'd somehow caused the whole thing.

"I'll take you up on that offer," the doctor said to Nathaniel. "But I'll need you to hold the patient steady while I set that bone. Can't have the ladies fainting on us now, can we?"

I clenched my teeth to hold back my irritation at his patronizing comment as the four of us made our way across the street and into Nathaniel's parlor. Irritation grew to annoyance when Nathaniel asked me to go cook breakfast for everyone while he and Doc Greely worked on Millicent's arm. Where did he get off assuming that just because I was a woman, I'd automatically know how to whip up a feast without gas or electricity, let alone a microwave?

A short while later, I wiped the sweat off my face from slaving over a hot stove—literally—and came out of the kitchen to find Millicent settled comfortably on the settee in the parlor. Nathaniel was holding her arm steady as she batted her eyelashes at Doc Greely, who was wrapping gauze around a makeshift splint fashioned from a board. Doc downed a glass of Nathaniel's whiskey and grumbled something about the pain in his leg, which apparently wasn't severe enough to keep him from returning Millicent's painfully obvious flirtations. Mabel was sweeping up the glass from the chandelier that littered the stairs and foyer.

"I can't get over how you knew about the earthquake before it happened," Mabel said, her eyes narrowing as she saw me come in. Pausing to lean against her broom, she glanced at Millicent, who was exchanging smiles with the doctor. "So tell me," she asked, "do you see wedding bells ahead for my sister?"

I groaned. How was I ever going to fit in here if everyone kept expecting me to foretell their futures? I couldn't, I realized, a knot tightening in my stomach. Sooner or later I'd have to figure out a way to support myself, find a place of my own to live. . . . Before I could come up with a polite answer to Mabel's question, I smelled smoke.

"Holy cow," I said. "Breakfast!" I ran into the kitchen and jerked the cast-iron skillet off the stove, burning my hand in the process. It had taken me half an hour to figure out how to build a fire in the wood-burning stove without benefit of matches, and then only with Mabel's help. But apparently it had all been for nothing.

My stomach sank as I prodded the burned bacon in the pan with a fork and discovered it looked like charcoal on the underside as well. Uncovering another pan, remembering to use a towel this time, I stared at the charred remains of the biscuits I'd tried to rewarm from yesterday's meal. I clenched my hands as I dumped breakfast into the trash can. I've never been very domestic, but I'd managed okay with toaster Pop-Tarts and microwave bacon. Fitting in here was going to be an even bigger adjustment than I'd imagined.

I set the burned pans in the sink and tried to turn on the faucet to soak them, but no water came out. Belatedly I remembered that the water mains were broken. I'd have to dunk the pans in one of the buckets Mrs. O'Hara had filled the night before. On second thought, I shouldn't waste water we might need for drinking or cooking to clean up the stinking mess I'd made, I realized glumly.

"Here now, let me take care of things," Mabel comforted me. "You go on and wait with the others."

I thanked her and left the kitchen, wishing I could just wake up and find out this was all really a nightmare after all. I wasn't cut out to be the domestic sort, and I certainly didn't want to become some stuffy society matron—the only acceptable roles for women in this day and age. I'd been wrong to think that I could fit into Nathaniel's time as easily as I could fit into a new set of clothes. I felt cold as snow inside. I didn't belong here, and I never would.

Needing to do something physical to vent my frustrations, I picked up a broom and began the long, tedious chore of cleaning up the debris scattered throughout the house. Why couldn't Dustbusters have been invented a few decades earlier? I wondered as I shoveled a load of rubble into the dustpan.

Twenty minutes later, Mabel served up a delicious meal of sourdough flapjacks. "Learned how to make these back when I was a new bride and my husband worked in the mining camps," she said, a look of nostalgia fogging her eyes.

Pancakes. She made it seem so easy. Would I ever be able to manage even a simple task like cooking breakfast without wishing I were back in my own time?

After breakfast, Nathaniel took me aside. "I've got to go check on my wharves and warehouses. Promise me you won't set foot out of this house until I come back."

"I'm coming with you."

He put his hands on my shoulders and faced me. "Taylor, for once in your life will you do as you're told? You've convinced me this house is the safest place in town. It's dangerous out there—fires and falling rubble, downed trolley cables, broken gas mains. . . ."

"I don't care." Before he could argue, I opened the door and walked outside, grabbing his camera off the half-moon table by the door on my way out.

Catching up to me, he cleared his throat. "Despite the fact that you're more stubborn than any other female I've had the misfortune to know, I'm proud of you. Doc Greely was right—it took great courage to rescue Millicent. Not many women would have been willing to crawl under that mountain of rubble to save someone they scarcely knew."

I raised my eyebrows in surprise. "You mean you actually *approve* of me doing something unladylike?"

"It was a brave act—though I'd prefer not to

see you take any more chances. You could have been killed."

"In my time, we have women firefighters," I told him. "They do that kind of thing all the time."

Seeing the skeptical look on his face, I felt my stomach fall. What if Nathaniel no longer believed I was from the future? After all, I didn't go forward in time when the earthquake hit. Other than one date-stamped bottle, he had no real proof that I wasn't just some psychic from his own time.

"This must be a terrible adjustment for you," he said as if reading my mind. "Knowing that you can't go back to your own time, your family. Before that shelf hit me in the head, I saw you—or rather, a swirl of light and shadows where you stood, growing dimmer, as if you were fading away. Damnedest thing I ever laid eyes upon."

"You saw that? Then you know—"

"I believe you. Taylor, I want you to know that I'm here for you—I'll always be here for you, if you need me."

Of course I need you, my mind screamed. I need you to hold me and tell me you never want to let me go, the way I want you, need you . . . love you. But I couldn't tell him that.

"Right now what I need is to get out of here," I answered, not about to spend the morning cooped up with Nathaniel's neighbors, worrying about the danger he might be in. If I was with him, my knowledge of the quake's aftermath might keep him out of trouble. "With or without you."

His jaw clenched at my words, but at least he stopped trying to talk me out of staying behind. We reached the carriage house doors, where he took my hands and stared at me with an intensity that made me shiver. "I'm sorry you couldn't go back," he said stiffly. "I know you only stayed because of me, but you shouldn't have troubled yourself."

Something tore in my chest. So he was sorry I hadn't gone off and left him. I'd become a burden to him, an unwanted houseguest who wouldn't go home.

"As soon as things settle down, I'll be out of your way," I assured him. "I can't stay on here any longer." I'd find a job, go to another city if I had to. Learning to live in an alien time period was bad enough, but if I had to be near Nathaniel every day, knowing I couldn't have his love, I really would go crazy.

The lines around his eyes hardened. "If that's what you want." He bent down and hoisted a large tree branch that had fallen in front of the carriage house doors, hurling it aside with more force than necessary.

After yanking open the doors, he ushered me into the car and cranked the engine. My gaze drifted out the open doors to the nightmarish landscape outside and a disturbing thought hit me. Although I knew some sketchy details about the fire's progress, neither Nathaniel nor I were supposed to be here now, after the quake. A tremor of fear rippled through me as I stared out at the billows of black smoke rising over the downtown district, blotting out the morning sun.

For the first time since I'd come here, I had no idea what the future had in store for him—or me. From here on out, all bets were off.

Chapter Seventeen

Scenes flashed by like visions in a horror movie, only shutting my eyes wouldn't blot them out. People trudging through the streets carrying children, bags, and bird cages, some pushing wheelbarrows or baby carriages filled with loaves of bread, blankets, and family photos, all headed toward the waterfront and a way out of the city that had become a living nightmare. I snapped photos with Nathaniel's box camera, whenever pedestrians clogging the street forced Nathaniel to stop the car. It made me feel a little like some sleazy tabloid paparazzi, but the historian in me felt duty-bound to record history in the making.

South of the Slot, a holocaust raged out of control, burning its way relentlessly toward the heart of the city. From all around, the sounds of weeping and praying carried over the dry crackle of flames. Smoke stung my eyes and burned my throat; glancing at Nathaniel, I saw that his head and shoulders were coated with ash raining down on the city.

Mobs of homeless San Franciscans crowded the streets, forcing Nathaniel to weave the car down side streets and back alleys. On Market Street, streetcar tracks looked as though they'd been twisted by a giant hand. Precious water bubbled to the surface from another broken main, running uselessly down swollen gutters. The Majestic Theater lay in ruins; smoke curled upward from the guts of several "fireproof" brick buildings.

Downtown, the domed top of City Hall teetered on naked girders above toppled pillars and layers of mortar dust. The sight of crushed arms and legs in tattered clothes wedged amid the rubble made me choke down vomit that rose in my throat.

"Tramps," Nathaniel said, shaking his head, a look of pity shadowing his face. He squeezed my hand to comfort me, but I found his touch more disturbing than soothing. "Poor devils must have been sleeping it off on the steps of City Hall when it collapsed."

Nearby, I spotted a pair of scumbags trying to wrestle an embroidered silk purse away from a young Chinese woman with an infant strapped onto her; two other frightened-looking children clung to her skirts. Nathaniel stopped his car and leapt out, decking one of the slimeballs before the guy knew what hit him. The other man let go of the purse and ran off into the crowd.

Nathaniel spoke to the woman in Chinese, a language he'd apparently picked up from his travels in the Orient. He pointed at the car. After saying something in reply, she climbed into the backseat, hugging her infant tightly to her chest. The oldest child climbed in beside her and Nathaniel lifted the middle child and deposited him in my lap.

"She says her husband was killed in the earthquake," he explained as he slid behind the wheel. "I told her we're heading for the waterfront and offered her a ride to the ferry landing. She wants to join her sister in Oakland."

The woman looked at me curiously, but if she wondered about my masculine clothes she said nothing, not that I'd have understood her if she did. I lost all track of time as we forged on, the child squirming in my lap. He clung to me, making frightened whimpering sounds as I stroked his silky tufts of black hair, murmuring what I hoped were reassuring sounds.

From the corner of my eye I saw Nathaniel glance at me, a wistful look on his face that startled me. I'd never thought of myself as maternal before, but the warmth of the child in my lap sent a sharp pang of longing through me. To have a child, Nathaniel's child . . . I wiped my eyes, hoping the others would think it was only soot from the ash raining down that clogged my vision.

At the waterfront we found even worse confusion than what we'd seen downtown.

"Long's Wharf—it's collapsed!" Nathaniel exclaimed, halting the car. We piled out, gaping at the sight of pilings half submerged beneath the bay. Several tons of coal belonging to the Southern Pacific Railroad had been dumped into the water, spreading a sickening black stain across the surface.

The Chinese woman said something to Nathaniel, glancing over her shoulder at the plume of black smoke snaking its way toward the waterfront. Nodding, Nathaniel took her oldest child and hoisted him onto his shoulders, piggyback-style, smiling playfully to calm the child, the way any proud father might act with his son. . . . Swallowing the lump in my throat, I held on to the middle child as I joined Nathaniel and the Chinese woman with her baby in the mass of humanity surging toward the ferry landing.

The gates were locked when we reached the landing, but hundreds of people stood outside, shouting and pounding on them. Others huddled beneath the docks. Suddenly a man unbolted the locks and spread the gates open wide. The mob surged forward, screaming and thrashing like a wounded animal. Nathaniel pushed the woman and me ahead of him, using his body to shield us from the wall of bodies pressing against us from behind. Smells of sweat and soot engulfed me, making me gag. To my horror I saw a man fall, and the crowd stampeded on ahead, trampling him. His screams of pain faded to a sickly gurgle, then stopped. I clutched my stomach, then felt

Nathaniel's solid warmth pressed against my back.

"Don't look," he urged. But I couldn't help it. It was too horrible, like one of those live newscasts of some crazy person setting himself on fire. You can't look, yet you can't look away.

Sun and soot drenched us as we waited for what seemed forever until the crowd pressed us forward to the water's edge. For a dizzying moment I thought we'd be pitched into the bay, but Nathaniel's steady hand on my shoulder calmed the panic inside me. The Chinese woman pulled a handful of coins from inside her silk purse and pleaded in broken English with a man at the docks to sell her passage to Oakland.

"Sorry, no room for Celestials," the man said, sneering.

Nathaniel stepped forward and slapped a wad of bills in the man's hand. "I trust this will convince you to change your mind," he said, looking as though he'd like to take the man's head off. Pocketing the money, the man agreed.

I took off my cloak and handed it to the woman. "Your children can use this as a blanket," I said. Her dark eyes moved from me to Nathaniel as she murmured words of gratitude in her own language. I saw her try to press her meager supply of coins into his hands, and felt my admiration for Nathaniel grow when he refused to take her money.

As the woman and her children waved goodbye and boarded the ferry, I nudged Nathaniel in the ribs. "Look!"

Enrico Caruso, the famed tenor we'd heard at the opera house—was it really only last night?—had used his considerable girth to push his way to the front of the mob, past old people and evacuees with children. Waving an autographed photo of Theodore Roosevelt over his head, he shouted in the booming voice that had made him famous, "I tell you, it is I, the great Caruso!" He shoved the photo into the hands of a dockhand. "The president himself has signed this, with my name," he shouted. "I'll trade it to any man here for passage aboard that ship!"

Uttering a swear word I didn't know was around in 1906, Nathaniel wrapped his arm around my shoulder and steered me away from the scene, skirting the crowd until we emergéd, breathless, on the street.

"This way." Taking my hand, he led me through the crowd until we came to a wood-frame building identified by a large sign as Westwind Shipping. Spotting a dockworker he recognized, Nathaniel pulled the man aside. "My ships—have you any news? What of the *Pacific Sun?*"

The man's ruddy face broke into a grin. "It's good t' see ye'r still with us, sir. Aye, the *Pacific Sun*'s sound as a whore's—"

Nathaniel broke off the man's colorful description. "You've had word from Antonio, then?"

"Aye. He docked the *Pacific Sun* at Monterey afore first light 'n' sent word on a northbound steamer. We jest got the word. Yer half sister's safe, though Antonio writes she's fit t' be tied for

285

missin' all the adventure here this mornin'.'"

"Adventure my eye." Nathaniel expelled a relieved sigh. "The little imp would sooner be in trouble than out of it any day, but this is one time I've outfoxed Victoria, for her own good."

I tugged at Nathaniel's sleeve. He leaned down and I whispered in his ear, "The fires—you haven't long before everything here will burn."

His face grew rigid. Turning to the dockhand, he fired off a series of rapid instructions. "Round up as many able-bodied men as you can find. Pay them whatever you have to for their services. I want everything from the office and the warehouses loaded onto the ships still docked. Sail within—" He glanced at me.

"One hour," I said, glancing at the advancing mountain of smoke.

Tracing the path of my gaze to the sparks arcing down from the menacing black cloud now only blocks away, Nathaniel clenched his jaw. "One hour it is."

"Aye," the dockworker answered. "Shall I round up a bucket brigade?"

"No need," Nathaniel said grimly. "Seeing as there's no more water. Mains are broken."

The man's eyes widened. "No water? But ye can't douse a fire this size without water. Saints preserve us."

For the next 45 minutes Nathaniel and I worked side by side with his men, salvaging what we could from his business until the heat of the flames grew too intense. As we rushed out of the company headquarters with our arms full of papers and supplies, we saw a shower of sparks cascade onto the rooftop. Dropping the load in his arms, Nathaniel grabbed my elbow and half-towed me to the dock. I looked back to see flames lick down the sides of his company headquarters, engulfing the building at the same instant his warehouse nearby erupted in a blaze of orange.

"The ships!" Nathaniel shouted to the ruddy-faced dockhand. "Cast off all those still moored. Take any men who want out of this hellhole with you aboard my fastest steamer and head south to a safe port. One more thing. You'll be taking Miss James here with you."

"Miss?" The dockhand arched his bristly eyebrows in surprise.

I whirled to face Nathaniel, feeling as if I'd been slapped. "I'm not going unless you come too," I said, stiffening my backbone as I fought down the pain. Still, I couldn't bring myself to abandon him in the middle of this disaster. What if something happened to him that my knowledge could have prevented? In a strange sort of way, by changing history I'd become responsible for him.

"Will you stop being so confounded stubborn and listen to reason?" His face was flushed from the fire's heat. "It's for your own safety."

"I don't care. I'll jump overboard. I'll—"

Before I could say more, a man in a black suit pushed his way forward to Nathaniel. "Nathaniel Stuart?"

"That's me," Nathaniel answered as I felt my

throat constrict. Was this man bringing some sort of bad news?

"Mayor Schmitz requests your presence at the Hall of Justice," he said loudly to be heard over the crackle of flames nearby. "He's assembling a committee of reliable citizens to help with this disaster."

"Schmitz!" Nathaniel looked ready to explode. "Everyone knows the weasel's on Ruef's payroll. I'll wager he's got orders to find a way to profit from the misery of others."

I cleared my throat. Motioning for the messenger to wait, Nathaniel took my arm and stepped just out of hearing distance.

"You're wrong about Schmitz."

"The man hasn't got a backbone in his miserable hide."

"Go to the meeting and you'll see. Ruef wasn't even invited. Schmitz has severed all ties. Eventually Schmitz will be indicted for his graft; he'll even go to jail. But this earthquake's changed him. He's going to go down in history as a hero of sorts."

"Of all the predictions you've made, this may be the hardest to swallow. But I'll hear the weasel out."

"We'll hear him out," I corrected.

"Taylor." He laid his palms against my cheek, burning my skin as he tilted my face up to meet his smoldering gaze. "Lord knows in the past few days I've come to respect you as an equal, a match for my wits as well as my wants."

I felt heat rush to my face at the memory of

those wants, heat coupled with shock to realize that Nathaniel Stuart, a man brought up in an era when women were treated like furniture, had actually admitted that I was his intellectual equal.

"But despite that," he was saying, "a female would never be allowed to attend a private political meeting among civic leaders."

"In case you haven't noticed, I'm dressed like a man," I said. "No one's even noticed I'm a woman."

His gaze dipped to the curves my shirt couldn't completely hide and his lips curved upward. "I've noticed. In fact, I'd say you're the most exasperating woman I've ever met. Still, I can't have you drowning yourself in the bay."

"Then you'll let me come with you?"

"If you untuck those shirttails and don't say anything, you may just get away with the charade. I'll introduce you as my cousin, James."

I should have felt grateful. But as I stared back into his smoke-filled eyes, all I felt was a sharp pang of desire and a gnawing emptiness that I feared would never be filled—along with a troubling feeling that the worst was yet to come.

"Fires are ravaging the city," Mayor Eugene Schmitz, wrinkled and sweat stained after touring the burning streets, stood grim faced before the 25 Committee of Safety members assembled in the candlelit basement of the Hall of Justice, the only portion of the building not demolished by the earthquake. "The Call and Examiner buildings are burning as we speak. City Hall is in ruins and several prisoners awaiting trial had to be let go when the jail collapsed. The fire chief's dead, killed in the quake," he went on. "Thousands are homeless, and the number's rising fast. With water mains broken citywide, we've run out of water—even the cisterns are nearly pumped dry. With no food or water, the threat of disease seems imminent."

A hush fell over the assembly as the full impact sank in. "What steps have you taken to restore order?" Nathaniel asked. The flickering candlelight deepened the furrows on his brow and magnified the shadows darkening his eyes.

"I've wired Washington for help and ordered in soldiers from the U.S. Army post at the Presidio to help keep the peace and battle the fires, though the latter is like trying to stop a charging bull with a popgun at this point. Police and soldiers are under orders to shoot looters on sight, and I've ordered all saloons closed until further notice."

"An admirable start." Nathaniel nodded approvingly.

"What else?" someone inquired.

"All gas and electric lines are shut down to prevent more fires from starting, though most were ruptured anyhow. I've also ordered a dawn-to-dusk curfew until order is restored. But none of that's going to take care of feeding all those homeless people out there, or keeping them warm through the coming night."

Rudolph Spreckels, Schmitz's longtime enemy, spoke. "What do you want from us?"

"To take charge of every homeless man, woman, and child in San Francisco. For starters, we need food, blankets, and the like. I'm asking for pledges from each of you to make the checks good in the event our city treasury runs out of funds."

"Count me in," Spreckels said. "Though with half the banks in flames already, there's no guarantee any of us won't be left paupers tomorrow."

The others gave their word, including Nathaniel, who pledged double to cover my share. Next Schmitz passed around public safety instructions and curfew notices for volunteers to distribute. A discussion was held as to the best ways to prevent the spread of disease and it was all I could do to hold my tongue.

Wiping the sweat from his brow, Schmitz continued. "I'm sorry to inform you that City Emergency Hospital caved in shortly after the earthquake, burying doctors, nurses, and patients." Over startled gasps and curses he added, "If anyone knows of a safe place to transport those patients still alive, I want to hear about it."

I jumped halfway out of my chair before Nathaniel pulled me back and elbowed me in the ribs. "Stuart House is undamaged," he informed Schmitz before I could spit the words out. "Dr. Greely, my neighbor, was treating a patient there this morning and we have some bandages and other supplies on hand. Any other injured are welcome."

"But we need antibiotics!" I blurted out. "To stop the infections—"

Schmitz spun toward me and his mouth dropped open. "Good lord. You're a female!"

I ignored the iron grip of Nathaniel's fingers tightening around my upper arm. "So what? I happen to know something about medicine. You'll need penicillin, sterile solutions, narcotics to ease the pain—"

"I've no idea what you're babbling about, young woman. But the men here have important business to conclude, so I must insist that you silence yourself or I'll have no choice but to cast you and your 'cousin' out."

"She has as capable a mind as any man present," Nathaniel challenged. "That is, if you aren't too close-minded to listen."

Before Schmitz could reply, a messenger came racing downstairs into the basement. "You'd all better get out while you still can," he shouted. "The buildings across the street are on fire and this one's likely to catch hold any minute!"

Nathaniel leapt to his feet, dragging me up with him. Schmitz hastily dismissed the meeting as the Committee of Safety fled upstairs and out into the nightmare scene beyond.

Across the street, flames darted out the windows of Pratwell Bank of Commerce. With a whoosh and a roar, the entire high rise erupted into a blazing torch. Fire fighters who had been battling the blaze with blankets and buckets of dirt backed away, giving up the bank as a lost cause.

A hard knot formed in my chest as I recognized a familiar figure heaving sacks of money into a wagon parked in front of the bank.

"Fenniwick," I gasped, covering my mouth with my hand to keep from choking on smoke. "He must've escaped when the jail collapsed. And there's Prudence's father—but what's he doing arguing with Fenniwick? And what are the two of them doing running *into* the burning building?"

"Emptying the vault, no doubt. Or in Fenniwick's case, looting it." Nathaniel's mouth brushed my ear as he pulled me tight against him, shielding me from the scorching heat.

"But that's crazy. The whole thing looks like it's ready to collapse."

A shriek split the air. Mortimer Pratwell staggered out of the bank clutching an armful of money sacks, his clothes in flames. Oxygen fed the blaze as he collapsed forward onto the wagon, dropping the sacks onto the loadful of money already there.

Nathaniel and I bolted forward in unison. I couldn't just stand by and watch a man burn to death, no matter what he'd done, and apparently Nathaniel couldn't either. Racing across the street, he ripped the jacket off his own back and shoved it over Prudence's father, but flames already were consuming flesh and blood and bone. I snatched a scorched blanket dropped by a fire fighter and rushed toward Mortimer Pratwell just as a trail of sparks landed on the money piled in the wagon and ignited it. Fire scorched my hands as I pushed forward and pressed the blanket over him, but it was too late. Mortimer Pratwell let out an agonized scream that died away to a rattling moan as the flames destroyed him.

Fenniwick raced out of the burning bank toward the wagon, carrying a bundle of stock certificates. He spotted Nathaniel dragging Mortimer's charred body from the wagon; then his gaze darted to the fire spreading across the load of cash. For a split second our eyes met and I felt consumed by his hatred, the same hatred I'd seen when he'd tried to push me off Nathaniel's roof.

Nathaniel pushed in front of me, barring Fenniwick's way. Judging from the white-hot anger on their faces, both men looked ready to kill. "Go on, you bastard," Nathaniel challenged, rolling up his sleeves. "Just try to hurt her again, so I'll have the honor of breaking your miserable neck with my own two hands."

A knife flashed in Fenniwick's hand. Fear stabbed me, sharp as a red-hot poker. Fenniwick's eyes narrowed and I had a horrifying vision of Nathaniel lying cut and bleeding, his body left to burn.

"No!" I shouted, tugging at Nathaniel's shirtsleeve. "He's got a knife. He'll kill you—"

Fenniwick's eyes blazed as he stood rooted to the spot, torn between revenge and greed. Then abruptly he whirled around and hurled himself across the back of the wagon, grasping handfuls of money and stuffing it into his pockets and waistband.

"Your hands!" The words escaped me without thought as I saw his palms, seared raw from the paper bills he clutched, bills curling black at the edges where they'd caught fire. A trail of smoke rose from beneath his jacket and I saw that it too had ignited.

Nathaniel ran forward, cupping his hands around his mouth to make his voice carry. "The money—for God's sake, drop the money!"

Fenniwick's eyes glazed as he backed toward the rear of the wagon, still clutching a fistful of burning bills. Frantically he beat them against his shoe, but succeeded only in igniting his sock. Flames shot up his leg and across his back; smoke spewed out from his collar and cuffs. A strangled cry twisted from his throat as he fell forward, facedown into the flaming pile of looted money that had become his funeral pyre.

Chapter Eighteen

Nathaniel pulled me against his chest, shielding me from the sight. I buried my face against his warm chest, inhaling the scents of smoke and salt water that clung to him. It felt so right to be in his arms. . . . My heart beat faster in my aching chest as my lungs struggled to breathe in air thick with smoke and cinders.

"The building's about to go!" Nathaniel grabbed me by the arm and yanked me away from the scene, half-towing me to where his car was parked two blocks away. He lifted me up and dropped me into the passenger seat, cranked up the engine, and leapt in. His hair was singed and his face glowed from the fire's heat, giving him a savage appearance that made my blood flow hot.

I followed the path of his gaze toward the waterfront, which was a solid tier of fire. Somewhere in the midst of it lay the ashes of what had once been his company.

"Two generations of Westwind Shipping up in smoke," he said, clenching the steering wheel, his mouth a grim line. "I only hope my men got out in time. I've seen death, but never one so grisly as what we've just witnessed."

I reached for his hand and squeezed it, wanting to comfort him. I had no right to complain, I told myself. After all, he'd never promised me anything.

"You're thinking of Prudence, aren't you?" I asked. "You want to go tell her about her father."

He nodded, his eyes registering surprise. "I didn't think you'd understand. I have no feelings left for the woman save for pity, but still I don't want her hearing about this from a stranger."

"No," I agreed, even though the thought of seeing Prudence again made my stomach churn. I glanced at my watch, remembering. Nob Hill wouldn't burn until shortly before dawn. "It's okay," I said. "We can drive up to Nob Hill and still have time to make it back to your place."

Gratitude and something more gleamed in his eyes as he reached for me and drew me against him, his mouth closing on mine hungrily. He tasted of smoke and flame; I closed my eyes and I felt a scorching heat that wasn't from the inferno close at hand.

"We've got to get out of here," he whispered, looking at me as if he never wanted to let me go. The pounding of his heart echoed in my ears. Was it really only lust? Part of me ached to believe it wasn't, yet I didn't dare dream anything else. Not in the middle of the worst nightmare of the century.

At the top of Nob Hill, the Pratwell mansion stood silhouetted against a pall of reddish smoke, a monument of doom. Paintings by old masters were lined up on the enormous lawn; servants were cutting masterpieces out of their frames and rolling them up to evacuate along with the family silver.

A butler opened the door and ushered us into the parlor. Prudence walked in; her face drained of color when she saw the grave look on Nathaniel's face. "If you've come to see me it can only mean bad news," she whispered.

Nathaniel's nod confirmed her fears. "I'm sorry to have to tell you this, but I didn't want you to hear it from a stranger. It's about your father."

"No—he isn't . . ." The words caught in her throat.

"His bank burned. Mortimer was trying to save his depositors' money in the vault when the roof collapsed." He took her hands gently. "I'm afraid he's dead. Fenniwick too."

She trembled, plainly struggling to control her emotions, and suddenly I didn't hate her anymore. Grace Pratwell lumbered into the room then and Nathaniel broke the news. Prudence's sisters, hearing the commotion, came in and soon all of them were sniffling and sobbing.

A sharp knock on the door interrupted the Pratwells' grief. The butler, looking apologetic for intruding, ushered in a handsome young military officer who halted in front of Mrs. Pratwell, his expression solemn.

"I've just received orders, ma'am," he said, removing his hat. "Nob Hill must be evacuated."

Prudence blotted her eyes with a lace-trimmed handkerchief monogrammed in gold thread. "N-not our home too! Surely, sir, you can see this family's suffered enough loss for one night."

Nathaniel took the officer aside. "The young lady's father, Mortimer Pratwell, died earlier in a fire downtown."

The officer ran a hand through his sandy blond hair, frowning. "Right sorry to hear that, Miss Pratwell." Stepping to Prudence's side, he offered her a dry handkerchief of his own. "Here now, miss, it's a powerful shame to ruin that pretty face of yours with all those tears."

"I—it is?" Prudence looked up at him, batting her silky eyelashes to blink away tears.

"Why, sure it is," he said, flashing a smile that could charm the stripes off a tiger. "Truth is, you're the nicest thing I've laid eyes on since this earthquake hit. Maybe ever."

Prudence smiled, dabbing at her eyes. "I declare, sir, if all the officers in the U.S. Army had such honeyed tongues, you boys would never have to fight off any enemies—you'd all just sweet-talk your way out of trouble."

The officer grinned, his face reddening to the roots of his hair. "It would be my pleasure to personally assist you and your family with your evacuating, Miss Pratwell. Do you all have someplace to go?"

Prudence looked down, poking out her lower lip. "None that comes to mind."

"In that case," he replied, "I reckon my parents can take you in. Did I mention they own a ranch down south of Monterey? Good-size spread, couple hundred head of cattle—with an adobe hacienda house plenty large enough to house your entire family."

"You're too kind," she said in a trembling voice. "After losing my f-father . . ."

He offered his arm, which Prudence quickly accepted. "Don't you worry about a thing, little lady. I'll see that you're taken good care of," he assured her as they strolled toward the door. "Did I mention that my hitch'll be up in another six weeks?"

Nathaniel and I exchanged a knowing glance. "I think Prudence will be okay," I observed.

"She does seem to be adapting remarkably well," he agreed.

Mission accomplished, we said good-bye to the Pratwells and headed out the door.

As Nathaniel held the door of his Silver Shadow open for me another soldier came racing across the street. "That's a fine automobile you've got there, sir," said the soldier. "But I've got orders to confiscate any motor vehicle I can find. For ambulances, you understand."

"But I'm on Schmitz's committee. This vehicle—"

"Is now an ambulance." The soldier pulled out

a Colt revolver and pointed it at Nathaniel.

"That's out of the question!" Nathaniel argued. "I must have my car to see this young woman safely home."

Home? The word struck me like a baseball in the chest. Did Nathaniel really think of his house as my home now, or was he merely saying so for the sake of convenience?

"I'm afraid you and the lady will have to find some other way there." The soldier shoved the barrel of the revolver against Nathaniel's chest. "You're not objecting, now, are you, sir?"

Nathaniel looked ready to pound the guy into the pavement, but I tugged at his arm to stop him from getting himself shot. "Let him have the car," I pleaded. "The injured need it more than we do."

"Taylor, you don't know what you're saying. What if the fire spreads to the hill before we can escape?"

"Out!" the soldier ordered, cocking the revolver.

Given no choice, Nathaniel nodded curtly. "Very well."

I took the camera out of the tonneau and hopped out, meeting Nathaniel on the curb. "It's for a good cause," I assured him as the soldier drove off, though I could see from Nathaniel's face that giving up his prized car was almost as painful as sending Victoria away.

"Never mind the car. Do we have time to make it off this hill before it burns?" he asked.

I met his gaze and saw concern etched across his face like weathered lines on granite. "I don't know," I admitted, trying to keep the fear out of my voice as I glanced at my watch. "I hope so."

He wrapped his arm around my shoulder and held me in silence for a long moment as we stood together at the top of Nob Hill, staring at the flames creeping upward from the burning city below.

My teeth chattered from the foggy dampness as we made our way on foot down Nob Hill, picking our way around ruptured pavement and piles of rubble. Flames glowed orange against the night sky in a dozen different places as we passed families evacuating possessions from doomed homes. On one street corner, incongruously, a man sat playing an out-of-tune piano in front of his burned-out home while a tattered group of survivors gathered around him, their voices rising in a fatalistic chorus of "We'll Have a Hot Time in the Old Town Tonight." I felt something twist inside at their brave attempt to drown out the tragedy unfolding around them all.

In the distance, an explosive blast shattered the night air. "Dynamite," I said under my breath. "Schmitz has ordered buildings blasted to create firebreaks."

Nathaniel tensed. "Won't that make matters worse?"

"I don't know," I confessed, ignoring my ankle, which was beginning to ache. Apparently it wasn't healed as fully as I'd thought from my run-in with Fenniwick. "I can't remember. I think it did, at least in some places."

He took my hand, forging a link strong as iron. His warmth radiated into me through the darkness, tugging at me like a lifeline as we ducked down a side street, then another and another, winding our way through a maze of destruction. Along the way we heard bits of news, all bad. The entire downtown district had burned; more fires were burning out of control along Montgomery and Kearny streets. A fire started at Delmonico's had spread, turning the Saint Francis Hotel into a fireball.

Around us, refugees clogged the streets, pressing against us in a swelling mass of humanity. A horse with blinders on reared up and let out a frightened whinny, nearly crushing the man trying to lead it out of a burning stable. I felt shell-shocked; no amount of research for my thesis could have prepared me for the terrible reality of living through this nightmare, running for our lives.

An hour or so past midnight, we found our way barred by a solid wall of fire stretching from Market Street to Chinatown, working its way relentlessly toward Powell Street and Nob Hill. Heat from the inferno seared our skin even from a two-block distance as we halted, stunned by the surreal spectacle.

"We'll never get through this way," Nathaniel shouted to be heard over the fire's roar. He grabbed my hand and pulled me away from the blaze. My heart beat faster as we turned and ran, veering off in a different direction, only to find our path barred once again by flames closing in on us from three sides. A shower of sparks rained down on us; one landed on Nathaniel's shirt. I suppressed a scream and pounded at the burning fabric with the edge of my sleeve. My efforts smothered the flame, but not before it burned a charred spot onto Nathaniel's bicep.

"Your arm—that wound needs attention."

"There's no time. The fire's spreading."

My heart pounded harder as we turned and fled back the way we'd come; I couldn't catch my breath. Nathaniel thumped me on the back to clear my lungs as I coughed, choking on the dense smoke. A tree branch caught the hat on my head and knocked it off, sending my hair flying loose to my shoulders. Glancing back, I saw the hat blazing, ignited from falling sparks. Prickles of fear made my skin clammy despite the intense heat sending sweat pouring down my back. A horrible thought gripped me. Had I changed history, only to cause Nathaniel to die by fire instead of murder?

Minutes passed, or maybe hours—I'd lost all track of time, running until my lungs ached and my legs felt like jelly. Fire blazed on three sides, when suddenly flames leapt across the street in front of us, deadly orange flashing against the ink black sky. Fear constricted my throat. "We can't get through," I gasped.

"In here." Nathaniel grabbed my hand and yanked me into a stable behind a burning house. Glancing around, he spotted a stack of horse blankets piled in one corner. Pulling two blankets from the stack, he ran outside and shoved them into a nearly empty watering trough. He threw a soggy blanket over my head and shoulders and draped a second one over himself. He grabbed my hand. "Run!"

We raced headlong into the blaze blocking the street, ducking down as flames caught the edges of the blanket with a horrifying sizzle. I held my breath and closed my eyes, feeling Nathaniel's strength flow into me as he half-pulled me through the flames. Emerging finally on the other side, we hurled off the burning blankets and kept running, hearts pounding, eyes burning, for blocks and blocks, until we were far from the flames.

"Are you all right?" he asked when I dropped to one knee, panting for breath.

"Just . . . winded," I managed to say.

We turned back and stared at the flames leaping against the predawn sky at the top of Nob Hill. Standing in silence, we watched as the fiery outline of the Pratwell mansion crumbled to ashes. The red glare gradually faded to a sickly yellow, spectral flames crackling against a sky as pale as death. A pall of smoke hung over the city like a huge black vulture, waiting to consume what was left.

"At least you know Prudence is safe," I said, wondering with a pang of jealousy if he still had feelings for her. She was, after all, drop-dead gorgeous, while I . . . I glanced down at myself, sorely aware of the poor comparison I presented, dressed in torn male clothing, caked in ashes, my hair probably looking as if I'd stuck my finger in a wall socket.

He took my hands and looked into my eyes with an intensity that melted my heart. "She was a foolish woman, though she didn't deserve all this. But when it comes to courage, decency, not to mention stealing a man's heart, she can't hold a candle to you, Taylor."

"She can't?" Did that mean he loved me? Was it possible, or was he only referring to our love-making? The memory made me tremble. But if he loved me, how could he have let me just walk into that attic and out of his life?

He bent toward me as though to kiss me, but before our lips touched, the wind changed directions, sending a shower of sparks down on top of us.

"Ouch," I yelped, brushing a burning ember off my cheekbone.

"Let's go." He grabbed my hand, pulling me forward. As we stumbled down one street after another, my ankle swelled and started to throb. My stomach was cramping, burned patches on my hands stung, and my mind floated in a daze, numbed by shock and too many sleepless hours. Only the presence of Nathaniel beside me kept me going; I felt connected to him after all we'd been through together—we were survivors, even if the whole world was burning down around us.

It was late morning when we finally reached Van Ness Avenue, only to see Spreckels's magnificent mansion in flames. Down the block, smoke curled upward from several other homes along the west side of the broad avenue. Despite my knowledge of history, I felt a wave of relief at the sight of Stuart House still standing across the street, though its turrets were scorched. Soldiers had cordoned off the street; firemen ran into the crowds and called for volunteers.

"Let's get you inside," Nathaniel said, pushing his way through the crowd to the steps of Stuart House. "If Doc's still here, I want him to have a look at that ankle."

"As long as you promise to let him treat that burn on your arm," I agreed.

On the porch, Mabel and Millicent stood holding each other, crying and watching helplessly as volunteers armed with wet blankets and soggy mops battled the fire threatening the two elderly sisters' home. Mumbling condolences, Nathaniel pushed past them and opened the door.

My knees wobbled and my stomach hurt from not eating anything since the day before; my eyes burned and my head felt as though I'd gone one too many rounds with Muhammed Ali. I ached for a hot meal and a soft bed—the same bed where Nathaniel had made love to me a night and a lifetime ago, I thought, trembling at the memory. But as I limped over the threshold, my eyes widened and I couldn't suppress a gasp. Nathaniel wrapped his arm around my shoulders and pulled me against him, trying to shield me from the sight. But I couldn't stop myself from looking.

The foyer and ballroom were covered with injured people, some with limbs bound in gauze, others with burned patches of oozing, blackened, and blistered skin. A soldier with his face wrapped in bandages lay moaning in a corner. Beside him, a woman in charred rags was trying to coax a baby to take a bite of a mushy substance on a spoon. The agonized wails of the injured filled the air; putrid smells of rotting flesh and burned skin made me turn away, gagging.

"In here. You need water." Nathaniel moved toward the kitchen doors, but before he could open them a strikingly beautiful woman, perhaps 35 years old, pushed them open from inside and marched toward Nathaniel and me. There was something vaguely familiar about her, but I couldn't put my finger on it.

"Nathaniel Stuart—finally, you've come home!" She spoke rapidly, her emerald eyes flaring in agitation. "I've been waiting here since yesterday. Where is my daughter—is she safe? Nathaniel, no matter what you may think of me, I demand that you let me see my little girl!"

Nathaniel's features turned to stone. "Jessica." He exhaled slowly, his lips forming a grim line. "So, my loving stepmother returns."

"Your s-stepmother?" I stammered in amazement.

"She's no blood relation of mine, thank the Lord," he informed me in a voice thick with sarcasm. "Though frankly, Jessica, I'm surprised even you would have the audacity to show your face in this house after breaking my half sister's heart. You lost all claim to Victoria when you abandoned her as an infant. If you think I'm going to let you anywhere near that child, you're even more foolish than I thought."

I stared at Jessica, dumbstruck. She had thick, curly red hair that hung loose to her waist and wore a shade too much makeup for daytime. Her plumed hat and tangerine-colored dress contrasted sharply with her vivid green eyes, but it was her face that was the real shocker.

It was a face I'd seen a thousand times before in the framed antique photo on Dad's dresser. A photo of Dad's grandmother, a legendary turn-of-the-century actress. I gaped at the woman before me, swallowing hard as comprehension hit me. Nathaniel had been able to forgive me when he thought I was a whore, but in fact my background contained something far worse—at least in his eyes. What would he say, I wondered with a tremor of dread, when he found out the truth?

The infamous Jessica Stuart who inspired such loathing in Nathaniel was none other than my own great-grandmother.

Chapter Nineteen

"Nathaniel." I tapped his arm. "Wouldn't it be best to air your family linen in private?"

Glancing toward the injured laid out in rows just a few feet away, Nathaniel clenched his jaw and pushed open the kitchen doors. "Ladies first." Glaring at Jessica, he added, "And I use the term loosely."

Two spots of color burned on Jessica's cheeks, but she pivoted and followed her stepson and me into the kitchen, giving me a curious look that made me wonder if she saw the resemblance between us.

"I'm Taylor James," I said, deciding it might be best not to add the cousin bit. After all, this woman probably knew enough about the Stuart family tree to spot me as a fraud.

"James?" Her copper eyebrows arched in surprise. "That was my maiden name, though few people know it. I changed it as soon as I took to the stage. Too many Jesse James jokes, you see. I don't suppose we're related, though there is a resemblance, wouldn't you say?"

"You've got thirty seconds to get your traitorous neck out of this house before I throw you out myself." Nathaniel advanced on Jessica, looking as if he'd relish the task.

Jessica's eyes sparked. "Nathaniel Stuart, you always were a strong-willed boy. But I see you've grown into an even more bullheaded man!" She lifted her chin defiantly. "I'm not leaving without seeing my daughter. I've been worried sick about her ever since the earthquake hit. Hate me if you will, Nathaniel, but you must know that I've never stopped loving my little girl. Never."

"Another of your lies. If you loved her so much, how could you run off and leave her?"

I pulled myself up and hobbled between the two, turning toward Nathaniel. "Whatever Jessica has done, she's still Victoria's mother. I think you ought to hear her out."

"Taylor," Nathaniel warned, "this isn't your business."

"Could we talk in private for a second?" I insisted.

He scowled at Jessica, but after a moment led me to a storage room off the kitchen. I cleared my throat, hoping he wouldn't throw me out the door along with Jessica when I told him my news.

"I've seen her before," I said, swallowing hard.

"In a photo on my father's dresser. Jessica is my great-grandmother."

His face turned the color of marble as he stared at me. "Good lord—those eyes, that hair . . . So that story you told me about coming from a family of thespians was true?"

Heat rushed to my face. "I even did a little acting myself, once." I saw my own turbulent emotions mirrored in his eyes—shock, confusion, doubt. "Maybe I'm biased," I plunged in, "but I've got a hunch that Jessica hasn't told you everything there is to know about why she left."

His eyes darkened at the mention of his stepmother's name. "I doubt that, but for your sake, I'll hear her out before I send her away."

Returning to the kitchen with me beside him, he turned to Jessica, his jaw set in a hard line. "Your daughter's safe. I'll tell you that much."

Her eyebrows raised in surprise. "Nathaniel," she said in a softer tone, "I know she isn't in this house. Half the city is ablaze. Victoria could be in dire trouble this very moment, and I won't rest easy until I've seen her. If she's safe, as you say, I promise I'll go away and not trouble you or her again."

I glanced down, unable to meet her pain-filled eyes, and noticed the swelling at her waist.

"As you can see, I'm with child," Jessica said, tilting her chin up. "I'm not married, in case you're wondering, Nathaniel. I've stayed a widow since Josiah passed on. But when I found out I was with child, I couldn't bear to rid myself of it—even though the father nearly had apoplexy when I told him. This one's all I've got"—she patted her stomach—"since I gave up my girl."

The unborn child . . . was it my grandfather? The thought chilled me to the bone. If I helped Jessica find Victoria, would she still feel as strongly about keeping the child growing inside her? If I interfered with history again, I might just keep my own grandfather from coming into the world—which meant I would never be born. I leaned against the table, silently praying my great-grandmother wouldn't change her mind and find some back-alley abortionist. Still, she didn't seem like the heartless woman I'd imagined Jessica to be. Something didn't add up. . . .

"Surely you don't expect me to applaud your moral fiber, Jessica." Nathaniel's cynical tone set my teeth on edge.

"Would you give her a break?" I said, torn between my loyalties to my blood relative and the man I loved. "Jessica's obviously worried about Victoria, and now she's got another baby on the way, with a deadbeat dad who doesn't sound like he'll qualify for father of the year. She's been through enough without you treating her like an ax murderer."

Nathaniel crossed his arms, scowling. "I'm sure you've made the best choice you could, under your present circumstances," he said. "But showing some vestigal maternal instinct over the child you're carrying doesn't excuse your abandonment of my sister."

Fire burned in her eyes, deepening the emerald green color that was so much like my own. "I never should have left Victoria all those years ago, no matter what he said!" She clapped a gloved hand over her mouth.

"What who said?" Nathaniel asked, frowning.

"No one. You wouldn't believe me anyhow. The only thing that matters now is finding my daughter."

I took a deep breath, gambling on my intuition. "Jessica, if you want to know where Victoria is, you're going to have to give Nathaniel reason to trust you. You could start by explaining why you deserted your husband and infant daughter all those years ago."

"Taylor . . ." Nathaniel shot me a warning look.

Jessica's chin wavered a moment. "Fair enough," she agreed. "I should have told Nathaniel the ugly truth years ago, but at the time he was too young to hear it. But I'm warning you, Nathaniel, I won't have my daughter's reputation sullied by any more gossip about me than has already been bandied about town."

Nathaniel nodded, his eyes wary. "Very well. But I'm warning you, Jessica—no lies."

"No." Removing her hat, she sat down at the table across from me and sighed. "I'm afraid it's not a very pretty story. As you probably know, when I met Josiah I was an actress. Still am, for that matter."

"A good one, from what I hear," I said, recalling Dad's stories of his turn-of-the-century grandmother who held her audiences spellbound—especially the men.

She shrugged. "Josiah thought so. He saw me

onstage and came to my dressing room afterward with his arms full of white roses. I thought he was the most charming man I'd ever met—it was love at first sight."

"What happened?"

Anger sparked in her eyes. "His brother."

"Ephraim?" Nathaniel frowned, the lines around his mouth hardening as I shuddered at the memory of my own experience at the hands of Nathaniel's uncle.

"Yes. He came to see me after a performance, not knowing I was engaged to his brother. He tried to seduce me, and when I refused, he—" She broke off, pressing white-gloved knuckles against her lips. "It's unspeakable."

"He forced you?" I said gently, exchanging glances with Nathaniel, who looked as if he'd been hit by a train.

She nodded, opening her eyes. "Yes," she said hoarsely. "God help me, yes. I tried to stop him, but . . . however did you know?"

"Because I caught my uncle trying to maul Taylor in this very house," Nathaniel said, his eyes widening in comprehension. "I wish I'd strangled the bastard—"

"But all Uncle Ephraim got for his efforts was a bruised jaw and a sore backside, thanks to Nathaniel and my dog," I chimed in.

She stared at me. "Serves the randy old goat right. You're fortunate my stepson put a stop to things in time, Miss James. So perhaps you *can* understand. I hated that man—I wished him dead."

"Why didn't you come to me years ago and tell me this? Or better yet, tell my father?" Nathaniel demanded.

"Who would you have believed—me or Ephraim?" she said bluntly.

Nathaniel shifted uncomfortably. "I don't know."

"You see? That's why I kept quiet—married Josiah and never told him what happened."

"Jessica." Nathaniel stepped forward, his voice strained. "I must know. Who is Victoria's father?"

"Oh, Josiah is—I'm certain of it. You see"—she reddened again—"I was already with child before Ephraim attacked me. But when Ephraim learned I was in the family way, he became obsessed with the idea that it was his. He hated me, wanted me out of his brother's life. So when Victoria was born three weeks early, he threatened to tell Josiah that we'd been lovers and claim the child was his unless I went away and never came back. I was damaged goods; he thought I wasn't good enough for his brother, even told me he'd accuse me of thieving if I wouldn't go. I refused, of course. I thought of taking her away with me, but what kind of life could I have offered her? Then he threatened to take custody of Victoria. I couldn't chance it! The thought of what he might do to her, especially when she got older . . ."

I squeezed her hands, horrified at what she'd been through. "I believe you," I said. "He's an awful man, and you did what you thought was right."

"I loved Josiah, but I loved my daughter more,"

she said, trembling. "Victoria was never out of my thoughts, not for a single day. But I had to protect her."

"And you did," Nathaniel said softly. "It seems I've been wrong about a lot of things lately, including you. To think that Victoria's grown up without her mother all these years because of my uncle's sins, damn his miserable blackhearted soul. I owe you more than an apology."

"In that case," she said, wiping her eyes, "now it's your turn to loosen your tongue, Nathaniel. Tell me where my daughter is."

He nodded, clearing his throat. "She's in Monterey. I sent her south on one of my ships. She's due back here in two days, and as Taylor here can tell you—the child needs mothering."

Jessica's face broke into a radiant smile. "Thank you," she said. "I promise you won't regret this."

Just then the kitchen doors slammed open and Doc Greely limped in. "Nathaniel Stuart—what's this I hear about you shouting at this good woman?" He gestured toward Jessica. "Why, she's been a godsend to me these past 24 hours, helping me tend the patients—holding their hands, bathing their wounds, even cooking up a fine stew to serve with the tinned goods in the larder—"

"Hold on!" Nathaniel interrupted. "This has all been a misunderstanding, nothing more. But I assure you, Doctor, this woman isn't going anywhere."

Doc Greely adjusted his spectacles. "Good. Glad to hear it." Bending forward he inspected the burned patch on Nathaniel's arm. "Got some salve you ought to put on that, young man."

"Later. First have a look at Miss James's ankle. And her hands—they're singed."

The physician grunted approval and ordered me to prop my ankle up on a chair. As he bent to inspect it, Nathaniel said something about going to check on things outside. I tried to stop him, but Doc Greely held me down, insisting that my ankle needed to be bound. I winced, suddenly aware of the painful throbbing, and decided to cooperate.

While Doc wrapped my ankle in gauze and rubbed some ointment on my hands, Jessica fussed over me like a mother hen, offering me a bowl of stew that she'd cooked up using water drawn before the quake. The warmth slid comfortingly down my parched throat and filled the ache in my empty stomach. Doc and Jessica urged me to lie down, even offering to move patients out of the spare bedroom upstairs to make room for me, but I refused, insisting on staying put until Nathaniel returned.

"Where'd he go, anyhow?" I asked, rubbing sleep from my eyes.

Jessica wrung a damp cloth and applied it to my palms, blistered from trying to save Fenniwick from his burning money. "No use fretting about him. Save your strength."

I sat bolt upright. "Where is he?" I demanded, grabbing the apron she'd put on.

Her expression softened. "I didn't want you to worry, but I see you're as stubborn as I am when it comes to finding out about someone you love."

"Is it that obvious?" My cheeks burned to think that a total stranger could read my feelings so easily.

"Afraid so. I must say I approve of my stepson's choice, not that my opinion's likely to count for much."

"I'm afraid you've misunderstood. Nathaniel hasn't chosen me for anything—I'm just a house-guest to him, and a troublesome one at that."

Her eyebrows shot up. "Oh, but he has chosen you, my dear. It's quite obvious."

"It is?" My heart skipped a beat.

"Why, it's as apparent as that red hair on your head that my stepson's in love with you. I take it he hasn't told you as much."

"No. Now tell me where Nathaniel's gone."

She gestured toward the window. "Joined the firefighters, trying to save your neighbors' house."

Cold fear shot through me. "He can't—"

Jessica placed her hands on my shoulders and pushed me back down into the chair I'd bolted out of. "Listen to me, Taylor. One thing I've learned is there's a time when you've got to let a man do what he has to do. That ankle of yours is swelled up like a rattlesnake struck it—why don't you just let me help you upstairs so you can lie down and rest a spell?"

"No," I said, pulling myself to my feet. Memories of conversations with Victoria flooded into my head, awful visions of what happened to the house across the street. . . .

"Is there a mop around here someplace?" I asked.

"A mop? I seem to recall seeing one in the closet there, but I don't think you ought to be on your feet cleaning up just now—"

I yanked open the closet and pulled out the mop, quickly drenching it in a bucket of water nearby. It wasn't much to fight a fire with, but it was better than nothing. Over Jessica's protests, I limped toward the door, using the soggy mop as a makeshift cane.

Outside, I squinted to see through the billowing black smoke as I pushed my way to the front of the crowd, using the mop as a battering ram. "Let me through," I screamed when I reached the cordons at the street.

"Too dangerous for ladies, ma'am," a soldier informed me.

"I know it's dangerous!" I argued, wishing I hadn't lost the hat that had hidden my long hair, a dead giveaway as to my gender. "That's why you've got to let me through!"

In answer, the soldier wrenched the mop from my grip while two other soldiers held me back and threatened to arrest me for disturbing the peace.

Swearing silently, I stumbled to a spot where a fire truck was parked. I spotted a fireman's hat and soot-covered coat on the back of the truck. Glancing around to make sure no one was paying attention, I grabbed the hat and coat and pulled them on, taking an ax for good measure. I ducked under the cordon unnoticed and slipped across the street, using the ax as a crutch.

A chain of volunteers was soaking the roof and porch of Mabel and Millicent's Victorian house with barrels of red wine. Others were battling smoldering trim with damp blankets. A wall of fire two stories high was already consuming the row of homes just behind. As I approached, sparks took hold of the turrets on Mabel and Millicent's home, and flames darted out an upstairs window. My gaze swept the perimeter of the property, then froze. Along the sides of the house, two soldiers were laying dynamite charges. My heart leapt to my throat. Nathaniel!

A firefighter ripped open the front door with an ax and went inside, shouting orders for everyone to get out. I followed him over the threshold, ignoring shouts from someone behind me to stop. Other firefighters ran past me, exiting the burning building.

"Nathaniel!" I called, panic tearing holes in my heart. I ran, or rather stumbled, from room to room, choking on the smoke. What if he was upstairs, lying there unconscious from the smoke?

Gripping the banister, I groped my way upstairs, hardly able to see through the smoke. I looked in the first room at the top of the hall. Empty.

Coughing hard, I tossed the ax aside and dropped to my knees, gulping in air as I crawled down the hallway toward a bedroom at the end. Suddenly the door opened and I saw him, carrying Mabel's calico cat in his arms. The cat was yowling, clawing at his shirt. His hair was disheveled and his clothes were coated in soot; a cut above his eye was caked with dried blood.

"Taylor! What the devil are you doing here?" he shouted as the cat bolted from his arms and ran downstairs. "Don't you know they're getting ready to dynamite this house?"

"I know," I gasped, struggling for air. "That's why I came . . . to warn you—"

An earsplitting crash boomed above me. Part of the ceiling had collapsed. . . . I looked up just in time to see a large wooden beam hurtling toward me before my head exploded with pain.

Chapter Twenty

"Taylor!" I heard Nathaniel shout. I tried to open my eyes but everything was blurred. I couldn't catch my breath. A crushing weight pressed down across the back of my shoulders, trapping me. The sizzle of flames crackled close to my ears and a cold chill shook me from head to toe as I realized the beam that had fallen on me must have caught fire.

"Taylor," Nathaniel's voice cried out as he reached my side, feeling for a pulse at my throat. "Thank God you're alive." His hands warmed me even as the fire's heat singed my hair and scalded my face. I opened my eyes and saw the fuzzy outline of him bending over me, flames leaping around him as he tried to free me. Fear constricted my throat. My dead brother's face flashed in my mind—was he waiting for me on the other side? I couldn't breathe. Smoke filled my lungs, searing my throat, my nose, my mouth. . . .

"Go—save yourself," I gasped, hearing the menacing sound of cracking timbers somewhere above us both.

"Damn it, woman, don't you understand? You might have been able to walk away from me, but I can't leave you—I love you!"

"You what?" The fog whirling in my head crystallized into picture-perfect focus. Was I hallucinating?

With a superhuman effort, he pried the heavy beam up an inch off my back and moved it off me, knocking it aside just as flames reached the section that had pinned my shoulders down only a moment earlier.

I rolled over and stumbled against him as I tried to get up, surprised at how woozy I felt, my shoulders screaming with pain. He, on the other hand, felt hard and strong and . . . heavenly, I thought disjointedly as he scooped me into his arms and against the protective warmth of his chest. He loves me, I thought, coughing for breath, fighting the black haze closing in at the edges of my mind. He risked his life to save me because he loves me! Joy surged through me, making me tremble uncontrollably.

"Hang on," he ordered as he carried me down the stairs, dodging the flames leaping up around us. I laced my fingers around his neck, inhaling the smoky smell of him, his words echoing in my mind. "Don't you understand? I can't leave you—

I love you." My heart thumped a disco beat and I closed my eyes, concentrating on survival.

He carried me outside, where I gulped in air, filling my lungs. Without pausing for breath, he marched across the street to Stuart House and pushed open the front door.

"Doc!" he shouted, spotting the physician. "Taylor's hurt—she was pinned under a burning beam."

The physician shook his graying head, gesturing toward the patients being lifted on makeshift stretchers and carried out by sweat-soaked volunteers. "No time to see to her now—we're evacuating. They're fixing to dynamite the west side of Van Ness Avenue to create a firebreak."

"Damnation," Nathaniel shouted, the veins in his neck throbbing. "You're a doctor! You've got to take a look at her!"

Shaking his head in a final apology, Doc Greely stuffed his medicine bag under his arm. "If you've got any sense, you'll come with us. Her too," he said, then disappeared out the door.

"We'd better go," he said, starting toward the door.

"No." I shook my head. "Your house will stay standing—we're safe here."

He paused only an instant before carrying me up the stairs to his room. "Are you all right?" he asked, a mixture of tenderness and concern in his eyes as he helped me out of the cumbersome fireman's coat and hat, then set me down gently on the edge of his temptingly soft bed.

"That depends." My voice sounded hoarse.

"Did you say what I thought you said back there?"

He knelt in front of me, taking my hands in his. "Taylor, my dearest, I've been in love with you since the moment I first found you banging on my bedroom door, screaming like a scalded alley cat."

"You have?" Joy flooded through me, washing over my pain.

He bent forward until his lips were a hair's breadth from mine. "You're the woman I've dreamed of all my life—warm, kind, considerate—yet braver and more daring than most men. Not many people would have gone up willingly in a flying machine, you know."

"I did it for you," I murmured. "Because I love you too."

His eyebrows shot up. "You what?"

"I love you. Since before I met you, even. I used to look at your photograph in a faded album and imagine what it would be like, waltzing in your arms."

"Good lord. If I'd known that, I would have locked the attic door and thrown away the key to keep you."

A smile radiated across his face as he pulled me into his arms and crushed his lips against mine, kissing me with the urgency born of disaster, long and deep, igniting a fire within me more intense than the flames from which he'd saved me. His hands caressed my back from shoulder to hip, pausing to cup the curve of my backside and pull me against him tightly. I buried my face against his chest, running my fingers over the rough stubble of his beard and through the thick tangle of hair at the back of his neck, the smell of wood smoke surrounding me. "I was so afraid. . . ." I began.

He pressed a finger to my lips. "I know. But you're safe now." My words died in my throat as he kissed me again. I closed my eyes, tears of happiness in them as he deepened the kiss and I responded with every ounce of strength left in me, aching to make love to him again . . . and again.

He released my mouth, his breathing ragged. "I don't know how I ever managed to let you walk back into that attic before the earthquake hit. It was almost more than I could stand."

"Why didn't you try to stop me? If you had I would have stayed. But I thought you didn't want me."

"Didn't want you?" His eyes widened, then streaked with guilt. "Good lord, woman, I've never wanted anything more in my life." He started to pull me toward him again, but as my weight shifted to my ankle, pain shot up my leg. I stumbled against him, unable to stifle a groan.

"What's wrong? Did I hurt you?"

"Just my ankle. It's nothing."

He helped me onto the bed. "You took quite a fall earlier, when that beam pinned you down. Are you sure nothing's broken?"

I moved my shoulder blades in circular test patterns. "Just bruised, I think. Nothing a hot bath wouldn't cure." In truth, every bone in my body ached as if I'd been run over by an 18-wheeler.

His hands moved expertly over my back and shoulders, his fingertips probing for serious injuries. His massaging touch made me ache, but not with pain. I leaned back, my eyes half-closed as his hands rested on the small of my back. He bent toward me to kiss me again, sending an electric jolt straight into my heart.

The instant our lips touched, an explosive blast roared in my ears, clanging my teeth together.

"Dynamite." Nathaniel swore and pulled me against him, shielding me with his arms as more charges went off in deafening succession until, finally, an ominous silence prevailed.

Groaning, Nathaniel let me go and pulled himself to his feet. "Much as I hate to let you out of my arms, I'd best make sure the house isn't about to burn down."

He moved to the pile of rubble blocking the attic door. After a few minutes, he'd managed to clear a path through the attic to the roof. Nathaniel handed me the box camera that he'd apparently brought upstairs earlier, when I was in the kitchen with Jessica. "Here. You may as well get one last shot of what's left of San Francisco."

Supporting my elbow to keep me from stumbling, he led me through the attic to the roof, where we climbed the narrow stairs to the widow's walk and looked out onto a panorama of destruction.

Across the street, once-grand homes lay smoldering in heaps of ashes as wisps of smoke curled upward from the rubble. But the fierce wall of fire that had threatened the rest of San Francisco was gone.

"It's over," Nathaniel said hoarsely. "The wind's shifted; the blaze is nearly out. But at what cost?"

His gaze swept the scene below. Everywhere, as far as the eye could see in three directions, from Nob Hill to the harbor, the city lay in ruins. Buildings had been leveled to ash; here and there burned chimneys jutted upward like stumps after a forest fire. I snapped a photo, then dropped my arms to my side, unable to look at anymore.

"The city's destroyed." Nathaniel stared outward, wind rustling through the thick tangle of hair on his head, reminding me of one of those early explorers standing at the helm of a sailing ship. "Gone . . . all gone. It'll never be the same."

"They'll rebuild—it'll be even bigger than before in just a few years," I said, laying a hand on his forearm to comfort him.

He pulled my head against his shoulder. "Thank the Lord I've got you. I've lost nearly everything else—my wharf, my warehouses, my airplane. . . . God only knows if Victoria will return safely."

"She will. She has to." I felt his losses as if they were my own, wishing I could find some way to take away the look of pain in his eyes.

A wistful tone crept into his voice. "I'm envious of you, you know. To have seen the future—it must be glorious. Tell me more about it."

"Well . . ." I hesitated, wondering where to start.

"Tell me," he insisted. "I need to know that all will be right with the world again."

"Okay." I nodded. "There are skyscrapers, tall buildings dozens of stories high—"

"Dozens?" A spark of interest lit his eyes.

"You bet. And they've built a bridge across the bay. It's called the Golden Gate."

"Phenomenal," he said, transfixed.

"I wish I had a computer to show you. You'd love one—it's a kind of artificial intelligence that you can even use to design 3-D models."

"Of aeroplanes?"

"Yes, even of airplanes," I confirmed, warming to the topic. "And we've made huge advances in telecommunications, what with TV, CDs, VCRs . . ."

"It sounds like alphabet soup."

"Then there's medicine. We've got vaccinations now for polio, mumps, measles, and they've cured smallpox—eliminated it worldwide. The only cultures left anymore are in laboratories."

"Amazing." He sighed deeply. "It's a comfort to know there's hope for the future, even though I won't see such wonders as you describe in my lifetime."

I thought of Mom and Dad then, wondering how they were, if they were worried about me— or if they'd given up hope of finding me by now and were sitting at home grieving. A pang of guilt hit me.

Nathaniel held my hands gently. "You miss it, don't you?"

I shrugged, looking down to avoid his gaze. "A little."

He tilted my chin up with his forefinger so that my eyes met his. "I must know, Taylor. Do you regret not going back to your own time?"

"Oh, no!" I protested a bit too quickly. "Being with you is worth giving up everything else. It's just that . . . well, sometimes I feel selfish for leaving my parents all alone. See, it's only been six months since my brother died and . . . you know, they took it pretty hard."

"Alex, the pilot." He nodded in understanding. "Was it a plane crash?"

"No. It was AIDS—an incurable disease. The plague of modern times, I guess you could say."

"I'm sorry," he said, squeezing my hands. "That must have been terrible for you. Thank the Lord you didn't catch it from him."

"Oh, that would be impossible. AIDS is spread, well, mostly by, ah—" I stopped, feeling my face redden.

"Oh," he said, looking flustered. "I see."

"Do you?" I asked, feeling a renewed surge of anger at Alex's old girlfriend, the one who didn't bother to tell him that she used to share needles while shooting drugs with her ex-lover. "After watching Alex die, I realized more than ever how important it was for me to wait until I met the right man."

"I'm honored that you chose me," he said, reaching for my hands, his thumbs turning circles in my palms that made it impossible to concentrate on his words. Suddenly I appreciated more than ever the treasure I'd found in Nathaniel, a man born a century before the first AIDS case was diagnosed. Talk about the ultimate in safe sex. . . .

He pulled me against him and hugged me tight, the corners of his eyes crinkling as he looked down and met my eyes. "See how you've managed to take my mind off my troubles? You're an incredible woman, Taylor James."

A quiver ran through me. "It's you who make me feel special. Before I met you, I didn't have much self-confidence. But since I've come here, I've accomplished so much. Only . . . now the earthquake's over, and I'm scared. I can't predict the future anymore."

"The only future I'm interested in is yours— and mine," he said, brushing the hair from my face as his thumb grazed my cheek. "Marry me, Taylor."

My eyes widened and my heart beat wildly. "Marry you?"

"I want you to be my wife. I was going to ask you the night before the earthquake, but then Antonio interrupted, and—"

"I'm a woman with no past. I don't have a pedigree, like Prudence. What will people say?" He loved me—he wanted to marry me even before we made love, when he thought I was a whore. . . .

"I don't give a damn what they say. You've already passed yourself off as my cousin—make that distant cousin. As for the details of your life history, I'll wager you'll not be the first San Franciscan to invent a new past after tonight."

"I could," I breathed, recalling stories of the thousands who'd risen to build new lives from the ashes of the earthquake, which destroyed records of everything, including births, marriages, and citizenship.

"You will," he said, tilting my chin up to meet his loving gaze. "Say yes, my love, and we can be wedded as soon as the dust settles enough to find a church still standing and a preacher to marry us. We'll build a new future together, just the two of us."

My heart soared above the city that lay in ruins—irrevocably destroyed, like my past. Tears of joy stung my eyes. It would be so easy to say yes, to forget all that I was before, or ever wanted to be. . . .

He lifted my hand and brushed his lips across my palm, sending a shiver of delight up my arm—and a jolt of reality into my brain. I pulled free, twisting away from him.

"Taylor, what's wrong?"

"I want to marry you, Nathaniel, but I can't. I'm only going to bring you trouble if I stay here—I don't fit in."

"What are you talking about?" He closed the gap between us. "You saved lives out there today—people respected you."

"Sure, when they thought I was a man," I corrected him. "Don't you see? I'm used to speaking my mind, to doing as I please, and none of the people who know you are going to accept me the way I am. I can't just forget everything I've been raised to believe—I never should have fallen in love with y-you. . . ."

Tears streaming down my face, I turned and fled down the rooftop stairs as fast as my wobbly ankle would permit.

"Taylor! Come back here!" I heard Nathaniel yell as I ran into the attic. His footsteps pounded in my head as he closed the gap between us and jerked me around to face him. "Don't you understand? I love you. I'll always love you. Just the way you are. No matter what happens, I want you more than I've ever wanted any woman—"

"I want you too. I love you, Nathaniel. But—"

A sharp jolt threw me against his chest as his arms closed swiftly around me. Abruptly the floor lurched underneath. "An aftershock," I gasped as I saw Nathaniel's eyes widen in comprehension.

I vaulted for the door, banging the camera against my chest. Nathaniel lunged toward me as we tumbled to the floor, the attic walls thundering around us. The noise was terrifying, rising and falling like waves crashing against a rocky beach, the floor rolling and pitching in sync with the earth three stories beneath it. My head throbbed; had I banged it when I fell?

"We've got to get out of here," I heard myself say—or rather, felt myself mouth the words. Sound crashed inward, becoming muted, as if my ears were clogged from flying. I felt Nathaniel's arms tighten around me, followed by a dizzying sensation of spinning through space that seemed to go on for an eternity, before everything skidded to a halt.

I opened my eyes, wondering how long they'd been closed. I saw that I was sprawled on the attic floor in Nathaniel's arms, one leg thrown over his thigh, my right arm cradling the camera.

"Are you all right?" His brow wrinkled with concern as he helped me to my feet.

My legs felt wobbly, but otherwise okay. Oddly, my ankle didn't hurt at all. "Yeah, I think so. And you?"

"Fine. That was a strong aftershock. We'd better get downstairs and see if any more damage was done."

"Right." I held on to his forearm for support, gripping the camera in my other hand as I pushed open the attic door and stepped into the light.

I rubbed my eyes, adjusting to the light in the bedroom, when I heard Nathaniel's startled intake of breath. He gripped my hand, a stunned expression on his face. I looked then, and froze as I saw what had captured his attention.

It was a bedside lamp with a clear glass shade—illuminated by the harsh glow of a bright white electric bulb.

Chapter Twenty-one

Nathaniel rushed forward and yanked off the shade, nearly burning his palms on the light bulb before I stopped him.

"Electric," he said, exhaling sharply. "I've seen it before, in large hotels. But . . ."

He stopped and raised his gaze to meet mine, a look of half-dread, half-wonder in his eyes.

I answered his unspoken question with a nod, then added, "I don't know what time period we're in, but something tells me it's not 1906."

"Are you telling me we've somehow come forward in time—to 1989?"

"I don't know, but I don't think so," I answered, trying not to let my own fear show as I dropped the camera on the bed and glanced around the room. The four-poster and armoire were the same as in Nathaniel's time, but everything else was different. Frillier. More feminine. Who lived here? And what would they say when they found us in their bedroom?

"What do you mean, you don't think so?" Nathaniel demanded.

"Everything's different," I answered. "Before I came back in time, this house was abandoned—empty."

He took a step backward, a look of determination on his face. "I've got to go back. Victoria—she'll need me . . . Good lord, what sort of Pandora's box have we opened up?" Grabbing my hand, he pulled me back into the attic, ignoring my protests as he hurriedly ran his hands over the interior walls, futilely searching for some escape.

There was none.

"Nathaniel." I laid a hand gently on his shoulder. "Face it—wherever we are, we're stuck."

He swallowed hard and slowly turned to face me. Wordlessly, he took my hand and we stepped together into the bedroom. My head pounded; what year was it, anyhow?

From outside I heard the sounds of traffic. Car traffic. I rushed to the window and threw open the curtains, Nathaniel close behind me.

"Motorcars . . . so many of them, and so strange," he gasped, staring at a man stepping out of the uplifted wing of a red sports car across the street. "And not a horsecart in sight. But the buildings—they're all different. Instead of houses, there are shops, and apartments. . . ."

"Those are modern-day cars," I said, my heart

beating rapidly as I recognized a late 1980s model, and something else—cracks in the sidewalk and fallen rubble that partially blocked the street in front of a nearby boutique.

"The damage to that store—it wasn't here the last time Apollo and I went jogging," I said, my excitement mounting. "So this must be sometime after the earthquake that sent me back to 1906."

Nathaniel glanced at the sun, squinting in confusion. "Before the aftershock hit, it was late afternoon," he said. "But now the sun's in the east." Instinctively, he reached for the pocket watch he'd given to me, but found an empty pocket. I fished in my fanny pack and handed him his watch. He snapped it open, staring hard. "Ten A.M.," he pronounced, snapping it shut with a decisive click. "But what date?"

I turned from the window and scanned the room, searching for a clue. Spotting a silver tray at the foot of the bed, my gaze came to rest on a pair of neatly folded newspapers. Ignoring the way my hands trembled, I picked up the one with the most recent date: October 18, 1989. "The day after the earthquake," I whispered, feeling Nathaniel's grip tighten on my hand as I met his astonished gaze. "I saved Stuart House—but everything's different. Nathaniel, what if it's been sold to someone else?"

"Impossible," he protested, though I could see doubt clouding his eyes.

"Not impossible," I insisted, lowering my voice. "What if they're downstairs right now?

And what do you think they're going to say if they find us here?"

"I don't know, but I sure as hell intend to find out." Still clutching the watch, Nathaniel charged out the door and onto the landing, forcing me to take the stairs two steps at a time just to catch up.

"Nathaniel, wait," I said in a stage whisper. "We could get ourselves arrested. You can't just—"

"I can do what I damn well must to find a way back to Victoria," he said as he stormed past the doorway to the turret room on the second story. He halted, an annoyed look on his face. "What the devil is that infernal noise?"

I fought down a smile. "Rock and roll music."

"I'll not allow such a commotion in my house."

"It's not your house anymo—"

Before I could stop him he banged open the door and barged inside, stopping dead in his tracks at the vision before him.

"Talking pictures?" he guessed, staring in fascination at a commercial on the television screen.

"Sort of. It's a TV," I said, stepping forward to flip the dial in hopes of picking up some news of the earthquake damage. An announcer delivered a grim pronouncement on the fate of several motorists still trapped under a freeway bridge that had collapsed in Oakland; next a sports commentator lamented the cancellation of the evening's World Series game but assured fans that any structural damage to Candlestick Park would be repaired as soon as possible. While I watched, Nathaniel picked the TV up and inspected it from all angles, interrupting his examination with detailed questions about how it worked. When another commercial came on, I flipped the dial again.

"Great Scott—who is that young woman? And why is she permitted to dress so brazenly?" Nathaniel demanded, staring at the on-screen image of Madonna wearing a cone-shaped bra, garter belt, and black lace tights, gyrating to the blaring strains of an MTV video.

"Times have changed. You've got a lot to get used to," I said. In his time, I was the virgin. But now he was the novice and ironically, I was the voice of experience—in every way but one.

A voice from behind startled us both. "Who's been in my room? I know I left this door closed . . . oh! Aunt Taylor—you're back! We've all been so worried about you, ever since the earthquake."

"Back?" I let out a startled breath, turning to see a young teenage girl dressed in acid-washed jeans and a Save The Whales T-shirt. While she wasn't quite a carbon copy of Victoria Stuart, the resemblance was uncanny. This was getting weirder by the minute, I thought, reaching a hand out to steady my fellow time traveler.

"This woman is your aunt?" Nathaniel said in an astonished tone.

The girl shrugged. "She's a cousin, sort of. We're related through Gram—my great-grandma, that's Taylor's great-aunt Victoria." She switched on a light. "At least the power's back on. It was the pits making do without it, like in the Stone Age."

"Victoria . . . ?" Nathaniel said, shocked.

The girl giggled, tossing back a headful of long, black hair held in place by a polka-dot banana comb. "Nobody's called me that in years, except Gram, of course, since I'm named after her. So Taylor, who's the dude?" Turning to Nathaniel she added, "I'm Vicky."

"What do you know of Victoria—your great-grandmother, the one you claim to be named after?" Nathaniel asked, an urgency in his tone as he stepped forward to within inches of the girl.

"She's—" The words stuck in her throat as she looked at Nathaniel closely. "Funny, but you remind me of someone, though I only know him from Gram's old photos. Like that one." She gestured toward a photo on the dresser of a young man wearing a leather jacket and a smile that bore a startling resemblance to Nathaniel's. "You've got the Stuart nose, all right," she said, staring at him. "But of course it must be just coincidence. . . ."

Her gaze dropped to his half-open palm and froze on the pocket watch monogrammed with his initials.

"I'm called Nathaniel," he said slowly. "Nathaniel Stuart."

She raised a hand to her mouth. "It is you, isn't it? Nate—Nathaniel. I guess you don't use your nickname anymore. Gram told me you must be dead, since you disappeared all those years ago." She flung herself at Nathaniel, who closed his arms around her automatically.

"How did you know about that?" Nathaniel asked, still holding her. "I'm still trying to understand it myself."

"Wow," Vicky said, a grin spreading from ear to ear. "Cool. So how'd you escape after your plane crashed, anyhow?"

"Plane?" Nathaniel asked, baffled.

"Amnesia," I ad-libbed, tapping a finger against my temple. "He can't remember a lot of things. It's common among trauma victims, you know."

Vicky flashed an impish grin. "Gram told me you were on a plane that crashed when I was a baby. But at least my big brother still remembers me. I could tell from the look on his face when he saw me."

"Brother?" Nathaniel's jaw dropped. "I'm not—"

I nudged him in the ribs. "Cool it," I whispered in his ear. "Go with the flow. Like this.

"Where exactly is your great-grandmother?" I asked.

Her smile faded. "Oh. I guess you haven't heard. She had a heart attack when the earthquake hit."

"Her heart?" Nathaniel asked as I felt my own pulse quicken.

"Yeah, but she's hanging in there. She's at the hospital, and she keeps asking to see you, Taylor. Wait'll she finds out you're okay, and that Nate's alive—"

"We'll go see her right away," I assured her.

Vicky cleared her throat. "Don't you think

you'd better change clothes first? Where'd you dig up those grungy old costumes, anyhow?"

I glanced down at my tattered outfit and Nathaniel's soot-covered, outdated shirt and pants. "Maybe later," I said, reluctant to explain our lack of clean clothes. "We need to get to the hospital. But first, I'd like to show Nathaniel the family album—just to refresh his memory."

"Sure thing," she said, motioning us to follow. She led us to the parlor downstairs and handed us a bulky volume. "Here you go. I still can't believe you're both here," she said before leaving the room. "It's like some kind of a miracle or something."

Nathaniel laid his hand across mine as I opened the worn leather volume to reveal yellowed pages filled with faded photos inside. "She's right, you know," I said, strengthened by the bond forged between us at his touch.

Nathaniel frowned. "I can't rest easy knowing Victoria will be coming home soon, needing me. . . ."

"Don't you see?" I said gently, pointing to an out-of-focus photo of Victoria—with her mother, Jessica. "She already has come home, years ago. Look." I pointed to a later photo, showing Victoria playing with an infant boy. "That's my great-grandfather. Victoria's half-brother."

Nathaniel's eyebrows shot up. "So Jessica stayed on after the earthquake and raised Victoria in my absence?"

"Apparently so. I'm so glad things turned out well for her after all—I didn't want to tell you everything before, but when I knew her she was a very lonely old woman, all scarred up, with no family at all. Oh my, here's a photo just a few years older, of Victoria in a wedding dress!"

Nathaniel traced his fingers around the edges of the photo, a nostalgic smile on his lips. "So she married Antonio. I should have known he'd take care of her."

"Quite well, I'd say, from the looks of this photo of the two of them with three kids," I said. "They look like a couple of lovebirds. I wonder what happened to all their children?"

Nathaniel closed the album then and cupped my chin in his hands, lowering his head to brush his lips on mine. I felt a warm surge flow through me as he kissed me again, and I savored the moment before he broke the spell.

"I say let's go to that hospital and find out."

"Right," I said, hopping up. "C'mon—we'll take the cable car."

Nathaniel's fascination with the sights and sounds of modern-day San Francisco was positively infectious. By the time we reached the trolley stop in front of the hospital he was ticking off names of automobile makes with the ease of a real pro.

We took the hospital elevator up, Nathaniel marveling at the fact that no operator was needed to make it work. On the third floor we got out and walked down the long hallway to his sister's room.

Victoria's head rested on the white pillow, looking frail and ephemeral as a wisp of dust. Her eyes were closed, but her time-worn face had a sense of serenity I hadn't seen before. Though lined with wrinkles reflecting her age, her face was unmarred by the horrible scars I'd once seen there. Or had I only imagined it? Had I really known this same woman before, on some other plane of existence, or was I the one detached from reality, confusing past and present? My mind swam as I pulled a chair close to Victoria's hospital bed and took her gnarled hand in my own.

Her eyes fluttered open; a ghost of a smile twitched on her lips. "Taylor," she croaked in her familiar reedy voice.

Nathaniel, standing behind me, came forward and knelt beside her. "I'm here, Victoria," he said quietly, clasping his hand around hers.

Her eyes widened. She doesn't remember him, I thought, feeling my stomach drop. How could she? It's been 83 years since she saw him, before he vanished in the earthquake. . . .

"Nathaniel," she whispered, her cracked lips turning upward into a painful smile as she lifted her gnarled hands to trace the contours of his face. "I always knew you would come."

Did she know what she was saying, or was she thinking of the other Nathaniel—the one who was in a plane crash? I couldn't tell, and somehow, suddenly it didn't seem to matter.

Her next words proved she was perfectly lucid, at least for the moment. "I named my firstborn

345

Nathaniel, you know," she said, sighing wistfully. "Ever since you went away, there's always been a Nathaniel Stuart in the family—I made sure of it. Insisted that my firstborn take my maiden name, since there was no male Stuart heir, though that caused quite a scandal." A ghost of a twinkle sparked in her eyes. "Antonio, God rest his soul, indulged my whims and taught me how to run the company, and ever since then Westwind Shipping has been passed down to the oldest child in the family." She paused as though struggling to catch her breath.

Nathaniel squeezed her hand. "Don't exert yourself. There's plenty of time for us to—"

"Oh, but there isn't!" Her pale eyes brightened momentarily, then faded. "My oldest boy died in World War II. He was a fighter pilot, you see. His eldest daughter ran the company for a while, but then she divorced her husband and moved off to Europe, leaving her son, my great-grandson, the third Nathaniel Stuart, in charge. But ever since he crashed one of our planes at sea—"

"Our plane? Westwind is a shipping fleet," Nathaniel pointed out.

Her eyelids drifted half-closed again. "You always were so rigid, Nathaniel. Times have changed, and we've changed with them. Nowadays Westwind is primarily an air cargo company, though we do keep on a modest fleet of cargo ships as well. Now as I was saying, after his plane went down, I stored all his personal papers, along with my will. What with all this nonsense about social security numbers and all,

I thought if you ever came back you might need some proof of identity."

"You *knew* I might come here someday?" Nathaniel asked, incredulous.

"Yes, of course," she said as matter-of-factly as if she'd been talking about a train that was late. "As I was saying, with my grandson gone, the burden has fallen back to me to keep the company together. . . . But my time is slipping away; I've been praying for someone capable of running things, at least until Vicky comes of age."

Nathaniel's eyes locked on hers. "Are you sure that's what you want?"

She nodded imperceptibly. "Oh, yes. Quite sure. Now then, Taylor, I do believe it's time for you to hear the end of my story."

"The end?"

"Why, yes. You see, when I was a little girl—"

"Victoria, how can a story about your childhood explain the end of anything?" Nathaniel asked with a touch of big-brotherly impatience.

She held a hand up. "Hush and you'll find out. Now as I was saying, when I was a very little girl, I used to play with my dolls up in the attic."

Nathaniel rubbed his chin thoughtfully. "Yes, I recall."

Her voice quavered as she continued, "Once when I was very small, perhaps four or five years old, an earthquake struck while I was in the attic."

"I remember the earthquake." Nathaniel said, frowning. "The whole household was frantic worrying about you, until you turned up an hour or so after the rumbling stopped. After that you refused to play in the attic again, so I built you the dollhouse."

I had an eerie premonition of what was coming next. "I ran out of the attic," she went on, "but everything looked strange. I ran into my room— at least, it should have been my room, only things were all different. Then I curled up on my window seat and looked out the window and saw the wedding."

"Wedding?" I asked as a ripple of warmth shot down my spine.

"It was lovely," she said, her voice fading as I sensed her starting to lose touch with reality. "In the gazebo, right in the middle of the flower gardens. Nathaniel was such a handsome groom, and Taylor, you were a beautiful bride."

"Me?" My cheeks felt hot; I looked down quickly, but not before Nathaniel saw me blush.

"Oh my, yes," she said, stifling a yawn with the back of her hand. "Dear . . . it is growing late, isn't it? At any rate, I didn't understand what was happening—the garden was filled with strangers and I was frightened, so frightened that I turned and ran back into the attic, not even realizing I'd forgotten my favorite doll until it was too late."

"The colonial doll, with the red gingham dress," I said, recalling a conversation we'd had once in her dollhouse.

"Yes, that's the one. At any rate, I hid in the attic for I don't know how long until an aftershock came along and jolted me to my senses."

Nathaniel stared at her, comprehension dawning on his face. "You're saying that you—"

A satisfied smile spread across her face as she closed her eyes at last. "Yes," she said. "I did. For a long time afterward I convinced myself it had all been a dream. But as soon as I met you, Taylor, when you came for my brother's wedding to that nitwitted Prudence, I knew that somehow history had gone awry—and you were the one who was meant to marry my brother."

She doesn't remember, I realized with a jolt. When I knew her before, when she was old and scarred and dictated her memoirs to me in that dingy old apartment . . . She doesn't remember, because everything's changed, and none of that existed.

"Good grief, Victoria," Nathaniel's voice intruded on my thoughts. "Why didn't you tell me before?"

"You'd never have believed it," she said, her voice so faint I could barely hear her next words. "But now you're here, both of you. And finally I can rest easy, knowing everything is the way it was meant to be."

I tugged at Nathaniel's sleeve and whispered in his ear, suggesting he needed a few minutes alone with Victoria. Fighting down the lump that swelled in my throat, I squeezed her hand and bent forward to kiss her on her cheek, soft as the leather of a well-worn glove. "Thank you," I whispered, blinking through a film of tears. "For everything."

Then I turned and tiptoed quietly from the room.

Epilogue

"You may kiss the bride," the minister said, smiling as he closed his Bible.

Looking handsome as a rake in his tuxedo and tails, Nathaniel bent toward me and lifted my veil. "With pleasure," he said, his lips turned up at the corners just before he pressed his mouth to mine.

A cool breeze refreshed me as I savored the sweet smells of lilacs and roses drifting from the garden around the gazebo; my senses exploded and I felt more alive than ever before. Time stood still as we held each other, Nathaniel kissing me as if he never intended to stop.

The unmistakable rumble of an earth tremor sent a startled gasp rippling through the audience of friends and family, but not even that disturbance could distract Nathaniel from his purpose in publicly claiming me as his own.

After all, ours was the love of a century.

The reception later was like a fairy tale, with me as Cinderella in the arms of my Prince Charming, gliding across the dance floor in the ballroom restored to all its former glory. Well, almost. The chandelier had light bulbs now, instead of gas lamps. But it was still the most romantic place I'd ever imagined—and now it was all ours.

Nathaniel twirled me across the ballroom for the first dance, drawing startled exclamations from the crowd, most of whom probably never saw anybody actually waltz before, except on TV. His breath warmed my ear as he whispered, "How does it feel to be mistress of the manor, Mrs. Stuart?"

"Wonderful," I replied, nestling closer against his shoulder. "I'm glad Victoria chose to leave her house to you."

"To us," he reminded me, pulling me closer. "And to our children, someday."

"How do you suppose Vicky will like the idea of a niece or nephew?" I asked, warming to the subject.

He cocked an eyebrow suggestively. "Not half as much as I'm looking forward to the idea of creating one."

After the dance, Vicky approached us carrying an enormous wrapped box with holes on the top and a big silver bow. "I thought maybe you'd want to open this wedding gift now," she said, a twinkle lighting her eyes.

Nathaniel took the heavy box from Vicky and held it while I lifted off the top. "Puppies!" I exclaimed, lifting out one of the wrinkled Shar-Pei pups that looked to be no more than six weeks old.

Vicky grinned. "I knew you'd like them. Gram made me promise to give you the entire litter."

"A whole litter!" Nathaniel's eyebrows shot up, no doubt picturing the chaos a whole houseful of miniature Apollos could cause.

"Gram used to raise them. Did you know that, Nate?"

"Somehow it doesn't surprise me," Nathaniel said, giving in to a good-humored chuckle as he tried unsuccessfully to stop two more pups from squirming out of the box before slamming the lid to keep the others inside. One pup bolted across the room and bowled into a waiter, sending a tray of hors d'oeuvres clattering onto the floor, while the other made a beeline for a potted palm in the corner. As Vicky and Nathaniel dove to retrieve the dynamic duo and put them in the kennel out back, I made a mental note to check out a book on the history of the breed, suspecting I'd find that the first-known Shar-Pei introduced in the United States would be a few decades earlier than before.

From the corner of my eye I saw Mom and Dad standing at the side of the room, smiling proudly as they welcomed more guests. If they still wondered about my whereabouts during the 24 hours after the October earthquake, they'd long since given up getting an answer. I'd told them I'd been stuck somewhere and couldn't get home, but didn't go into the details, insisting they'd never believe it anyway.

"Being in the limelight certainly seems to agree with your mother." Nathaniel rejoined me and nodded toward Mom, who looked younger than I'd remembered. Did I mention that after the 1906 earthquake, Jessica claimed her inheritance from Nathaniel's late father—whom she'd never officially divorced—and went on to establish the James Theater? These days, Dad was running the old place, directing plays in which Mom often had a starring role. He still drinks a bit too much, but what the heck. I couldn't fix everything, could I?

"Mom always wanted me to be an actress," I admitted.

"I'm curious," Nathaniel said. "Just why did you leave the stage?"

"Because I'm a lousy actress."

A grin creased his tanned face. "Your gypsy fortune-teller act did leave something to be desired."

I rolled my eyes. "Don't remind me. Okay, okay, so I'm not exactly star material."

"You certainly seem to be a rising star in the San Francisco State University's history department."

I grinned, recalling the high praise I'd received when the academic community got a look at my master's thesis. "True," I agreed. "Thanks to those never-before-seen original photos of the 1906 earthquake that I dug up in my 'research.'"

"Ah, but you're forgetting about the most mysterious figure in those history books," he said, brushing his lips sensuously across my forehead. "The elusive red-haired beauty last seen being carried into Stuart House by its owner just before he disappeared. Perhaps you've seen her? It's rumored she ran off with the master of the house after the quake."

• "I believe," I said, my voice throaty, "that she's ready to run off with the master at this very moment."

Later, after the guests cleared out and Vicky took off to stay with my folks for the weekend, Nathaniel and I climbed the stairs arm in arm.

"Everything was so perfect today," he said, sifting his fingers through my hair as he paused on the second-story landing outside Vicky's room. "If only Victoria could have been here to witness it," he added, a wistful look on his face.

I pushed the door open and peered inside, then felt a shiver run up my spine. "She *was* here," I whispered, motioning toward the window seat in the turret overlooking the gardens. On it sat a forgotten doll, wearing a colonial-style red calico dress.

Nathaniel's jaw fell open. "That rumble earlier . . . then, that means Victoria could still be here—frightened, hiding in the attic. Don't you see?" He rushed past me, taking the last flight of stairs two at a time.

I ran to catch up with him and grabbed his arm. "Nathaniel, wait."

"Wait? There isn't time." He bolted toward the attic.

I pushed in front of him and pressed my back against the attic door. "Think about what you're doing. If you stop her from going back in time, you'll be changing her whole life. She won't marry Antonio, the man she loved, or get to know her real mother. She'd grow up in a different world, one that's tough enough for an adult to adjust to, let alone a child. Speaking of which, her children and grandchildren will never be born."

Nathaniel stood still as a statue. "And great-grandchildren," he said, as my meaning sank in. "Vicky."

"She won't exist," I said softly. "None of this will. This house, your air cargo company— they're all here today because of Victoria."

"She's led a good life," he said, emotional battle lines drawn on his face. "A happy one. Do I have the right to change that?"

"I don't know," I admitted. Seeing as I'd messed around with the future myself, I didn't feel right giving him the opposite advice. "I can't answer that. Only you can."

As if on cue, the earth started to rumble in yet another tremor. Nathaniel and I exchanged wide-eyed stares before I stepped aside and presented him a clear path to the attic door. "You can go back with her," I said, feeling my heart break at the very thought. "I'll understand, if you need to go."

He stood motionless, as though frozen in time, an agonized expression on his face as he waited for the earth to stop trembling. "She's gone," he said when it was over. "My home is here now. With you."

I stepped into his welcoming arms, letting out the breath I'd been holding. "It seems everything's come full circle," he said quietly.

I lifted my arms to encircle his neck. "Yes," I agreed, smiling. "It has."

He picked me up then and swept me onto the four-poster bed in the room where it all began.

"Tonight," he whispered, brushing my neck with his lips, "I intend to savor each moment with you as if this night will never end." His lips found mine and branded me with a century-old fire as his fingers found the zipper on the back of my bridal gown and guided it downward with practiced, unhurried care.

"Take all the time you need," I murmured as the gown slipped to my ankles and Nathaniel's bare hands stroked the sensitive skin on my back. After all, I thought as contentment spread through me like warm honey, we have the rest of our lives to spend together.

Nathaniel looked around him in eager fascination as we climbed the steps of Westwind Shipping's private corporate jet the next morning, bombarding me with technical questions I insisted only a mechanic could answer. I wondered where he found the energy, after our near-sleepless wedding night.

"You still haven't told me where we're bound," he said, buckling up his seatbelt. "Los Angeles? Monterey?"

"Keep guessing," I said as the steward poured champagne for us both. "I had in mind something a bit farther afield."

"Mexico? Hawaii? Siam?"

"Thailand," I corrected. "Siam went out with Anna and the King. That's a Yul Brynner movie."

"We'll have to rent the video when we return," he noted.

"Sure," I agreed. It was amazing how fast he was adapting to modern-day life, I thought as the pilot started up the engines. Victoria was right—Nathaniel certainly was a man ahead of his time.

"A toast to our future," he said, raising his glass to clink it against mine before lifting the rim to my lips. Champagne fizzed in my mouth and slid down my throat, making me feel light-headed and warm inside at the same time. I offered my glass to him and he took a sip, savoring the vintage, then set his glass aside and pulled me into his arms. The taste of champagne lingered on my lips as he kissed me long and lovingly, the engines roaring in our ears as the Lear Jet taxied down the runway.

I watched the satisfied expression on his face as the plane became airborn. He leaned toward the window; together we watched the earth fade away beneath us and the clouds give way to blue skies above.

"I give up," he said at last, turning to face me. "Precisely where are you taking me for our wedding trip?"

I smiled, then told him. "To show you the world."

Dear Readers,

I hope you have enjoyed reading *Apollo's Fault* as much as I've enjoyed researching and writing it.

Descriptions of the devastating 1906 San Francisco earthquake and fire in the novel are based upon news reports, survivors' memoirs, and other written records of the era. Stuart House is a fictitious creation; however, dynamite charges were set off and the fire's westward spread did halt at Van Ness Avenue. Whether the fire stopped because of the dynamite or merely shifting winds, however, has long been a matter of debate.

Boss Ruef, Mayor Eugene Schmitz, Rudolph Spreckels, and Enrico Caruso were real historical figures. All conversations involving these individuals are fictitious, although the events in which they are depicted are genuine. Rudolph Spreckels did attempt to establish a trolley company that would run on underground cables. Those plans, like so many others, were derailed when the earthquake struck. The quake devastated existing transportation lines, necessitating funding to swiftly restore and expand above-ground lines. Shortly after the earthquake, Boss Ruef was convicted of graft and served time in prison. Mayor Schmitz, though also indicted, later had his sentence commuted. Disdained by many of his contemporaries, Schmitz drew praise even from his critics for his leadership during the earthquake crisis. Enrico Caruso, shaken by the disaster, fled San Francisco in the quake's aftermath, never to return.

All other characters depicted in the novel are entirely fictitious and any resemblance to real individuals, living or dead, is entirely coincidental.

In describing the 1989 earthquake, I've relied on news reports and—fortuitously—on an eyewitness account provided by a member of my writing critique group who survived the terrifying quake.

Miriam Raftery

Don't miss these passionate time-travel romances, in which modern-day heroines fulfill their hearts' desires with men from different eras.

Traveler by Elaine Fox. A late-night stroll through a Civil War battlefield park leads Shelby Manning to a most intriguing stranger. Bloody, confused, and dressed in Union blue, Carter Lindsey insists he has just come from the Battle of Fredericksburg—more than one hundred years in the past. Before she knows it, Shelby finds herself swept into a passion like none she's ever known and willing to defy time itself to keep Carter at her side.

_52074-5 $4.99 US/$6.99 CAN

Passion's Timeless Hour by Vivian Knight-Jenkins. Propelled by a freak accident from the killing fields of Vietnam to a Civil War battlefield, army nurse Rebecca Ann Warren discovers long-buried desires in the arms of Confederate leader Alexander Ransom. But when Alex begins to suspect she may be a Yankee spy, Rebecca must convince him of the impossible to prove her innocence...that she is from another time, another place.

_52079-6 $4.99 US/$6.99 CAN

Dorchester Publishing Co., Inc.
65 Commerce Road
Stamford, CT 06902

Please add $1.75 for shipping and handling for the first book and $.50 for each book thereafter. NY, NYC, PA and CT residents, please add appropriate sales tax. No cash, stamps, or C.O.D.s. All orders shipped within 6 weeks via postal service book rate. Canadian orders require $2.00 extra postage and must be paid in U.S. dollars through a U.S. banking facility.

Name _____
Address _____
City _____ State _____ Zip _____
I have enclosed $_____ in payment for the checked book(s).
Payment <u>must</u> accompany all orders.☐ Please send a free catalog.

ELIZABETH CRANE

TIMESWEPT

Don't miss these passionate time-travel romances, in which modern-day heroines journey to other eras and find the men who fulfill their hearts' desires

Reflections In Time. When practical-minded Renata O'Neal submits to hypnosis to cure her insomnia, she never expects to wake up in 1880s Louisiana—or in love with fiery Nathan Blue. But vicious secrets and Victorian sensibilities threaten to keep Renata and Nathan apart...until Renata vows that nothing will separate her from the most deliciously alluring man of any century.

_52089-3 $4.99 US/$6.99 CAN

Time Remembered. Among the ruins of an antebellum mansion, young architect Jody Farnell discovers the diary of a man from another century and a voodoo doll whose ancient spell whisks her back one hundred years to his time. Micah Deveroux yearns for someone he can love above all others, and he thinks he has found that woman until Jody mysteriously appears in his own bedroom. Enchanted by Jody, betrothed to another, Micah fears he has lost his one chance at happiness—unless the same black magic that has brought Jody into his life can work its charms again.

_51904-6 $4.99 US/$5.99 CAN

Dorchester Publishing Co., Inc.
65 Commerce Road
Stamford, CT 06902

Please add $1.75 for shipping and handling for the first book and $.50 for each book thereafter. NY, NYC, PA and CT residents, please add appropriate sales tax. No cash, stamps, or C.O.D.s. All orders shipped within 6 weeks via postal service book rate. Canadian orders require $2.00 extra postage and must be paid in U.S. dollars through a U.S. banking facility.

Name _____

Address _____

City _____ State _____ Zip _____

I have enclosed $_____in payment for the checked book(s).

Payment <u>must</u> accompany all orders.☐ Please send a free catalog.

BITTERROOT

VICTORIA CHANCELLOR

Bestselling Author Of *Forever & A Day*

In the Wyoming Territory—a land both breathtaking and brutal—bitterroots grow every summer for a brief time. Therapist Rebecca Hartford has never seen such a plant—until she is swept back to the days of Indian medicine men, feuding ranchers, and her pioneer forebears. Nor has she ever known a man·as dark, menacing, and devastatingly handsome as Sloan Travers. Sloan hides a tormented past, and Rebecca vows to use her professional skills to help the former Union soldier, even though she longs to succumb to personal desire. But when a mysterious shaman warns Rebecca that her sojourn in the Old West will last only as long as the bitterroot blooms, she can only pray that her love for Sloan is strong enough to span the ages....

_52087-7 $5.50 US/$7.50 CAN